James W. Brown, Robert W. Stewart

An Italian Campaign

The Evangelical Movement in Italy, 1845-1887

James W. Brown, Robert W. Stewart

An Italian Campaign
The Evangelical Movement in Italy, 1845-1887

ISBN/EAN: 9783337235772

Printed in Europe, USA, Canada, Australia, Japan

Cover: Foto ©Andreas Hilbeck / pixelio.de

More available books at **www.hansebooks.com**

AN ITALIAN CAMPAIGN;

OR,

THE EVANGELICAL MOVEMENT IN ITALY.

1845–1887.

FROM THE LETTERS OF

THE LATE

REV. R. W. STEWART, D.D., OF LEGHORN.

BY THE REV.

J. WOOD BROWN, M.A.,

Gordon.

𝔏𝔬𝔫𝔡𝔬𝔫:

HODDER AND STOUGHTON,

27, PATERNOSTER ROW.

—

MDCCCXC.

Butler & Tanner,
The Selwood Printing Works,
Frome, and London.

CONTENTS.

BOOK I.

IN THE OLD WORLD.

BOOK II.

THE NEW ORDER.

v

BOOK I.

IN THE OLD WORLD.

INTRODUCTION.

"Lì si vedrà la superbia ch' asseta,
  Che fa lo Scotto e l' Inghilese folle
  Sì, che non può soffrir dentro a sua meta."
                    —*Dante, Paradiso*, xix. 121-3.

AT the end of one of the streets of Leghorn—the
"Via degli Elisi," or "Paradise Row," as we
might call it—and near the square which bears the
name and effigy of Cavour, there stands a great block
of building no larger nor loftier perhaps than its
neighbours, yet distinct from them by the more
ornate style of its design, the Gothic arch above the
door, and the narrow lancets of its windows. Some,
as they passed by, struck no doubt by these pecu-
liarities, have been heard to name it "Il Convento";
but the British traveller has a key to the mystery
in the significant words "Scotch—Church," which he
may read engraved in zinc, one on each side of the
ample *porte cochère* leading to the garden. This
gate stands hospitably open of a Sabbath morning:
and entering, we gain access to a handsome Church,
which occupies in a surprising way the rear of the
building. Once within the door which shuts out the
garden with its oranges, its fig and pomegranate trees,

3

and its camellias, it is easy to forget that we are no longer in the native land of Presbytery. Pulpit, precentor's desk, pews, all are there, and of orthodox pattern, and the very light of these sunny Southern skies only reaches us through glass that is bright with the heraldry of Scottish families. There, as at home, we can join with our countrymen in the worship of God according to the simple Presbyterian rite, endeared to us of the North by so many sacred associations.

When the minister has pronounced the Benediction, he disappears through an archway to the right. Were we to follow him past these red baize doors, we should find ourselves in a large and lofty apartment, one of the rooms of the Manse, which, by an arrangement not uncommon in these Italian Stations, forms part of the same building as the Church. The room of which we speak, contrived to serve the double purpose of vestry and study, was occupied (and not infrequently seventeen hours in the twenty-four) for well-nigh forty years by one of the most devoted and successful ministers of the Free Church of Scotland, the Reverend Robert Walter Stewart, D.D. His library it is that stands in these cases which cover the walls, and it contains, besides the more ordinary volumes forming the stock-in-trade of the ecclesiastical profession, much that is curious and interesting—fine early editions of the Latin and Italian Classics, rare black-letter Vulgates and service-books of the Romish Church, as well as works of the Italian Reformers seldom to be met with. The presses, too, upon which these book-cases stand, are full of correspondence—for Dr. Stewart was a prodigious penman—some of it preserved on the slight pages of quarto copying-books such as merchants use : fifteen volumes there are of these containing five hundred pages each—the rest, being letters received, lie in bundles, docketed by month and year with scrupulous care. What suggestions does this, the incoming part of the correspondence, afford in the very outward guise of it! Quaint foldings marked by fragments of broken seals ; addresses inscribed upon the letter itself; these are strange to us of the younger generation, who have never written without using the convenient envelope. We stare at the enormous demands for postage scrawled on letters from Scotland. Here again is a sheet of the delicate ivory-white " Bath Post " once in such vogue, covered with the straggling characters of a masculine Italian hand. It is a letter from a refugee priest, partly written in curious Latin, partly in still more curious English, announcing his safe arrival on British shores. Look at this blue stamp bearing the name of a well-known and much respected Leghorn house—Henderson Brothers. It is impressed on a letter from Scotland, dated some time in the early fifties : the oil which formed the vehicle of the colour has spread itself in a dull stain round the characters of the stamp. Vividly we see the time of surveillance, when so closely was the Scotch minister watched that it was necessary to send letters relating to the work of evangelisation from one safe hand to another, and by private opportunities, in case they should be tampered with in the course of post. Here, too, are many sheets bearing widely different dates, but alike in this, that they are pierced and slit as might be done by a knife passed through all the thicknesses of envelope and letter together, in several places. It is the sign of disinfection, and of those dread years of cholera, only too frequently recurring, when the work, never without trial, was carried on under shadow of death itself.

The same stores, were we at liberty to search them fully, contain, we should find, much that bears upon Dr. Stewart's personal history. Here, for example, is a diary kept by his saintly mother, the Hon. Margaret Stuart, in which are many details of his earlier life from 1812, when he was born in the little rural manse of Bolton, through the time of his education at Glasgow University, and of years when he accompanied his parents in their travels and residence abroad. Turning these faded pages, we seem to see the Via Pontefici of Rome, where for nine months in 1829 the family was established, and the Reformed Church, Geneva, where Dr. Stewart—then a young man—received the Holy Communion for the first time from the hands of César Malan. Here too, in a packet by themselves, lie all the papers relating to his settlement in 1837 as colleague and successor to his father, the Rev. Andrew Stewart, M.D., of Erskine.

One of these is the deed of presentation to the living, signed by the trustees of his cousin, Lord Blantyre ; another the " call," bearing the names of many who now sleep peacefully in that green churchyard by the Clyde.

If we wonder at the change which brought him, like another Columbanus, from the shores of the Western sea to those of the Mediterranean, God's leading of His servant becomes plain to us from the same abundant source. We live over again in these letters the noble year of the Disruption, in which, like many others, he sacrificed position and income for his faith and principles. We read with regret how his health, already impaired, broke down altogether under the arduous and successful efforts he then made to put the cause of the Church on a proper footing in his parish and district : and we rejoice with his friends as, at the moment when it became plain that his work in Scotland must cease, a way was opened up for further labour and usefulness by the call he received to minister among the Scottish colony in Leghorn. Other letters there are, conveying the various invitations he had to become the pastor of this or the other London congregation, or to take charge of the Colonial and Continental work of his own Church at head-quarters in Edinburgh, not to speak of the correspondence relating to the Moderatorship of the General Assembly, a position which he was honourably called to occupy in 1874.

To use this material in writing a biography of Dr. Stewart would be a natural and a grateful duty, were it not that his own positive and often-repeated prohibition stands in the way. "Let no life of me be written," he was accustomed to say, as one and another of his old companions attained this somewhat doubtful and dearly bought distinction. But surely there is no reason why these stores should not find their use in expounding and illustrating the work to which his life was given. His friends know well that while he lived every personal feeling of his was put resolutely aside when it came into competition with the great cause of God's truth in Italy. In the like spirit, then, the author desires to work while penning these pages. Those who read them must be content to catch what glimpses they can of the workman through the plain record of his manifold labours, and of those great movements in which he played no insignificant part. Perfumes that are unbearable indoors may give a piercing pleasure when burnt in the open air, where they mingle with the scent of a thousand flowers. So be it here. May the glory of man be lost in that of God; yet so as by that loss to be found unto praise and honour at the appearing of Jesus Christ!

We find the first evidence of the movement we are about to study in an Act of the Scottish Assembly's Colonial Committee of 1840. In that year a sub-committee was appointed, and charged with the interests of the Continent of Europe. If any one

be inclined to smile at the assumption of such a responsibility, let him rather reflect how gallant a sight
it is which shows us this Church of Scotland, small in
numbers and far removed from the larger centres of
Western life, unrolling the map of Europe, careless of
Czar or Pope, and laying an appropriating finger upon
places remote from each other as Riga and Leghorn,
Cronstadt and Corfu, Malta, Messina, and Rome,
with the express purpose of setting up chaplaincies
at some or all of them. The name of Leghorn
appears in this list probably in consequence of a visit
paid to that place about this time by the Rev. Mr.
Robertson of Logie. He had supplied the Presbyterian pulpit at Gibraltar for some weeks, proceeding
thence to various towns on the shores of the Mediterranean and in France as the Committee's agent of
inquiry.

Leghorn in 1841—to present the substance of Mr.
Robertson's report upon it—was inhabited by a considerable British colony, numbering from 170 to 200
souls, the majority of them Scotch. There was also a
large number of English-speaking sailors in the port:
sometimes as many as 300; and—to complete the
survey of possibilities—at certain seasons of the year
a tide of travellers flowing to or from Rome made
Leghorn their resting-place for a time. It is true
that an English chaplain was settled in the town, and
had recently got a handsome Church built (it stands
in that same Via degli Elisi of which we have
spoken); but Mr. Robertson, who preached to the

Scotch residents during his visit, and found that even at the shortest notice he could gather a congregation of fifty persons, reported it as his belief that were the Committee to send out a Presbyterian clergyman, he would be heartily welcomed, and would soon establish himself in a promising sphere of labour.

This report was so satisfactory that the Committee lost no time in looking out for some one to occupy the post. While they were doing so, it happened that the well-known Dr. John Duncan, then acting as Jewish Missionary at Pesth, found that his health required him to seek a warmer winter climate than that of Hungary, and left Pesth on the 10th of November, 1842, with the purpose of spending the colder months in Leghorn. When there, he carried out the plans formed by the Committee; gathering a congregation and performing Divine Service with every sign of success till his departure in the spring of 1843. All who know the history of the Scottish Church are aware what a crisis she then passed through. The little congregation at Leghorn had been informed by Dr. Duncan of the conflict, and what it meant; and when the famous Protest was given in, and the Disruption became an accomplished fact, these Scotch people dwelling far from home threw in their lot unhesitatingly with the Free Church, and waited with patience for two years till a regular ministry could be established among them.

During this time they were not forgotten at home. It is noted in the *Record* for July, 1844, that "an association has been formed in Glasgow similar to the Ladies' Colonial Association of Edinburgh, whose views are directed to Leghorn as a station which it would be desirable to occupy. The general anxiety indeed which has been expressed with regard to the Mediterranean stations has induced your Committee to request the Rev. Mr. Stewart, late of Erskine, to visit these stations, to inquire into the religious condition of our countrymen ; to suggest what provision may be made for them in the meantime ; to ascertain what difficulties will require to be overcome, and what probable good will result from their occupation." Dr. Stewart (let us call him so from the first, though in fact the Degree in Theology which was conferred upon him by Princeton College only dates from 1849) had special qualifications for the task thus assigned him. Besides his more ordinary ministerial training and experience, he had a rare familiarity with the French and Italian languages, gained in those early years of foreign travel and residence at Geneva and Rome, to which we have already alluded. More lately also, in 1842, the state of his health had made another visit to the Mediterranean .necessary, during which he made proof of his ministry, both at Malta and Constantinople. Bound on a mission then for which he was eminently fitted, Dr. Stewart sailed in 1844 from England by the *Liverpool* to Gibraltar, and thence proceeded to Malta and Corfu. At this latter place, Lord Seaton, the Lord High Commissioner of the Ionian Islands,

received the representative of Free Church Presbyterianism with the most flattering attention, and from
Corfu he returned home by Malta, Naples, Leghorn,
and Marseilles.   There seems to have been some
delay consequent on Dr. Stewart's report being presented, for we find him acting for nearly a year as
secretary to the London Missionary Board before
the appointment was finally made ; and it was on
the 12th of June, 1845, after visiting on his way
the Reformed Churches of France and the Vaudois
Valleys, that he landed in Leghorn—the first missionary chaplain of the Scotch Church established on
the Italian mainland.

A caution that was both national and natural
marked the beginning of this novel enterprise.   In
a little square by the canal and overlooking the port
—now called Piazza Cappellini—stood the well-known
" Thomson's Hotel," and there, in a room used by
Dr Duncan two years before for the same purpose,
the first services were held.   One can understand
that the situation of this infant congregation and its
pastor with regard to the Church of England chap-
laincy was one of extreme delicacy.   Fortunately a
prudent and Christian disregard of offences (even
when these took the sad form of direct opposition
and excommunication) prevailed, and soon Dr.
Stewart was able to report that he had the pleasure
of seeing " those who opposed at first now occasionally dropping in to Church."

Three matters of pressing importance there were

which came up for settlement in these early years of the Mission. The first—that of proper Church organization—was put on a right footing with the least possible delay. Soon after Dr. Stewart's arrival, it happened that three other ministers of the Church of Scotland found themselves together in Leghorn. The occasion was one too rarely fortunate to be missed, and accordingly the Rev. Messrs. Gray, Keith, Makellar, and Stewart constituted themselves into a Presbytery, *in hunc effectum* as the legal phrase runs, for the single purpose of ordaining office-bearers over the newly formed congregation. We note with pleasure the names of those who were thus appointed—Messrs. Henderson, Thomson, Rae, and Robertson—for theirs was no ornamental office ; they formed the staff of which their pastor was the commander. Seldom has a minister worked with more efficient helpers ; and as we shall presently see, the Kirk Session of Leghorn, which they composed, was not only efficient in establishing and guiding the Presbyterian cause in that city, but gave much valuable aid in mission work among the Italians.

Provided with a proper Church government, the congregation at Leghorn yet lacked an adequate place of worship. When the number who attended the services in the hotel became so large that Mr. Thomson's room could no longer contain them, they found accommodation for a time in the Swiss Church, kindly lent for that purpose in the afternoons. The hour however being an unsuitable one,

a hall in the Via Castelli was taken on lease and
properly fitted up for public worship. This place
had been a granary, was low in the roof, and ill-
ventilated ; and as the congregation still increased,
and the heats of summer drew on, so great was the
consequent discomfort, that it became plain something must be done to provide a suitable Church.
Those immediately interested subscribed liberally,
money was got from friends in Scotland, and the
result appears in the handsome building—Church
and Manse under one roof—to which the reader has
already been introduced in the opening sentences of
this chapter.

The new Church was opened in 1849 ; but before
that event took place, another matter of importance
had emerged and been dealt with satisfactorily. As
soon as death broke for the first time the ranks
of Dr. Stewart's congregation, the question arose
whether these Scotch people had the right of burial
in the British Cemetery of Leghorn ; or rather, to
state the matter more exactly, whether they could
be buried there by their own clergyman, or whether
the service must be conducted by the English chaplain of the place. The original British burying-
ground is extremely ancient, having been ceded by
the Italian Government some three hundred years
ago. But shortly before the time of which we write,
the Bishop of Gibraltar had performed the ceremony
of consecration upon a new cemetery, and it was
contended that since that event no burial could take

place there except under the rites of the English Church. On the other hand, Dr. Stewart and his session held the view that this burial-ground was in fact a part of Great Britain in Italy, and that the North Briton should have his rights in it, and among them his national Church privileges, recognised as freely and fully as were those of his Southern neighbours. A memorial embodying these facts and presenting this plea was sent home, and after nearly a year of vexatious delay the matter was settled by Lord Palmerston, who wrote directing the Consul to see that no hindrance was offered to the members of the Free Church or their minister in using the burial-ground with whatever rites they chose.

It was probably inevitable that in the first beginnings of an enterprise such as we are examining, those who conducted it should be obliged to fight their way against many opposing influences to a position of stability and respect ; and Dr. Stewart and those who supported him in Leghorn were to be heartily congratulated when, as early as the year 1849, they found themselves fully organized, equipped, and established.

CHAPTER I.

TAKING THE FIELD.

" Se Tosco se', ben dèi saper chi e' fu."
—*Dante, Inferno*, xxxii. 66.

WHEN a congregation is first gathered, nothing can be more natural than that the energies of pastor and people should for a time be confined, in large measure at least, to the service of their own immediate needs ; but sooner or later when these have been provided for, the same energies, if the spiritual life of the Church be maintained, will be found neither declining nor dormant, but earnestly engaged in work of a wider kind and of a more or less missionary character. So, at least, it was in Leghorn. We have seen how the Church there met both stoutly and successfully the difficulties connected with her own rise and establishment ; we are now to trace the triumphs of the same energy and sagacity in a larger field.

The circumstances of the time gave a wonderful opening and impetus to this wider purpose. In 1848 constitutions more or less liberal were granted to all the Italian States, even to those under the power of the Pope ; and with regard to that in which Leghorn was more immediately interested, we find Dr. Stewart writing as follows, on February 23rd, to the convener of the Glasgow Ladies' Committee : " The constitution of Tuscany was published on Friday last amid great and general rejoicings, firing of cannons, Te Deums in the churches, and general illuminations at night.   Two years ago there was a general illumination as a thanksgiving to the Madonna of Montenero for having preserved Leghorn from utter destruction by the earthquake ; but I would not illuminate for such a cause.   On Friday night however I obeyed the order with alacrity, for the constitution granted to this country is a most liberal and satisfactory one. The Roman is of course the religion of the State, but all the other forms of worship at present existing are declared to be tolerated according to law, and among the rest of course the Scotch Presbyterian Church.   And as we have been now three years in existence, and are known to the Government as peaceably disposed, there would be no objection on the part of Government to the establishment of a Free Church at Florence—an event I most anxiously look for, and pray that God will put it into the hearts of the Colonial Committee to accomplish, both for the sake of our countrymen and the Italians.   I hope the time is coming when they may seriously think of it." |

There was another circumstance besides the con-

stitutional liberties of 1848 which seemed to open
the door for an extension of work among the Italians.
The Free Church in Italy was not merely tolerated
in her immediate work—that of supplying ordinances to the Scotch residents—but (and the point
was noted by the Committee and their agent with
keen appreciation of the use that might be made of
it) no restriction was placed upon her, nor any pledge
required such as that exacted from all the chaplaincies of the Church of England, that they should
abstain from attempting to proselytise among the
Italians. This forbearance was but the result of an
oversight; for the Romish authorities both knew
and dreaded the aggressive tendencies of Presbyterian
ministers. Yet none the less welcome was the liberty
in which with all good conscience Dr. Stewart found
himself free to preach the gospel to every creature;
and no long time elapsed before he made trial of the
extent to which he would be suffered to proceed in
promoting the work of evangelisation.

Dr. Luigi Desanctis, a priest who had taught in
one of the theological chairs in Rome, left that city
for Malta, that, under protection of the British flag,
he might safely profess Protestant principles. This
happened in 1847; and on the 9th of April in the following year, having come to Leghorn, he conducted
evening service in the Free Church there, the congregation including on that occasion some twenty Italian
Roman Catholics. Two days afterwards he preached
again in the same place; and at the invitation of Mr.

Henderson, one of the elders of the Scotch Church, he addressed a congregation of forty-two Italians on the following Sabbath at a villa in the neighbourhood of Lucca. Those who arranged these services, with such courage and address, were not the men to let the movement drop when it had been fairly begun. Dr. Stewart and his session opened the Scotch Church for occasional preaching of the gospel in Italian during the year that followed this first attempt; and when the new church was ready for Divine service in April, 1849, the sermon of dedication then preached by the pastor was in some sort a challenge and declaration of the intended propaganda. As such it was translated into Italian, printed, and widely circulated among the people. Thus then the voice of Protestant truth, silent in Italy for more than two hundred years, was again heard in the very district where Burlamacchi, Diodati, and Calandrini had lived and laboured, and the Free Church of Scotland stood honourably and openly committed to the work of Italian evangelisation.

All this did not take place without exciting the attention and awakening the resentment of the Roman clergy. The parochial authorities, within whose bounds the Scotch Church in Leghorn was situated, became alarmed when they saw the unexpected use to which that place of worship was put. They summoned the beadle, who happened to be a Romanist, and questioned him closely as to what had taken place on the occasion of Dr. Desanctis' preaching. An espionage, which had for some time been carried on in the Manse by means of the Italian servants there, was made more close and vigilant than ever ; and when Dr. Stewart's sermon, to which we have already alluded, was committed to the press and circulated among the people, the Government itself—so serious was the matter thought by its clerical advisers—made a secret inquiry into all that was being done, and embodied the results in a State paper preserved in its archives. We may here refer to an article in the *Dublin Review* for 1853, which was credibly attributed to the pen of Cardinal Wiseman. In it the writer mentions this very State paper, which, he says, had been communicated to him by the kindness of a friend ; speaks of the Scotch minister at Leghorn by name (p. 213) as a chief enemy of their cause ; and proceeds in such a painful strain of invective as discovers very plainly to any one who can read between the lines what alarm was felt in the highest places of the Roman world at the bold and successful operations carried on in connection with the Leghorn Presbyterian Mission. Were further proof of this panic needed, it might be found in such a passage as the following : " Confessions were made about this time to two Scottish noblemen—one by the Pope's chamberlain, the other by a cardinal—that the Free Church of Scotland was the only Church they feared, and the only one in Britain they respected : that they knew all her missions, and watched them jealously." " This," says

Dr. Stewart, " I had from the fountain-head in both cases."

What made the situation in 1849 a serious one, however, was not the natural suspicion and enmity of the Roman clergy so much as the fact that circumstances combined to put a dangerous power into their hands. Before the year was out, Time's wheel again brought great political changes in Tuscany, and a new order of things arose which was destined to persist in more or less rigour for another decade, and to prove during that time a serious obstacle in the way of those who sought the diffusion of Protestant truth among the Italians. We have seen how the Liberal constitution of 1848 was ushered in with loudly blown trumpets and *feux-de-joie.* Hardly were twelve months gone when under Austrian influence and protection a reaction set in : the *statuto* was suspended, and with the very breath of spring were blown the trumpets of war, and under the bright sun of May flashed murderous fusillades, when some four hundred recusant Liberals of Leghorn were shot in horrid butchery beneath the town wall. The curious visitor of to-day is shown a marble tablet set to mark the spot and record the infamy. It looks out, laurel-hung, from the grim masonry, an unimpeachable memorial of the time when the fortress of Leghorn was hastily occupied by Austrian troops, and when its crumbling bastions, lately in process of peaceful demolition, were crowned anew with dread circles of shotted guns pointed against the town.

Under this reaction, when constitutional liberty was recalled, and the freedom of the press abolished, the Roman clergy attained an unexpected command of the secular arm ; and those who know how freely that Church has always availed herself of the power by which kings rule, will readily believe that no hesitation was shown in doing so on this occasion. The sad and threatening events we have been speaking of occurred in May. During the following September Dr. Stewart was summoned to appear before the Leghorn police, and was subjected to a close examination. In the Appendix will be found an account of what took place, written at the time, from which the general tenor of the questions may be gathered. One of these was directed to discover the nature of the religious service commonly used in the Scotch Church ; and Dr. Stewart used to tell how astonished the officials seemed when, in detailing the simple rubrics of our Scottish rite, he mentioned that prayers were regularly offered for the Grand Duke and his Government. This unexpected display of loyalty to the powers that were may have had something to do with the fact that no further steps were taken by the authorities ; but in letters of the time Dr. Stewart mentions another reason, which excited his liveliest thankfulness, so providential did the circumstance seem. He had gone to Scotland in the autumn of 1848, and had been detained there during the following winter collecting money for his new church. Much against his will, he saw, month by month, the precious time of liberty slip away; and hardly had he returned to his post when the days of terror commenced. It was not until the summons and inquiry of September made this enforced absence appear in its true light, that it came to be recognised for what it was—a gracious leading of God's own hand. Had Dr. Stewart remained in Leghorn, he would certainly have used the brief days of freedom to the uttermost, both by distributing Bibles and other Protestant books, and by entering into some arrangement for the regular preaching of the gospel to Italians in the Scotch Church. In that case his answers to the questions of the police must have been of a different nature, and in all probability the Tuscan Government would have closed the church and given its pastor his passport for Scotland at a few days' notice.

The work was thus by God's good hand preserved ; but there is more to record ; for it was even extended. In his letter of February, 1848, from which we have already seen a quotation, Dr. Stewart expressed an earnest wish to have another station of the Church established at Florence. Hardly a year passed before this desire was fulfilled. The Rev. R. M. Hanna, minister of Girthon and Anwoth, had been obliged to reside at Pisa on account of his health. During 1847, when he first went there, he was unable to undertake any duty ; but in the following year he supplied the pulpit at Leghorn, while Dr. Stewart was absent in Scotland. Having thus acquired a familiarity with the Italian work, and a liking for it, Mr. Hanna resolved to seek some appointment in his adopted country rather than return home. On leaving Leghorn he went for a time to the station at Malta; but finding the great heat there prejudicial to his health, he came north again. By this time the Colonial Committee had agreed to set up a station at Florence, and Mr. Hanna was settled there in "his own hired house," on the 26th of September, 1849, at which date we find him opening his apartment to a little congregation of visitors and engineers who came to him for Divine service. Of this humble beginning the present Scotch Church, handsomely lodged in its palace on the Lung' Arno, is the issue. Even in these earliest years the enterprise had a place and a use peculiarly its own. Besides affording an invaluable base of operations for work among the Italians, it supplied ordinances to many of our own exiles, and gathered, in genuine appreciation of Presbyterian simplicity and fervour, such teachers of the English-speaking world as the Brownings, Mr. F. Tennyson, and Mrs. Beecher Stowe.

No one, seeing this bold advance by which an aggressive Protestant Church was planted beside the very palace of the Grand Duke, and at a time when retreat might have seemed more natural, will readily accuse of cowardice those who were responsible for it. But fortunately the leaders of the attack knew how to combine caution with their courage. In illustration of this it is enough to record a somewhat picturesque incident which occurred in 1850. A young friar from the Dominican Convent in Leghorn, habited no doubt in the black and white robes of his order, visited the Scotch Manse, to seek a private interview with the Presbyterian pastor. He came asking news of Dr. Achilli, with whom he was acquainted, and desiring to find out whether his own expenses as a refugee would be paid him were he also to leave the Church of Rome. The reply he received was that, if he were sincere in his purpose of becoming a Protestant, a well-known door stood open to him in the town,[1] but that the Scotch minister as tolerated by Government could not interfere in such a case.

Other facts of the time give reason to believe that Dr. Stewart would not have assumed such a forbidding attitude had he not shrewdly suspected what seems to have been the case—that the Dominican was a clerical spy, sent by his Superiors to entrap their deadly enemy and procure his banishment from the country. The visit of Keith and Bonar in 1839 (see " Narrative of a Mission to the Jews ") was not forgotten, and helped to increase the suspicion and animosity felt by the Roman clergy against Scotch ministers ; while incidents such as that just mentioned made Dr. Stewart and Mr. Hanna feel it impossible to take any open part in the work of evangelisation

---

[1] That of Mr. T. Bruce, whose zeal and success in Bible Society work and in aiding the escape of refugees will be again referred to.

without running an unjustifiable risk of being forced to quit Italy altogether. They must keep in the background, content to direct the efforts of others and supply means for the enterprise without appearing in it themselves. While the freedom of the press was denied, it was their purpose to work hard in preparing translations of suitable books to be issued as soon as liberty was again given. Such were their hopes ; but before we inquire how, and how far these were realised, let us examine for a little the religious condition of the country, noting what was already done in the evangelical cause, and what materials lay to hand for the use of those who sought to win a further and wider acceptance for Protestant truth.

Even before 1848, while the press was still subject to control by the " Index," and no Italian was allowed to profess any faith but that of Rome, Protestants interested in the religious state of Italy found means to introduce secretly considerable numbers of Bibles and religious tracts. These were printed in Great Britain, put into the pockets or baggage of travellers, and quietly distributed where they were likely to do good. Messrs. Keith and Bonar, to whom we have already alluded, did something in this way while travelling to the Holy Land. Their ship touched at Leghorn, and they employed the time there in distributing books on the quay. The police—half ashamed of themselves—executed a brief arrest on the persons of these ministers, who were carried up to Florence for examination ; but truth has ever survived the operation of oppressive laws, and the good seed thus sown by many different hands produced its natural fruit in a harvest of conversion, which seems to have abounded in Tuscany above other places. These happy effects were seen among all classes of the people. The well-known Count Guicciardini, heir to an ancient and honourable Florentine name, was one of the first converts, and many others of every rank became Bible readers and inquirers after the way of life.

Two years after the Presbyterian Church was established at Leghorn, a new opportunity occurred for extending these efforts. The Pope granted a measure of liberty—a good example which was imitated by both Sardinia and Tuscany. Under this foretaste of the constitutional freedom soon to follow, the demand for Bibles in Leghorn became such that there was a difficulty in meeting it, and from that town the precious volumes were carried by those who purchased them into many parts of the interior. The edition of the Scriptures which was provided to meet this demand was that of the British and Foreign Bible Society, printed in 1841, which sold at three pauls (about 14*d.*) a copy. A translation of McCrie's "Reformation in Italy" also excited great interest, and was most useful in creating a demand for Bibles. One of the sergeants belonging to a regiment then quartered in Leghorn used to read it aloud to his comrades after mess; and Count Guicciardini came down to ask Dr. Stewart if something could not be done to give the book a yet wider circulation in the country—so valuable did he think it. About the same time a volume of " Protestant Discourses," containing among others a sermon by Chalmers, issued from the press in Florence, and had a good sale. As the censorship was now become merely nominal, advantage was taken of this favourable state of affairs to publish a number of useful books. One of these was a telling tract, with the title " Dove andate," and it is interesting to note that the Westminster Confession of Faith appeared in a translation executed by two young Scotswomen —the Misses Rae and Pate—who belonged to the Free Church Bible Class at Leghorn.

In all this we find history repeating itself very remarkably. When the Reformation dawned, and during the century which followed, many were the Italians who came under the power of the truth. All over the country societies were formed, based on the re-discovered principles of the faith, and graced by such names as those of Contarini, Nardi, Bruccioli, the Colonna, and many others. The reaction in favour of Romanism destroyed, indeed, this fair promise ; nor could much be hoped from the eighteenth century with its widely felt weight of spiritual indifference ; but when the evangelical movement had fairly developed itself in the countries of the North, and those under its power had scattered the good seed of the Word, as we have seen them do, then in more hopeful circumstances the former results

appeared as surely as if by the operation of a spiritual
law. Italy answered to the truth, and many converts
were made by the reading of the Word. As these
Protestants gained confidence, they began to draw
together; and little societies, in which may be seen
a real resemblance to those of the former age, were
gathered for the mutual reading of the Word of God.
Thus matters ripened rapidly towards the formation
of a regular Italian Protestant Church.

Much had been done to promote the movement
by Italian political exiles.[1] When the brief liberty
of 1848 shed its light on Tuscany, it was proposed
to send some of these men back to Florence, that
they might work there under the direction of an
"Italian Evangelical Publication Society," in preparing and printing editions of the Holy Scriptures
and other Protestant books. The reaction of 1849
hindered the accomplishment of this plan, and it
might have seemed as if once more Reforming truth
was to be suppressed and Papal error to triumph.
But a new force was now by God's providence in the
field. The Presbyterian ministers of Leghorn and
Florence, supported by a courageous band of office-
bearers and other workers, laboured with unwearied
devotion; and the maintenance of the good cause
under persecution, not to speak of its ultimate
triumph in the brighter days which followed, was

---

[1] Magrini and Ferretti are the names most frequently mentioned at this time.

due in no small degree to their continued and zealous efforts.

The most pressing duty was naturally that of securing for the country, against all opposition, a continued supply of Bibles and evangelical literature. It is true that Admiral Pakenham, an Englishman then resident in Florence,' and deeply interested in the Protestant movement, had just been banished from Tuscany upon the discovery of a store of Bibles in his house. Yet this plain warning of what might be expected at the hands of the Government only served to impress a salutary caution upon those who still endeavoured to make the truth more widely known. They fell back in the emergency with comfort and security upon the two Presbyterian stations ; and now was seen the practical wisdom of that appeal which had insisted upon the establishment of these as a foundation for mission work among the Italians. Leghorn, as the port of Tuscany, was charged with the duty of introducing Bibles into the country. Florence, central among the scattered groups of converts, presided over the distribution of these books.

Even the details of such a traffic are interesting, and we may find in them a vivid picture of times and scenes that have passed away, let us hope, for ever. The Bibles or other books, packed in bales like ordinary merchandise, were addressed, as "Stationery," to the Messrs. Henderson in Leghorn. They remained stored in the office of that firm, or in Mr.

Bruce's house, until, in small parcels or as single volumes, they could be gradually conveyed in the pockets of private passengers to Florence. As may be supposed, the Leghorn custom-house was a great hindrance to this traffic, and curious means were sometimes used to evade its restrictions. Thus when Trevier's " Reasons for Quitting the Church of Rome "—a book much used in the evangelical work —had been printed at London in an edition of 5,000 copies, 500 of these were made up by the publishers, Messrs. Partridge, Oakey & Co., into a firm bale covered with sacking, then with tarpaulin, and bound over all with iron hoops. When the steamer conveying this instalment of the book reached port, these precautions had their use ; for the bale was quietly lowered over the vessel's side, and towed to shore under water, thus escaping observation.

Many were the willing hands which helped in this work, and not a few godly women were of the greatest service in the way of conveying the books from Leghorn to Florence by rail. The task was one which had a certain danger in it, and curious tales are told of the narrow escapes that were sometimes made. One conscientious smuggler, after repeatedly passing the Florence custom-house with her pockets full of Bibles, was at last suspected and searched. What was her wonder and thankfulness to find that—of all days—this had happened on the very one when by some oversight (for which she had blamed herself on the journey) her usual cargo of

contraband literature had been left at home! This
is but one instance out of many which might be
given ; for often had those busied in the work reason
to thank God and take courage, feeling that He was
guarding their labours and making their cause His
own. The superintendence of what was done naturally remained in the hands of Dr. Stewart and Mr.
Hanna. Theirs it was to arrange and counsel and
direct, and a lively correspondence—carried on for
sake of security in a kind of jargon—passed constantly by private hand during these years of oppression between the Manse at Leghorn and the Scotch
minister's lodging at Florence. In these letters Dr.
Stewart is addressed as " Dr. Erskine," Mr. Hanna
as " Sir Girthon Anwoth," while " Bannockburn " and
" Kempenfelt " represent respectively Mr. Bruce and
Admiral Pakenham, and Bibles are alluded to as
" incorruptible seeds." In the Appendix will be
found a specimen of these curious letters.

The translation, printing, and circulating of these
books involved no little outlay of money. We are
now to ask whence these funds were derived, and
how they were applied to the work in hand. In
April, 1850, Dr. Achilli paid a visit to Edinburgh,
where a number of those interested in the religious
condition of Italy assembled to meet him at the
house of Sheriff Jamieson. Achilli was asked how
the cause of the gospel could best be served in his
native land. " Let Bibles and other good books be
circulated there by means of colporteurs,' he replied ;

and forthwith those present constituted themselves
into the "Italian Evangelical Publication Society,"
with the view of raising money to carry out this plan
of operations.   This was not enough ; for there must
be a corresponding society in Italy itself, composed
of men conversant with such work as was proposed,
who could both advise regarding the best manner
of employing the funds raised at home, and become
responsible for their application as might be directed.
Before the 26th of October a " Committee of Correspondence and Agency" had been formed for this
purpose in Tuscany, consisting of Dr. Stewart, Mr.
Hanna (who acted as secretary), Sig. Malan, and
M. Colomb.

There were many reasons which prevented the
Committee of Agency from being content to work
merely in the way of importing such literature as was
required, and these reasons were at last so cogent
as to induce them to attempt, in spite of prohibitive
laws, the production of Bibles and Protestant works
in Tuscany itself.   The dangers of a secret press were
great ; but even in this respect the enterprise com-
pared favourably with the constantly recurring risks
of importation through the various custom-houses ;
while as to positive advantages, those who promoted
it knew well the nation they had to deal with, and
calculated, not in vain, on the larger measure of
acceptance this literature of their propaganda would
win among the sensitive Italians if it could bear on
its titles the impress of Florence rather than that

of London or Edinburgh. In fact before the year was out a secret press was actually set up in the city of the Grand Duke, and poured forth an almost ceaseless stream of evangelical books. A volume of " Family Prayers," the " Companion to the Bible," and the " Scripture Catechism," were issued in this way ; and last but not least the invaluable " Pilgrim's Progress," for the translation and printing of which funds were furnished by Mr. Lenox, of New York, a constant and munificent supporter of the evangelical cause in Italy. Thus those who sought to establish their work against difficulty and opposition had reason to regard the problem as solved, so far as an abundant and easily accessible supply of Protestant books was concerned.

CHAPTER II.

THE VANGUARD.

"Enayma que nos aman la Santa Trinita,
  E lo proyme ; car Dio lo ha comanda :
Non sol aquel que nos fay ben, mas aquel que nos fay mal.
  *   *   *   *   *
  Car lo regne del cel li sere aparelha al partir d' aquest mont,
  Adonca aure grant gloria si el ha agu desonor."
  —*Nobla Leyczon.*

WE have already noticed the success which
attended the distribution of Bibles and other
Protestant books, the converts that were made, and
the meetings that began to assemble for the reading
of God's Word : each of them an incipient congregation. Those who had laboured long for such a result
could not at sight of it but thank God and take
courage. On this very account, however, they felt
that new efforts were demanded of them. Privileged
as they had been to supply the Scriptures to Italy,
they were bound to see that the ministry of the
Word according to a true and pure Church order
was not wanting to that country. But where was
such a ministry to be found ? Not among the con-

verts themselves, most of whom were, like the vast majority of the population from which they were drawn, men of little or no education. Those who thus made the cause of Protestant Italy their own certainly looked forward to the time when converts from every province should themselves serve their brethren in holy things ; but whatever change the future might bring, for the present this was impossible. Nor was it to be thought of for a moment that the Presbyterian ministers of Leghorn and Florence could themselves supply this want by acting as pastors to the converts. More than one reason made this impossible. We have already noted how delicate the position of these clergy was with regard to the Tuscan authorities, and how the work they did among the Italians had to be of a kind which offered nothing to attract the attention or provoke the interference of those in power. Not that the Government was itself so anxious to prevent them from interfering with the people ; for had this been the case, an excuse could easily have been found for requiring them to leave the country. The instincts of the Government were still in a measure liberal, and the vigilance they exercised over these Presbyterian stations was instigated by the Roman clergy. But Dr. Stewart and Mr. Hanna felt themselves bound on this account to use every precaution which discretion could suggest, and to refrain for the sake of the work itself from engaging too openly in it.

Another reason there was for this abstention,

and one even more native and prohibitive. This lay
in the jealous temper of the converts themselves.
Foreign aid they welcomed ; but any interference
on the part of foreigners they resented and refused, and this peculiarity had to be studied and
allowed for by those who sought their good. "The
principle on which this Mission is conducted by
us," wrote Dr. Stewart in 1851, "is that laid down
by Carlo Alberto, ' Italia farà da se,'—' Italy will
do for herself.' I have been long enough in this
country to know the feeling of jealousy and dislike with which the poor Italians regard anything
foreign, whether religion, politics, or bayonets, and
sympathise with it. It is by humouring not by
thwarting it that we are to do any good, and therefore we put those forward whose birth and nationality
can excite no prejudice, and we keep in the background and in a certain measure direct those who are
put forward. God has blessed this mode of acting in
Florence, and unless we would be summarily packed
off, as Captain Pakenham was, there is no other way
we can act here." The *non possumus* of the Scotch
pastors is thus fully accounted for.

Unable to entrust this task to converts who had
need to be taught instead of capacity to teach ;
equally unable to engage in it themselves ; where did
these leaders find the fellow-labourers and agents of
whom Dr. Stewart speaks : men of Italian blood and
speech, yet sound Protestants, and qualified to act
as shepherds to these scattered sheep in Tuscany ?

They found them where United Italy found her king—in Piedmont. From the valleys of the Waldenses, from the bosom of that ancient and apostolic Church, whose purity and constancy have won tributes of admiration even at the hands of her enemies and persecutors, there came at the summons of the Tuscan Presbytery those who, in spite of personal risk, stood in the front rank of the religious war, rallied their fellow - Protestants round the standard of the gospel, and led them even under the galling fire of persecution to the peaceful triumph of a bloodless victory.

In these days it was almost universally believed by the Waldenses and their friends that this people had never been " reformed," because they never needed reformation. Safe in their remote and sheltering hills, they had been privileged to keep pure and entire from the first ages the primitive apostolic doctrine. Recent speculation claims to have thrown doubt upon this pleasing tradition. We are now told that the Waldenses were not distinguished from the general body of the Church until the eleventh or possibly even the twelfth century. Then it was that Waldo and his " poor men of Lyons " became " reformers before the Reformation," gradually emancipated themselves from the growing corruptions of Christendom, and found a retreat from the heavy hand of those who could persecute as well as apostatise in the eastern valleys of the Cottian Alps. What concerned our Scotch ministers however was not the past history of the

Waldenses, interesting as are the problems which it offers, but rather their present condition, and above all their fitness to become God's instruments in feeding and guiding His little Italian flock. As to this last qualification there appeared to be no doubt. Of unimpeachable orthodoxy, holding a confession of faith which resembled in all essential points that of the Westminster divines, and living under a Presbyterian Church order, they were especially careful in the selection and training of candidates for the ministry; and last, but not least estimable, they had a character not uncommon among mountaineers at once honest and immovable, ruled by principle and tenacious of purpose. Everything seemed to mark out the Waldenses as instruments appointed of God for the Italian work.

As such did Dr. Stewart at least regard them. Interested from his earliest years in their romantic history as touched for children by the skilful hand of Mrs. Sherwood in her "Fairchild Family," he visited the Valleys in 1845, and kept up during the years that followed a constant correspondence with their leading men. One of the earliest letters indeed which he received in Leghorn was signed by the members of the Vaudois "Tavola," and contained a passage which we may render as follows: "We are truly grateful to you, dear brother, as well as to Mr. Henderson, for your proposal to write a book on the Waldensian Church, with the purpose of exciting an increased Christian sympathy in your fellow-country-

men for the Church to which we belong."[1] Such
being the relation of our first Italian missionary to
the ancient Church of the Valleys, we cannot wonder
that when circumstances arose which created a need
for fully qualified native workmen, he should as by
instinct have applied to his friends in the North for
this necessary help.

The man who was called to commence this work
in the South was Sig. B. Malan, of Torre Pellice. Dr.
Stewart had obtained from the Edinburgh Italian
Committee a grant of the necessary funds for his
support, and in October, 1848, he left the Valleys to
spend the few remaining months of liberty in preaching the gospel at Pisa and Florence. This visit,
brief as it necessarily was, gave the Tuscan converts
an opportunity of becoming acquainted with Sig.
Malan's gifts; and when the first severities of the reaction from constitutional liberty were over, and the
Protestants began to recover some confidence, Count
Guicciardini and Dr. Chiesi went in deputation to ask
the "Tavola" that Sig. Malan might again be sent
among them as their minister. This request was most
favourably entertained. Sig. Malan left Piedmont
in the spring of 1850, and proceeded to his post in
Florence by way of Leghorn; at which halting-place

---

[1] The book to which this extract refers was one of a series of
"Lectures on Foreign Churches," and appeared in May, 1845,
under the title of "The Present Condition and Future Prospects
of the Waldensian Church."

he was heartily welcomed by the Scotch congregation, and commended to God for the work of evangelisation in the solemn prayers of a communion Sabbath.

In a few weeks the Waldensian missionary was fully engaged in his interesting duties. Almost daily meetings were held from house to house, and two regular services every Sabbath. Soon the work assumed such dimensions that it could not be overtaken by one man, however devoted ; and accordingly another young Waldensian—Sig. Geymonat—was sent to Sig. Malan's assistance. This relieved him of the larger and more public meetings, leaving him free to use all his time and energy in visiting inquirers and converts in private, that he might build them up in the faith. Such abundant labours, so wisely divided and ordered, it pleased God to crown with plentiful fruit. " One of the converts," writes Malan on July 26th, " is in correspondence with a friar of Luther's order—the Augustinian—an augury of good." Even the Jews of Florence began to feel the rising tide of spiritual impression. Some of them were seriously affected by reading the letter addressed to Israel by " Rabbi " Duncan, and eight or ten came one Sabbath evening to the Waldensian pastor for instruction. Everywhere indifference was yielding to earnest inquiry, and the labourers in this interesting field only regretted that the *régime* under which they lived did not afford them larger opportunities than those they actually enjoyed.

Before many months a wider door of usefulness

was opened. The Tuscan Government had for long allowed Italian preaching in the Swiss Church at Florence for the Protestants of the Grisons and Ticino. In September, 1850, M. Drouin, the Swiss pastor, who had hitherto performed this duty, left Florence ; and the consistory invited Sig. Malan to supply the vacant place, so far at least as an Italian service was concerned, by preaching once a fortnight in that language. It is difficult to over-estimate the advantage which this invitation brought to the struggling cause of Protestant truth. In the opening of the Swiss Church to their pastor the converts found an opportunity of worshipping God openly according to their conscience. Besides, they could freely invite their Roman Catholic friends to this public service, though they dared not trust them with the secret of their more private reunions ; and who could tell what an effect the sight of an orderly, imposing gospel ordinance of this kind might have in the way of winning men to join the evangelical Church ? Such were the hopes with which this new aspect of the work was viewed by those who engaged in it ; nor were these hopes entertained in vain. From the first the audience was numerous ; the little church and its very vestibule were crowded with attentive worshippers, and it was reckoned that each Italian congregation was composed of not less than four hundred persons.

This new interest was not in the least degree prejudicial to those other departments of the work

formerly established; rather did they share in, and
benefit by, the access of zeal and courage which it
brought. In January, 1851, Sig. Malan had no less
than eight district meetings of the converts under his
charge—one of them outside the Romana gate. In
one or other of these there was a daily Bible-reading,
where the people put questions, the pastor gave ex-
planations, and all united in prayer.

One can imagine what care and sagacity were
required to carry on so extensive a work without
attracting the attention of Government. Dr. Stewart
noticed with alarm that various British periodicals
were publishing detailed accounts of what was being
done, and addressed warm remonstrances to the
editors, informing them of the sinister use which was
like to be made of their ill-judged communications
by those who were on eager outlook for records of
names and facts which might serve to put the fore-
most men in this movement under arrest. Danger
was felt to be in the air, and every means was used
to avoid it. Here is part of a letter which Sig.
Malan addressed to Dr. Stewart. It gives a vivid
picture of the nets and snares among which these men
moved. "I think it my duty to send you a word
or two about S. P. of P. . . . His look, his careful choice of words and sparing use of them, in short
something hard to express exactly, has left me in a
most unwelcome state of doubt regarding the purity
of his motives. I paid another visit to P[isa], and
saw Ch[iesi] and Gd. The latter gave me exact

information. . . . The man is a spy of the Government and the Jesuits, whom everybody is afraid of . . . he keeps up a constant correspondence with Rome." In another communication the same writer reported that a friar in disguise had come to one of the Protestant meetings in Florence, and added that the man had been warned never to do so again in case of compromising the work, but rather to go and talk with Sig. Malan privately. "Be cautious" was evidently the order of the day.

In spite of these precautions, most unwillingly adopted, the Protestant movement made constant and wonderful progress. This was due in great measure to the happy art of organisation possessed by the leaders, and used to set each new convert at work in gaining others. The means chiefly employed was the original one of colportage. "They are busy," writes Malan, "in circulating good books." The volumes most used at this time were (besides the Scriptures themselves) "The Shorter Catechism," "Barnes on the Acts," and the famous "Lucilla." This last book attained a great popularity. A priest was heard to say of it, "This is indeed powerful! I know not how we shall find an answer to it." But though the answer of sound reason was necessarily absent, that of force was always ready ; and before long the clouds which had been gathering and darkening, broke in a storm of sharp persecution on the infant Church of Tuscany.

Signs of what was impending had begun to appear

some time before the actual event took place. During the latter months of 1850 the sons of an Italian marquis were summoned, and warned by the police that they must no longer attend the Protestant service. But no decisive step was taken till the commencement of the following year, when the success of the Waldensian Mission became yet more distinctly marked. On Christmas Day no less than forty Tuscans openly abjured Romanism, receiving the Sacrament at Sig. Malan's hands in the Swiss Church. This, the Roman clergy felt, was too serious a matter to be overlooked. They demanded of the Government that the Italian service should be suppressed.

All now depended on the Grand Duke, and the Grand Duke, unfortunately, was a mere tool in the hands of the Jesuits. A complaint was accordingly made in proper form to the Prussian *chargé d'affaires* that the Italian services held in the church, for which his Government was responsible, were being conducted so as to give offence. They were too frequent, it was said, and the music was made too prominent a feature; in short, they must either be greatly modified or cease altogether. These remarks were communicated in course to the consistory, who very properly fell back upon their ancient rights, and refused to submit to any dictation in the matter. In this way the diplomatic "incident" fell out rather for the furtherance of the gospel, as the service thus gratuitously advertised was more largely attended than ever. On the following day however fifty Florentines were summoned before the police, and, on their refusing to promise that they would not again attend the Swiss Church, were formally served with interdicts which prohibited their doing so under pain of prison. Some were bold enough to tear up these papers openly, and soon all Florence was talking with sympathy of the "Evangelici," and the firm stand they made for liberty of conscience.

A new element in the case appeared within a few days, when the Prussian Envoy, on whom great pressure must meanwhile have been brought to bear, threatened to withdraw his protection from the Swiss Church if the consistory continued to authorise these services. Betrayed by one at whose hands they might rather have expected support, those who opened their place of worship to the Italian Protestants had no choice but to withdraw this accommodation from Sig. Malan and the converts. They flew their colours to the last, however ; and a moving sight it must have been when, on the last Sabbath of January, *gendarmes* entered with the morning congregation, and the Swiss pastor intimated that because of *force majeure* no Italian service could be held in the afternoon. Thus, amid general disapproval, in the expression of which even Roman Catholics were heard to join, this, the widest door of usefulness they had enjoyed, was closed to the evangelicals in Florence.

The meetings of converts in private houses still

continued, and were attended with an interest which
the sense of growing danger helped perhaps to in-
tensify. Nor was this interest confined to Florence,
or even to Tuscany. English papers—*The Times*,
The Globe, *The Record*, and *The Examiner*—took the
matter up, and told their readers how matters went
in the Tuscan capital. Mr. Hanna had just proposed
to collect and translate these notices, with the idea
that they might serve to encourage the converts;
when, perhaps in consequence of this foreign criti-
cism, the authorities in Florence were provoked to
a further step. The chief of police summoned Sig.
Geymonat to appear and undergo examination.
Fortunately for the gospel cause, this labourer in
it was not only an earnest evangelist, but a man
of courage and astuteness. Nothing of a seriously
compromising character was elicited by the officials,
and Sig. Geymonat was only warned to be more
careful in future, if he wished to be allowed to remain
in the city.

Every new event, indeed, made a further necessity
for caution felt. Sig. Malan, who, as we have already
noted, took charge of conducting the services held in
private houses throughout the city, resolved to give
up this duty as now too dangerous. He proposed,
instead of preaching by word of mouth as before, to
prepare a discourse, or other edifying matter, every
fortnight, which might be printed and circulated in a
thousand copies among the converts. Two numbers
of this periodical were issued. The first contained a

discourse on the Lord's Prayer; the second a collection of prayers for family and private use; and the secret press was busily producing this and other articles of evangelical literature, when, in the month of March, the Government, at an end of its patience under clerical pressure, struck a blow that was meant to be decisive.

Sig. Geymonat, though watched by the police, seems to have been considered by those in charge of the work as less obnoxious to suspicion than his fellow-labourer. It is certain, at any rate, that he began to take charge of the private meetings in Florence at the time when Sig. Malan withdrew from that duty. This change worked well for a time, but soon Sig. Geymonat learned that spies sent by the priests were dogging his steps. He took every precaution to avoid discovery that was consistent with the continuance of the work in which he was engaged. The places of meeting were constantly changed from the house of one convert to that of another. All however was in vain. One Sabbath the police, guided by an informer, found the evangelist holding a Bible-reading in the third storey of a house in one of the most retired streets of Florence. He had been invited to meet there with twelve young men who wished to hear the truth from him, and he sat, Bible in hand, expounding the words of Jesus, "I came not to send peace on earth, but a sword." "My friends," said Sig. Geymonat, "we must not expect things to go smoothly with us if we confess and follow Christ; we must be prepared for opposition, trial, and even imprisonment." At the very word entered a company of *gendarmes* with smiling faces (one wonders if their ears had caught the last sentence of the preacher), well pleased, it seemed, to have made out an undoubted case against one who had so long troubled them while he cleverly avoided capture at their hands. The meeting was hastily dispersed, and now indeed the sword of the law hung suspended over the evangelist's head.

During the week which followed, Sig. Geymonat worked with redoubled zeal. Knowing that the time of liberty would soon be gone, and anxious to make the best use of his freedom while it lasted, he held three or four meetings with the converts every day. Then came the summons; the short informal trial, and the sentence—one of exile from the Grand Duchy. Pending its execution, the convict was imprisoned in the Bargello—the common gaol of Florence; nor was he even permitted to return home for an hour to gather his effects for removal. Worse trials than this however were in store for him. On the second day of his imprisonment a person of prepossessing appearance entered his cell and commenced a conversation on religious subjects. This was done with no honest purpose, but with the design, it would seem, of obtaining information which might lead to the arrest of others; for the man was a detective, under whose charge Sig. Geymonat presently travelled comfortably enough to Pisa. At that place he began to experience more rigorous treatment. To the shame of the Government be it said that this preacher of the gospel, whose sentence was no more than one of exile, was confined there in the common prison with five felons, whose disgusting company he endured for three days. At the end of this time all were taken out, handcuffed together in couples, and marched in the maddening sun to Pietra Santa, under a military guard. At this last town Sig. Geymonat suffered his greatest trials. Those in charge of the prison were aware of the offence for which he endured banishment, and seem, like St. Paul's gaoler at Philippi, to have resolved on making his punishment as severe as they possibly could. The "inner prison" there was a low-roofed cell, hardly admitting a ray of light, and approached by a hole so small that the prisoner was forced to creep to his confinement on hands and knees. There he lay for some days in lonely darkness—an experience which raised his joy to a transport when at last he reached Spezia and found himself on the free soil of the Sardinian States. With all speed he travelled to Genoa, where Admiral Pakenham, himself a refugee from Tuscan oppression, received the young Waldensian most kindly in his villa at the Bernardino gate, and provided means for his return to the Valleys.

It would have been strange had the police of Florence been content to take one Waldensian and leave the other. When Sig. Geymonat was apprehended, Sig. Malan received his passport, accom-

panied with an order to quit the town within three
days.   This breathing-time afforded an occasion
which many gladly took advantage of to prove
their gratitude to the Waldensian Mission, and their
affectionate attachment to the persons of the missionaries. Sig. Geymonat indeed was not accessible—
the Bargello had him in ungentle keeping—but Sig.
Malan was still in his lodgings opposite the Pitti
Palace ; and the Grand Duke, had he cared to look
out of window, might have seen at any time during
these three days a constant *vai vieni* of citizens from
every rank of the people, paying their farewell respects to this representative of persecuted religious
liberty. When the term of grace was expired, Sig.
Malan carried home with him a letter of thanks
addressed to the Venerable Waldensian Table, and
signed by two hundred Florentines : so far was the
arbitrary action of Government from commanding
universal approval in the city.

CHAPTER III.

"Non disse Christo al suo primo convento:
  Andate, e predicate al mondo ciance;
  Ma diede lor verace fondamento.
  E Quel tanto sonò nelle sue guance;
  Si ch' a pugnar, per accender la fede,
  Dell' Evangelio fèro scudi e lance."
         —*Dante, Paradiso*, xxix. 109-114.

WE are now to trace the history of trying times, and it may be well that we should first review, as calmly as our feelings permit, the exact position which Tuscan Protestants occupied with regard to the law of the land and in view of the government under which they lived. We shall thus be able to appreciate at their true value the apologies which have been offered for the conduct of the Grand Duke and his police, and shall at the same time be prepared to understand what was done by the friends of religious liberty to secure toleration for those who needed it so sorely.

Let us begin by making the admission that in the Tuscany of these days no law existed expressly prohibiting freedom of conscience. Roman Catholic·

ism was of course the only form of religion recognised by the State ; but so far as the code went, a man might hold any religious opinion, or none, as best pleased him. He might even possess and use an Italian Bible without thereby incurring any civil pains. This is the fact relied on by those who try to defend the Grand Duke and his Government from the charge of religious intolerance which legitimately lies against them ; and it is disappointing to find Mr. T. A. Trollope, in his recently published "Reminiscences," repeating the same worthless plea—how worthless and how ungenerous we shall soon be in a position to judge.

This pretended liberty of conscience was in fact a mere empty name; for as soon as any one in Tuscany tried to avail himself of it, he came under view of the law, and exposed himself to its penalties. Any one might possess and read an Italian Bible ; but what value can we attach to that concession when we find that the law was invoked, and with too great success, to punish the man who ventured to make such an act possible by bringing the Italian Scriptures within reach of the Tuscans ? To introduce Bibles from abroad was contraband ; to print them within the duchy was prohibited ; there was not a copy of the Scriptures in a convert's hands but by the goodwill and courage of those who ventured to smuggle Bibles into the country in spite of the custom-house, and to print them there in spite of the police. Those who assert that Tuscans were free to

read the Bible must do so in face of the significant
fact that on the 18th May 1849 three thousand
copies of Martini's version of the New Testament
were seized by the police, and the circulation of the
Scriptures without note or comment was declared
illegal.

Waiving this preliminary question, and supposing
the converts in possession of Bibles, as in fact they
were, we ask how these could be used without breaking the law. They might be read, no doubt, but not
aloud nor in company ; or the reader became guilty
of an attempt to make proselytes, and as such might
be severely punished. Even in the bosom of his own
family the Protestant was not safe, and that "religious
liberty" which Tuscany enjoyed was too narrow to
avail a convert who might venture to conduct family
worship. His children had been baptised in the
Church of Rome, and Roman baptism was a rite
which carried in its benign bosom far-reaching con-
sequences of pain to those who dissented from the
religion of the State. Take the case of the Mortara
family, for example. These people were Jews, and
not Protestants, yet their sad story has a direct bearing upon the point before us. They lived in the
Ghetto of Rome, and employed, like many others of
their nation, a Roman Catholic maid-servant. This
woman, abusing the trust reposed in her, took her
charge—the infant son of the house—to a priest, and
had him secretly baptised. The boy was now claimed
as belonging to the Church of Rome, and, under

pretext of preserving him from being brought up in
Judaism, he was torn from his parents and removed
to Alatri, a remote town on the Neapolitan frontier.
When the unhappy father and mother travelled
thither, they were denied access to their child; and
even under the remonstrances of the Emperor of
France, who interested himself in the case, the Curia
stood firm to their point; only issuing an edict that
all Christian servants employed in the Ghetto should
immediately quit their situations—a measure apparently designed to remove them from the temptation
to get Jewish infants secretly baptised.

If such claims were made upon a case of clan-
destine baptism, it is not likely that less value
would be attached to the rite when celebrated in
the ordinary way, as it was in the case of the
Tuscan converts. But why, it will be asked, did
these Protestants not avoid the difficulty by keeping
back their children from Roman baptism? Even
had this been possible, it would not have met the
case of those who had children born and baptised
before they left the Church of Rome. But, in fact,
no other baptism than that of the Roman Church
was allowed by law to these unfortunate men. Had
they carried their children to a Waldensian pastor
or Scotch minister, they would have been punished as
proselytisers, and whoever performed the rite would
have been banished the country. Nor could children
remain unbaptised without enduring a life-long persecution. To secure admission to any school or

university; enrolment in the army, or honourable discharge from its ranks; entry to any trade or profession; at every turn of life, in short, the *fede di nascita*, or baptismal certificate, was required. It is not easy to see how the father of a family could live under these conditions; keep true to his Protestant faith, and yet escape the penalties of the law.

The same oppressive legislation shadowed every scene of life for these unfortunate people, who, we are told, enjoyed under the paternal government of the Grand Duke "full liberty of conscience." Did two converts desire to take each other as husband and wife, the rite of marriage, like that of baptism, could only be performed by a priest of the Roman Church, and the parties to it were bound to confess and receive absolution. So far indeed was this principle carried in practice, that a case is on record of a mixed marriage celebrated between a British subject and an Italian in the British Consulate, which was followed by the expulsion of the newly made bride and bridegroom from the town where they resided : the civil authorities alleging in support of this action that so bad an example of parties *living together without marriage* was prejudicial to public morals. If this could be ventured in such an instance, what mercy was the law likely to have for poor Italian Protestants in like circumstances?

Worst of all, the very deathbed of the convert was not free from this legalised revenge. Let us examine the typical case of Beretti, which happened

at Florence in 1856. He was an invalid, languishing
under the sickness of which he died, when it came to
the knowledge of the *curato* that he and his wife
had separated from the Church of Rome. Forthwith
began a long trial of the convert's constancy. Sisters-
of-mercy brought him delicate and nourishing food
such as poverty did not allow him to procure for
himself. They requested that he would consent to
see the priest ; and when he refused, they and their
dainties disappeared together. Finally, at the visible
approach of death, the *curato*, accompanied by two
other priests, entered the sick-room, where, in spite
of the patient's remonstrances, they remained for
several hours discussing the articles of the Roman
faith, and urging Beretti to return to his old obedience. Hardly were these gone, in high displeasure at
the convert's obstinacy, when two others came in and
attacked Beretti's wife, plying the poor woman with
arguments and entreaties, and meeting with the same
firm refusal. Next day the sick man died, thus escaping from further suffering ; but his wife was left in the
desolation of her recent widowhood to become the
victim of new tortures. Her first visitor was a priest
named Buratti, who had already put himself forward
in an evil cause by becoming a prominent and justly
dreaded accuser of the Protestants to the police. He
questioned the poor woman sharply, demanding why
she had allowed her husband to die without the
viaticum. To her assertion of the Protestant faith
he made the brutal reply, "Vostro marito è dannato

e voi sarete dannato con lui," and, sitting down at the table, wrote out and signed a formal repudiation of the corpse as that of a heretic which could not be buried in consecrated ground. This paper the widow had to take to the police, who abused her roundly, asking what she intended to do with the *cadavere dannato*, for they would certainly give her no help to remove it. Finding however that the poor woman stood firm, and threw on them the responsibility of allowing the corpse to remain unburied, they sent a cart under cover of night, upon which the body was removed to the dead-house. Thence it was presently cast into a wayside enclosure, lying rank and uncared for by the road to Bologna: a grim and forsaken spot used for the interment of suicides and unbaptised persons, yet, as we think, hallowed for ever by receiving the body of one who was thus "faithful unto death."

Another incident, which happened at Leghorn in 1856, shows in a remarkable way how far the Roman priesthood were prepared to press their claims in case of death. A member of the Scotch congregation in that city married an Italian lady belonging to one of the Roman Catholic families of the place. The marriage was first performed by Dr. Stewart at the British Consulate, and shortly afterwards repeated in Switzerland according to the Roman rite. Mrs. —— then became a British subject, and more, a true convert to Protestantism, showing her change of faith by attending the Scotch Church with her husband. While she was being prepared by Dr. Stewart to partake of the Communion for the first time, a fatal illness attacked her. The other members of her family, who were still Romanists, insisted upon the attendance of a priest, and when this was refused they informed the *Parroco*. As soon as Mrs. —— died, the priest sent to claim her body as that of a Romanist, and being informed of the mistake, he went to the Bishop, who demanded evidence that the deceased had become a Protestant. The Consul, when appealed to, refused to recognise the Bishop so far as to send him a certificate, but informed the authorities that he would go with his men the next evening to remove the body to the cemetery, and added that he would like to see who would venture to take it away! The Bishop telegraphed to Florence, and on the following afternoon a sergeant of police was sent to the house to announce that the funeral would be allowed to take place! When a firm use of Consular authority was needful to rescue the body even of a British subject from priestly interference, can we wonder that the poor Italian converts who enjoyed no such protection had much to suffer in their moments of sorrowful bereavement? A dying man was free according to that "liberty of conscience," so much insisted on, to profess his reformed faith; but the law obliged his medical attendant, when death drew near, to warn the rest of the family that they might summon the priest, and even to lodge the information himself should they refuse to

do so. One can readily understand then—and many
instances besides that of poor Beretti confirm the
conjecture—that the profession of another faith than
that of Rome in face of the parish priest with his
viaticum would be but the signal for an assault of
mingled solicitations and threats, entreaties to abjure
heresy, and assurances of pains to follow obstinate
persistence in it, by which the last hours of the Protestant might become a very agony of faith both to himself and his relations. They too, should they venture
so much as to support and encourage the dying man,
might be denounced to the police as proselytisers.
This crime of "proselytism" indeed it was of which
the clerical party made use to empty the "liberty of
conscience" which nominally existed of all real sig-
nificance, and to bring under penalty of the law any
and every Protestant, excepting only such, if such
there were or could be, who were content to hide
their faith in their hearts and act in every respect as
if they had it not.

It seems certain that the Government, while unable to resist the pressure put upon them by the
Church of Rome, had at least the grace to feel somewhat ashamed of the part they were forced to play
against their Protestant subjects. Publicity, such as
must result from a regular trial, was what they
desired to avoid; and accordingly on the 25th of
April, 1851, the Grand Duke issued an edict em-
powering the police to arrest on suspicion and local
judges to condemn summarily to prison or exile

without the delay and other unwelcome accompani-
ments of a formal process. It is too plain what use
might be made of this new power by men willing
to become instruments of clerical anger against the
Protestants. The mere possession of a Bible or
other evangelical book, much more any meeting to
read God's Word with prayer, might be construed
into an evidence of proselytism, and the persons so
engaged might without more ado be hurried off to
immediate prison or exile. That this is no fancy
picture of the state of things which existed in Tuscany, many facts attest beyond reasonable doubt or
question. We have already had occasion to speak
of Count Guicciardini as an illustrious convert to
Protestant principles. On the Government assuming
this threatening attitude, he, who might have tried
to temporise and to purchase safety by his wealth
and influence, made up his mind to seek no advantage for himself which his poorer brethren could not
share, and by a voluntary exile to find in some other
land the liberty which his own denied him. On the
eve of putting this plan into execution he happened
to meet with a convert named Betti, one with whom
he had been intimately associated in the getting and
circulating of Bibles. To him Count Guicciardini
mentioned his proposed journey, and added that he
would gladly come to pay a farewell visit at Betti's
house that evening. This he did, and not alone
either ; for he brought with him a convert named
Guarducci, who met him on the way. Magrini too,

another of those that sought the kingdom of God
secretly according to the reformed faith, came to
Betti's house; for, as he passed through the street,
he observed the others entering. Meanwhile Betti
on his part had invited three more—Solaini, Borsieri,
and Guerra—to bid Guicciardini God-speed; so that,
partly by design and partly by accident, six persons
in all were assembled with the master of the house.
The talk, as one can easily fancy, ran on what was
nearest these men's hearts—the state and prospects of
evangelical religion in Florence; and naturally too,
in view of Guicciardini's departure, they desired to
join once more in the worship of God. Hardly however had a Bible been opened, when the police, who
had meanwhile traced these men to their meeting-
place, broke in upon their devotions. Then occurred
a curious scene and a singular escape. Count Guicciardini had with him a copy of the Italian New Testament, and the proof-sheets of a work then passing
through the secret press; both of which he concealed
hastily beneath his waistcoat when the alarm was
given. The *gendarmes* searched the party, and,
coming to Guicciardini, requested him to undo his
waistcoat. With quiet composure he did so—button
by button—till his fingers touched the last, and all
was about to be discovered—a result which would
have placed the hidden source of evangelical literature at the mercy of the Government—when, as if
ashamed of his task, the officer of police turned away,
saying "Enough," and for a time the danger was past.

Again however in the prison, to which Betti and his guests were immediately hurried, their persons were searched; and again, as if by a miracle, the concealed pages escaped detection. When sentence was passed, the prisoners were given their choice of two punishments: either imprisonment for six months at Volterra or exile from Tuscany for a like period. Only one of the converts, Giuseppe Guerra, chose the prison; the others went into exile, to Piedmont or elsewhere. It was observed by those interested in the gospel cause that this sharp sentence had the happiest effect on two of those who endured it— Magrini and Guarducci. These men had hitherto been far from making a full profession of the reformed faith, and still less did they ever dream of suffering for it; but the circumstances in which their sentence left them made them study God's Word with a new and personal interest; so that they returned from banishment not merely confirmed Protestants, but ready to become zealous workers in the evangelical movement.

The case however which gained a European fame was that of the Madiai. It has been so fully dealt with in publications of the time that we need only give a hastily drawn outline of what happened: such as may be enough to show, in a palmary instance, how easily a charge of proselytism could be proved before the Tuscan courts. Francesco Madiai had been a courier, but was then retired from that way of life, and, with his wife Rosa, kept a boarding-house

in the Piazza Santa Maria Novella at Florence. These
people were converts to the gospel, and occupied a
somewhat important place among the Protestants of
the city; for, if we are to believe the accusation
against them, their house was one of those chosen
by Sig. Malan for the purpose of holding religious
services. The Waldensian evangelists had already
been driven from the city; but some facts which
came to the knowledge of the authorities seemed to
show that these meetings were still continued, and
on the 17th of August, 1851, the police entered the
house of the Madiai. Three persons, one of them
an Englishman, were discovered seated at a table
with Bibles open before them, and they, together with
Francesco Madiai, were immediately lodged in prison.
The arrest of Rosa Madiai was effected on the following day. Arthur Walker, the Englishman, was
set free almost at once upon an application from the
British Embassy. Two of the Tuscans—Manelli and
Fantoni—after lying for eight days in the Bargello,
were sent into exile as "accomplices"; while—to an-
ticipate by ten months the tardy course of Tuscan
procedure—it was at last found that the Madiai were
guilty of proselytism, and they were sentenced, the
husband to hard labour in Volterra, and the wife
to a house of correction at Lucca. After nineteen
months of suffering they were exiled from the duchy,
and we may here note a curious circumstance which
took place at the time of their release. The Government had given strict orders that it was to be kept

as quiet as possible, to prevent anything like a demonstration being made ; but in spite of all precautions the news was communicated to Mr. Macbean, the British Consul at Leghorn, who, accompanied by the chaplain, visited the exiles on board steamer, and conveyed to them a much-needed supply of clothing and other comforts. The chief of police at Leghorn tried in every way to discover how this information had leaked out, and failing to do so, made a direct appeal to Mr. Macbean, saying that his superiors had severely censured him for allowing the fact to become known, and that he was most anxious to learn who had told the Consul of it. Mr. Macbean however was quite unable, even if he had been willing, to throw light on the matter, as the communication made to him was an anonymous one.

Returning then to the arrest ; it is plain how suspicion was made to take the place of proof in the case of the Madiai. The police suspect—not without reason—that this household is deeply concerned in the work of evangelisation ; they watch the entry, and, when a favourable occasion offers, they attempt a surprise. But they are unfortunate in the time they have chosen ; no more than three persons besides the master of the house are met together; it is evidently, to judge from the official process itself, a mere friendly gathering of those who are already lost to the Church of Rome ; for, if the Madiai are proselytisers, and if Manelli and Fantoni are their accomplices, who pray is the victim of these

nefarious arts ?—not surely Mr. Walker ? and yet he
is the only other person discovered in the company
with them. But Bibles are on the table ; Protestant
works—some of them in several copies—are found in
the house ; there is a servant, too, of weak intellect
who has become a Protestant, evidently by the
solicitation of her master and mistress ; and so these
dangerous characters must suffer the penalty of their
misdeeds ! One can respect, without approving it,
the action of a Government which, conscientiously
deciding to hold illegal all forms of religion but
the one it approves, proceeds with impartial rigour
against heretics ; but far otherwise was it in the
Tuscany of 1851. On the Grand Ducal chair sat one
whose " Highness " was certainly not "serene" save
by courtesy, for he did not possess even the negative
merit of a consistent purpose, being by turns, when
left to himself, a foolish nonentity—the " Gran' Ciuco "
of the Florentines—and, when wrought upon by the
Jesuits that surrounded him, a despot filled with the
most relentless cruelty of all : that which springs from
religious fear. In 1850 he is all for liberty of conscience ; in 1851 he has a bad dream, of which his
spiritual advisers know how to make use : he sees
amid smoke and flames the figure of a beloved
friend apparently suffering the pains of purgatory.
How is it then that his prayers, and the masses he
has ordered, are ineffectual ? Those that have his
conscience in keeping tell him it is because Protestants are tolerated in his dominions ; forthwith follows

the edict of May, 1851, and next year the constitution is withdrawn. Religious liberty is not formally denied, indeed, but means are made available whereby converts may be arrested on suspicion, and dealt with summarily; and thus really, if not technically, to become a Protestant is to underlie the pains of the law.

We have examined sufficiently the relation of Protestantism to the laws of Tuscany, and have noted in this connection the first beginnings of persecution; let us now ask what efforts were made on behalf of the converts, and with what means and success the work of evangelisation was continued under these trying conditions. The places left vacant by the enforced departure of Sig. Malan and Sig. Geymonat were filled in a temporary way by two other Waldensian youths—Sig. Charbonnier and Sig. Torino, whom the "Tavola" sent to Florence that they might perfect themselves in the Italian language, and so be fitted for a wider usefulness as preachers of the Word. Dr. Stewart, who was the author of this plan, and had obtained funds to carry it out from the liberality of friends in Scotland, wrote to these young men in July, 1851, offering them salaries from the Edinburgh Italian Committee, if they would consent to act as evangelists among the Florentine converts. In declining this proposal for his fellow-student and himself, Sig. Charbonnier explained very honestly the difficult position in which they were placed. Sig. Torino had already been summoned before the police and cautioned : they were afraid of being banished from Florence before their purpose of acquiring Italian in its best form and accent was fully attained ; and for these reasons they could not venture to assume any official connection with the mission work in Tuscany. It was all the more to these men's credit that, while thus acting with what may seem exaggerated caution, they yet in practice did all that was required of them without fee or reward. The times rendered it impossible to hold regular meetings, but from their lodgings in the house of Bianciardi—a man connected with the secret publication work—these devoted evangelists visited the converts from house to house, learning Tuscan from those they taught, and in turn communicating to them the true language of heavenly things. In this way the scattered flock was fed until the recall of Sig. Charbonnier and Sig. Torino, which took place when they had spent but a few months in Florence ; yet not before an affecting scene was witnessed at a farewell service held in December, when Holy Communion was dispensed to twenty-two persons.

This constant change of labourers, inevitable as the circumstances of the case made it, was most unfortunate for the stability and progress of the work in Florence. The results would have been disastrous indeed, had not Mr. Hanna done all that prudence allowed to serve the converts as pastor while they were deprived of a native ministry. Much was also effected at this time by means of the secret press.

Restricted as the Scotch pastors were in their direct dealings with Italians, they here found a full occupation for their desires and energies ; while the converts themselves, to whom for the most part a vocal and personal ministry of the Word was wanting, nourished their souls in private on the literature thus provided, and were able at the same time to testify for their faith by circulating these books among their friends and acquaintance. A letter addressed to the Glasgow Ladies' Committee explains the way in which this branch of the work was carried on. Dr. Stewart and Mr. Hanna, aided by Italian literary men,[1] busied themselves in preparing and perfecting translations of suitable books. These, when they were ready for the press, were handed to one of the converts in Florence, who conveyed them secretly to the printer. So great were the precautions taken, that probably not even Mr. Hanna knew where the press was, or the name of the printer ; and certainly Dr. Stewart carefully kept himself ignorant of both. Thus, though the police were on the alert, and did on one occasion fall upon a store where copies of the various books were kept previous to distribution, yet the press itself was never discovered. Narrow escapes, however, were not uncommon. M. Colomb, the Swiss pastor at Florence, who, it will be remembered, was one of the Committee charged with this publication

---

[1] Such as Villari, now well known as the author of a most excellent life of Savonarola.

work, had in his house two hundred copies of an edition of the "Lucilla" printed in 1852. An alarm was raised that the police were at the door, when, without waiting to see if it were true or not, the panic-stricken man lost his judgment, and heaped the precious pages on his fire. How many readers, one wonders, would discover this curious incident in the veiled language which Mr. Hanna used to convey intelligence of what had happened to Dr. Stewart. Here is the extract: "Poor Mr. Dove was sadly frightened, and burned about a hundred of Mrs. Lucille's new dresses. Did you ever?" This incident, like many another, bears witness in a painful way to the conditions of fear under which the good work was carried on.

While efforts were thus being made to support and extend the agencies already established, those who were busied in this way could not overlook the persecutions to which the converts were subject, and the peculiar needs under which they lay on that account. Sufferings of the same kind had been endured shortly before by Portuguese Protestants in the island of Madeira; and Dr. Stewart took advantage of this by translating and circulating the touching accounts of these people's courage and constancy, that their Tuscan brethren might be animated to endure with a like resolution whatever they might be called on to suffer. But mere sympathy was not enough to meet the necessities of the case, and it was felt that no means should be left untried which might seem

to promise any alleviation or correction of the civil
disabilities under which these poor Italians lay.

Something of the sort was done in connection with
the notable case of the Madiai.   These "prisoners of
Jesus Christ" were as we know committed to gaol in
August, 1851, and lay in their cells untried and un-
condemned till June of the following year.   During
this time every means was used by friends of the
truth to give publicity to what had taken place.
Lord Shaftesbury came out from England, and, after
seeing Dr. Stewart at Leghorn, went on to visit the
Madiai in the Bargello, returning to give the weight
of his great influence in favour of the agitation which
had been commenced in Great Britain.   Yet this was
but a prelude to what followed.

When the servant of the Madiai, who it seems had
fallen conveniently ill, was recovered, and had her
memory refreshed by the present of fifty scudi and
five new dresses from the Archbishop of Lucca;
when, in a word, the trial took place, and the Protestant world was shocked to hear that, after enduring
ten months' imprisonment already, these converts
were sentenced, the one to three years and nine
months, the other to four years and eight months'
additional confinement; then indeed it was felt that
every effort must be made to undo what had been
done, and to prevent if possible the renewal of such
an outrage in the future.   An appeal was at once
taken to the superior court, and Mr. Scarlett, the
British *chargé d'affaires* at Florence, did all he could

with the Grand Duke on behalf of the prisoners.
All was in vain, however: the appeal proved unsuccessful, and the Madiai were sent to their places
of confinement in Volterra and Lucca. But the
general indignation instead of disappearing only
increased. Lord Palmerston, then in power, did not
indeed repeat Cromwell's gallant threat to make
British guns thunder in Italy on behalf of the
oppressed, but he imitated that example as far as
the sadly degenerate spirit of our times would allow
by ordering Mr. Scarlett to pay all the expenses
of both trial and appeal. In October a deputation
composed of several persons of rank and influence
left England for Florence to intercede with the
Grand Duke on behalf of his oppressed subjects;
and, that it may not be supposed that this feeling
was confined to Protestants, we may give ourselves
the pleasure of noting—to his deserved praise—that
a well-known Canon of Volterra interested himself
in the Madiai upon information conveyed to him by
Mr. Montgomery Stuart. This ecclesiastic was an
intimate friend of Pio Nono, having been educated
with him in the college of the Padri Scolopi under
Orselli and Inghirami; but in spite of his training
and position, he showed the most disinterested kindness to these poor people, visiting Francesco in the
prison of Volterra, and even undertaking the journey
thence to Lucca, that he might see Rosa and inform
her of her husband's welfare.

These efforts were not altogether in vain. They

had at least the good effect of encouraging the converts, and convincing the Jesuits, who surrounded the
Grand Duke and prompted his actions, that public
sentiment in Europe was against what had been
done.　But the immediate result was what might
have been expected, considering the want of tact
displayed in the conduct of the negotiations and
the character of the sovereign with whom they were
attempted.　The deputation had unfortunately contrived to offend Sir H. Bulwer, the British Envoy at
Florence, by ignoring his position altogether and
going directly to the Grand Duke.　They were
easily put off by that exalted personage with a few
fair words ; and, as soon as their backs were turned,
new measures—the fiercest and foolishest that a
weak rage and wounded pride could suggest—
were at once taken to make the situation of the
Protestants still more intolerable.

Even before this time the state of affairs had
suffered serious aggravation.　In January, 1852,
Florence was startled, not by a new dream of the
Grand Duke, but by an undoubted deed of darkness
which daylight revealed.　The Madonna's best neck-
lace, valued at 12,000 francesconi, had disappeared
from the Cathedral.　Here was another cause of
offence, which must be met, not by a new edict,
but by a sterner and more sweeping application of
the law already in force against Protestants.　It is a
sign of what was then done that a decided increase
took place at this time in the number of arrests

made among the converts; and this new onset of
persecution was not confined to Florence itself, but
spread, as by some ill infection of bigotry, throughout
the entire duchy. At Leghorn, for instance, a station
of carabineers was established on the first floor of the
tenement immediately opposite the Scotch Manse,
where a lieutenant and his men sat at the windows,
in constant outlook upon all that was done there,
and ready to arrest any Italians who might be seen
on their way to visit Dr. Stewart. But all this was
as nothing to what followed. About a month after
his capital had been relieved from the vexatious presence of the heretic deputation, the Grand Duke, to
purge Tuscany as it were from Protestant pollution,
published a law denouncing the penalty of death
itself against the unfortunate converts. This, it will
be said, was some sorry jest; but as regards the mind
of the ruler himself, it would appear that he actually
intended to carry out this grim revival of departed
horrors, for he at once proceeded with an admirable
consistency to appoint two executioners who should
deal with any whom the courts might convict under
the new statute. At the same time increased powers
were given to the prefects and sub-prefects of police,
who might now imprison for any period not exceed-
ing five years *without trial.* This of course was
intended to avoid that unwelcome publicity which
had made the Tuscan Government a gazing stock to
Europe in the Madiai case; and so immediately and
fully was it acted on, that in March, 1853, no less

than thirty Protestants were lodged in prison for offences connected with their religion.

It is remarkable how little effect these violent measures had in checking the life and progress of evangelical religion in Tuscany : another proof, were any needed, that persecution is a political mistake as well as a moral iniquity. For a fortnight indeed after the penalty of death had been denounced against them, the Florentine converts suspended their accustomed meetings for worship ; but soon their courage revived, and all went on as before. Religious services were held from house to house by Sig. Gay, a Waldensian student, for whose support Dr. Stewart procured means from the Edinburgh Committee, as he did in the case of former evangelists. Sig. Gay's short term of labour in Florence was marked by a circumstance to which we must again return. He was ordained as evangelist to the Florentine converts by the Free Church Presbytery of Italy, and thus received power to dispense the Sacraments ¦among them. Unfortunately he was recalled by his own Church some two months after his ordination, so that once more the care of the growing cause came upon the Scotch ministers.

We may take it as a proof of the faithfulness with which this sacred trust was discharged, that in the year following Mr. Hanna was warned by the Grand Duke's Government, through Sir H. Bulwer, that they suspected him of encouraging converts to come to his house, and otherwise aiding the spread

of heresy, and that this must cease. Instead of
ceasing, however, it continued, though under all the
precautions which Christian wisdom could suggest.
In 1855 one of the inquirers was "a most interesting Roman Count," who ended by embracing the
reformed faith. There was a difficulty in his case
which may be mentioned here, as it illustrates the
delicate questions with which these ministers had to
deal. He was a widower; and his deceased wife
had made him her executor. One clause of the will
provided that a sum of money should be devoted to
the payment of masses for her soul. We see the
new heart and tender conscience of the convert in
his question: "Can I conscientiously administer
this bequest, believing, as I now do, that there is no
such place as purgatory and no efficacy in prayers
for the dead; nay, that the mass is an abomination?"
His spiritual adviser gave him the wise answer that
Naaman got regarding the house of Rimmon, and,
like Naaman, this interesting character disappears
from our sight with the words, " Go in peace."

Dr. Stewart, fortunately, was left without interference—an immunity which he owed rather to his
residence at Leghorn than to any want of activity
on his part—and could thus render valuable service
in matters of the greatest importance which then
emerged. The first of these was the case of the
converts at Pontedera. This town is a place of some
importance, situated where the tributary valley of the
Era sinks gently into that of the Arno. The gospel

had gained a hearing there about this time, probably
by means of converts who came from Florence. The
chief name in the evangelical movement at Pontedera
(would that it had never lost its honourable importance!) was that of Scipione Barsali, the carpenter and
theatre door-keeper. In October, 1854, he came to
the Manse at Leghorn, pleading the case of a poor
Protestant family in Pontedera who were in actual
destitution since their father, Eusebio Massei, had
been cast into prison on account of his religious
principles. Dr. Stewart sent Barsali on to Mr.
Hanna, as it was he who kept the Committee's purse,
giving him at the same time a letter of recommendation to the treasurer. Mr. Hanna had just received
his warning from the Government, and was obliged
to dismiss Barsali for the moment without seeming
to pay much attention to his plea. Shortly afterwards
however he sent money to Pontedera for the support of Massei's family : an act which involved the
cause in grave difficulties. Landucci, the Tuscan
Home Secretary, heard what had been done, and
sent at once to complain to Lord Normanby, the
new British Envoy, that Mr. Hanna was bribing the
Italians to become Protestants. Here we have
another exhibition of the crooked ways in which
Rome led the Tuscan Government. They reduce a
poor family to beggary by imprisoning the bread-
winner as a Protestant, and then pretend that converts
are bought, because these innocent sufferers receive
aid from Great Britain ! Mr. Hanna made a satis-

factory explanation at the Embassy ; but the natural result of this repeated interference was to throw the charge of Pontedera and the Protestants there almost entirely upon Dr. Stewart. It will be readily understood that the persecuting spirit of the Government made that charge a heavy and an anxious one.

In the autumn of 1855, just a year after Massei's imprisonment, a process was instituted against no fewer than sixteen inhabitants of Pontedera who were accused of Protestantism. This sweeping measure occasioned a petition to Lord Normanby, signed by twenty-nine persons of the place, asking that the British Government should interfere on the converts' behalf. Acting upon this appeal, Lord Normanby obtained from the Tuscan Government an assurance that the process should be stopped ; but after a few months' delay, intended to blind those who were taking so troublesome an interest in the case, prosecution was resumed under the Prefecture of Pisa, and was directed by the relentless hand of Cardinal Archbishop Corsi, who openly expressed his determination to make an end with these heretic inhabitants of his diocese. Corsi appointed a synodical visitation for the month of April, 1856 ; and in the searching series of questions drawn up by him for the use of the parish priests in preparation for his coming, we see the net that was spread to catch, if possible, all the converts in Pontedera. "We cannot escape," writes one of them to Dr. Stewart ; and again, " all we evangelicals of Pontedera appeal to your wise counsel ; do what you can to obtain from the Tuscan Government our freedom to enjoy gospel ordinances."

It will be readily believed that such an appeal was not made in vain. The minister who at this very time sent home the joyful news that his own servants had turned Protestants, and that he was giving them daily instruction in the hope that they might yet become the nucleus of an evangelical congregation in Leghorn, was not likely to neglect the converts at Pontedera. But it was doubtful what plan of action afforded the best hope of success. Should recourse again be had to the Embassy at Florence ? This indeed was done, and at once ; but Lord Normanby could not see his way to effect or even to attempt anything till the process was concluded and sentence actually pronounced. Then, said he, something may be tried in the way of getting the penalty modified or remitted. Dr. Stewart was not content to wait so long, nor was he satisfied that the proposed line of action was the right one. He had set his heart upon no capricious toleration, granted to this case or refused to that, according to the activity or supineness of British Envoys in troubling the unjust judge of Tuscany ; but upon a large, wise, and well-founded measure, which should recognise the ten thousand Protestants of the duchy (for to that respectable number they had now, even by their enemies' testimony, attained), and should allow them such religious liberty as was enjoyed—say by the Jews—under this very government. The means which its promoter hoped might be effectual in winning this measure for Tuscany was a serious and pointed remonstrance from the Government of Great Britain. A title to interfere, he thought, might be founded on the fact that religious liberty was granted to Romanists by that Government, whether coming from abroad or changing their faith at home ; and that such interference might be the easier, he proposed that a memorial to the Foreign Office in London should be signed by the Tuscan Protestants, detailing their disabilities and the persecutions they suffered for their faith, and asking the Government of Great Britain to obtain for them that freedom in the worship of God which they conceived to be their right.

Various circumstances contributed to deprive this well-laid plan of the success it deserved ; and in order to see how this came about, it is necessary we should remark that a plague of Plymouthism had already affected the Protestants of Tuscany. Less than six months after Malan and Geymonat had been banished from the duchy, three Englishwomen, who held more or less strongly these peculiar opinions, came to reside in a villa at no great distance from Florence ; interested themselves in the evangelical work, and, very naturally, endeavoured to turn what was doing in the direction which they had themselves been led to prefer. This they were the more easily able to do as the converts were inexperienced in Scripture, and at the particular time we are considering—August, 1851—were deprived of the pastoral care which Mr. Hanna gave them; as he was then absent in Scotland. To such a length were matters carried that, one Sabbath, Miss Johnstone—the eldest of the three Plymouth sisters—assembled some of the converts at her villa, and actually dispensed the bread and wine of Communion to them with her own hands. Dr. Stewart had early notice of what was being done, and a number of matters to which we have already alluded, were undertaken with the view of correcting these disorders. The volume of Family Prayers was hastily brought out, and Barnes' Notes on John 15th were hurried through the secret press, as well as some other treatises on Church government which it was conceived might arrest the growing evil. Application was also made to the Waldensian Church to ordain one or more of the students they sent to Florence, and on this being refused, the Free Church Presbytery, as we have seen, took the extraordinary step of themselves ordaining Sig. Gay, believing it absolutely necessary in the circumstances to secure in this way an orderly administration of the Sacraments among the converts.

This unfortunate collision raised a natural, if considerable, degree of heat in the feelings of both parties. What Mr. Hanna describes as a *burrasca*, or "row," took place at one of the meetings of converts held in Florence towards the end of 1853. Sig. Gay had dispensed Holy Communion to the congregation, and at the close of that ordinance Miss

Johnstone congratulated him on having come over to her way of thinking. "Not at all," he replied ; " do you not know I have received ordination from the Presbytery?" On this Miss Johnstone set herself to alienate the converts from his ministry, and began to conduct an opposition meeting. Such being the state of affairs, it will be readily understood—to return to the proposed memorial—that when Dr. Stewart brought forward his plan, there were some who viewed it with jealousy and suspicion merely as coming from the chief promoter of that Church order which they denied and opposed. Unfortunately too there was something in the proposal which —little as its author suspected or intended such an offence—was capable, one now sees, of being interpreted in a way quite fatal to its success with people who in the fervid force of their late revolt from Rome were ready to go too far in the direction of individualism and the repudiation of even a simple and scriptural form of Church government. The obnoxious word which proved such a stumbling-block was " Patriarch " ; and if any one wonders how it came to be employed by Dr. Stewart, there need be no difficulty in satisfying so natural a curiosity. He was anxious that the converts, in approaching the British Government, should breathe no mere vague aspiration after liberty of conscience, but that an express and feasible scheme for securing at once the rights of the Government and the liberties of individuals in religious matters should be sketched out ;

which the British Government, if they approved it, might press for acceptance on the authorities of Tuscany. In looking about to find an actual instance of what he desired, Dr. Stewart thought of Turkey, and of the liberal treatment which the Armenian subjects of the Porte met with at the hands of that Mohammedan power. "They are represented," he told the Tuscan converts, "by a Patriarch, who is responsible for them with the Government, and under that sensible arrangement they enjoy full religious liberty." "Do you," said he, "ask the British Government to propose that you be allowed to elect from among yourselves a similar official, who may in like manner be accepted as your representative with the Grand Duke." No one who considers the matter calmly and without prejudice can fail to understand the honest meaning of this proposal, which was as far from aiming at any ecclesiastical tyranny as it was earnest in seeking the removal of civil pains ; and when we add that Dr. Stewart wrote to Count Guicciardini, saying that he had thought of him as the first representative of the converts, it will be seen that there was no want of a tolerant charity either, for by this time that nobleman had identified himself with the Plymouth party. All however proved in vain. The leaders of the opposition had little difficulty in persuading the converts who adhered to them that the proposal aimed at the re-establishment of a hierarchy over them, such as that of the Armenian Church, while with those who refused to be thus

hoodwinked, the argument of fear was employed with
the worst effect. They were told that to sign a
memorial would be to mark themselves out for fresh
persecution : that the police would then have no
difficulty in knowing whom to arrest ; and that a war
of absolute extermination, with exile or even death
as its issue, would immediately be proclaimed against
all within the duchy who should thus denounce themselves as Protestants. We should err indeed were we
to suppose that all the converts were thus deluded.
Many were anxious to sign the memorial, and especially was this true at Pontedera, where the evangelicals
unanimously approved of the plan ; though one Fab-
broni, a Florentine convert, had written to dissuade
them from this course of action. But it was felt that
unless a large majority of those concerned were willing to give their names, so that the memorial might
be a true index of the strength of Protestantism in
the duchy, it could not be successful, and should not
be persisted in. Acquiescing then with regret in the
only course left open to him, Dr. Stewart abandoned
the plan which at one time promised so well for the
interests of the suffering Protestants of Tuscany.

Fortunately there was still much to cheer those
who had suffered this disappointment. At Leghorn, for example, the evangelical movement was
making a gratifying progress, and already a semi-
public service was organised there under the care of
Sig. Comba, the Waldensian pastor who had been
put in charge of the infant congregation : a little

household of faith which numbered at this time some
eight or ten communicants. The political world too
offered encouragement to those who then watched
the signs of the times with a view to the interests of
Italian Protestantism. They had dreaded a concordat
between the Pope and the Grand Duke of Tuscany
which would have bound the latter potentate to excel
his former efforts against heresy in his dominions.
The Grand Duke, in fact, left Florence for Rome with
the purpose of signing this agreement ; but shortly
after he arrived in the Eternal City, a change came
over the political horizon, caused by the proposals
which were then issued from Sardinia. At the same
time the Austrian ambassador concurred with
Baldasserone, the Tuscan Minister, in advising that
the concordat should not be signed : telling the Grand
Duke what an annoyance his Government had found
it. The Grand Duke accordingly—to the high
satisfaction of his Protestant subjects—returned to his
capital without entering into any agreement with the
Pope. A public entertainment of great splendour
was given in the British Embassy at Florence on this
occasion. The Grand Duke was there, and the
Papal Nuncio ; who might almost have overheard
some whispered words which passed between the
host, Lord Normanby, and Mr. Hanna on the subject of Pontedera and what was doing there. That
little congregation of faithful souls seems to have
profited by the persecution it suffered ; for its
members showed a ripeness for regular organisation

which had not appeared before. They met and elected three elders, two deacons, an assessor, and, for pastor, Dr. Tito Chiesi, a respected advocate of Pisa. This was a great encouragement to Dr. Stewart in his labours to win liberty for those who thus began to show themselves deserving of it.

Forced to give up the hope of having a memorial signed by Italian converts, Dr. Stewart still sought to reach his purpose by other means, and proposed that his own Church should approach Government on the subject. Sheriff Cleghorn drew up an able and temperate memorial of every important case of persecution which had occurred from the withdrawal of liberty to the year 1856, and this was signed by many both in the Free Church and out of it ; as witness the names of Lord Shaftesbury and the Primate of England, which stand in support of the appeal. It cannot be said that Lord Clarendon, to whom this memorial was addressed, showed the interest in it which might have been expected ; but he forwarded the document to the Embassy at Florence, with instructions to do whatever might be possible in the circumstances. The very fact that the British Government had taken the converts' case into consideration no doubt had its influence in procuring for them that alleviation in their hard condition which began to appear about this time and continued till the days of liberty dawned. During these years occasional arrests were made, and one sentence of eight months' imprisonment was passed ; but an unwonted restraint certainly began to mark the proceedings of the police. Inflammatory harangues were delivered from the pulpits, the people were encouraged to mob their Protestant neighbours, and then the prefect stepped in to arrest those whom he ought to have protected. Such were the new tactics employed against the evangelicals, who, when arrested, generally suffered banishment from the town or village where they lived for a few days under pretence of public order. Here was certainly a great and welcome change from the old heroic times when any excuse was enough to condemn a convert to actual exile or lengthened imprisonment.

Nor should we overlook the fact that even those measures which were now used, contrary to law and still more to justice as they were, had in some cases at least been provoked by the attitude of the converts themselves. This remark applies to an arrest more vexatious than serious which occurred at Leghorn during 1856. Two Waldensian schoolmasters—Sig. Costabello and Sig. Giordano—had reached that port, *en route* for Florence, where they intended to perfect themselves in Tuscan. The custom-house officers found Bibles upon them; and after being detained for three days in prison they were sent back to Piedmont. This unfortunate affair was the result of gross imprudence on the part of those whom experience should have taught to be more careful. An evangelist in Genoa, himself it seems an exile for his religion, had asked the young men to convey these

books to friends in Florence, forgetting that the
errand they were on should have excused them
from being exposed to such a risk. Worse than this
however, another convert had entrusted them with a
letter to Dr. Stewart. It is needless to say that had
the police fallen upon that, which providentially
they did not, the result would have been most serious
for the Scotch Church, and the work which it supported.

Not long afterwards, a letter was actually discovered and opened while passing by rail between
Leghorn and Florence. The police thus had information enabling them to seize a number of Bibles
which a canal-boat was conveying to Miss Johnstone.
The curious in such matters will value Mr. Hanna's
cryptographic communication of this incident to Dr.
Stewart. "Have you heard," he says, "that a letter
from גימינאני to בארסלי has been opened on the
rail ; and, in consequence, soap sent by a canal-boat
to the she-bread-breaker seized ? "

A more direct culpability too marks the occasion
of an arrest which took place at Pontedera in 1857,
when four converts were banished from the town for
eight days. It appears that the evangelicals in that
place had most unwisely given offence to the civil
and religious authorities by boasting openly of
British protection afforded them through the ambassador at Florence and the "Scotch Priest" at
Leghorn. We cannot fail to note however, even
from these incidents, a decided change in the con-

dition of the converts, and also the direction in which their gratitude looked while they gave thanks for their improved position. Others too were of the same way of thinking; for when the Pope visited Florence a few months afterwards, he put a marked slight upon the British Ambassador; to show, it was believed, how he resented what had been done on behalf of the Tuscan Protestants.

The days of active persecution then were over; but a curious mistake happened in 1859, which for a moment made some Florentine converts believe that the good old times of the handcuff and the cell had returned. They were met in some considerable number at a private house for the purpose of holding a religious service; and when they left the dwelling, what was their amazement to find a company of *gendarmes* at the door ready to conduct them to prison; while the officers of justice on their part were no less astonished at the mistake they had made. It appears that a family of Neapolitan refugees had taken rooms in the flat immediately above that in which the Protestants were assembled, and, being of strongly Nationalist opinions, had hung out from their balcony a board bearing the significant word "Verdi"—not, be it understood, in homage to the popular composer of that name, but as a political manifesto; for all over Italy in those days "Verdi" was the accepted abbreviation for the name of the coming king— *Vittorio Emanuele Re D'Italia*. Misled by this

sign, the police had supposed that the meeting which
assembled under it bore a political, not to say a
revolutionary character. It is hardly necessary to
add, that when a few words had explained everything to the satisfaction of the authorities, the
converts were allowed to depart quietly to their
homes.

We should expect to find that with less to fear the
Protestants of Tuscany would show some decided
advance, and that the evangelical cause in that
country would make distinct progress. So in fact
it was. The Manse at Leghorn formed in these days
a rendezvous for many who there received spiritual
nourishment. Gimignani, the leader and catechist
of the Leghorn converts, was under Dr. Stewart's
regular instruction along with two others ; the little
congregation in the city had doubled its membership ; and, in spite of the danger which attended
such an act, a day was appointed—the 11th of June,
1857—on which the converts from Pontedera were to
assemble in the Manse, that Dr. Stewart might celebrate Holy Communion with them. He felt it impossible to refuse this service, great as the risk was,
if he was still to dissuade these people from following
the Plymouth way and *breaking bread* among themselves.

Plymouthism indeed began sensibly to decline
from the time when the adverse circumstances
which had fostered it in Tuscany gave way to more
free and healthy conditions. We have remarked

what gratitude was felt by the converts for British interference on their behalf, and it may well have been that a feeling of the opposite nature animated them towards those who had done all in their power to prevent any such action being taken. This change of temper became at length so marked that in 1858 there were distinct signs of a purpose among the Florentine converts to range themselves under an orderly Church government. The Plymouth party naturally opposed this tendency, and Count Guicciardini wrote an irenicon which veiled under certain concessions a position substantially unchanged ; but a majority of the converts were determined to carry out their new ideas of what was fitting, and, separating amicably from the rest, they formed themselves into a regular Protestant congregation.

Taking then a brief review of these ten years' labours in Tuscany, what results do we find ? Many thousand Protestants, not entirely free from Plymouthism indeed, but beginning to shake it off, organised congregations at Florence, Pontedera, and Leghorn, besides many scattered groups of converts in the villages ; persecution nearly given up, though by no good will of the priests, who go in deputation to the Government, but get this answer to their complaint, " What can we do with eight thousand people ? " a press ever active and of late preparing to issue a new edition of the Italian Bible in four thousand copies ; and, not to speak of Waldensian and Tuscan evangelists, two Scotch Ministers at

Leghorn and Florence, through whom all this varied evangelical work is kept in closest and most helpful relation with the sympathetic and liberal Protestants of Great Britain and America. Truly all interested in this wonderful movement had reason to say, like the Psalmist : "The Lord hath done great things for us, whereof we are glad."

CHAPTER IV.

"THE HOUSE OF MY FRIENDS."

" E come donna onesta, che permane
  Di sè sicura, e per l' altrui fallanza,
Pure ascoltando, timida si fane,
  Così Beatrice trasmutò sembianza ;
E tale eclissi credo che in ciel fue,
  Quando patì la suprema Possanza."
—*Dante, Paradiso*, xxvii. 31-36.

THE difficulties and dangers to which the gospel cause was subject in Tuscany made those who promoted it seek other fields, where their labours might at once be less restricted and more fruitful. One of the earliest chosen lay at a great distance, being no other than the ancient capital of the Eastern Empire, now the city of the Porte. In Constantinople there was a population of some thirty thousand Italians, who lived there under a government which would offer no opposition to any work of evangelisation among them; and this city was already the seat of British and American Missions, the members of which would readily hold out helping hands to any one who might be sent to co-operate with them

94

in preaching the gospel. Dr. Stewart pressed these points upon the Italian Associations of Edinburgh and Glasgow, and in the latter months of 1851 the Glasgow society united with that of London to carry out this project. Means being thus provided, the man was not long of making his appearance in the person of Sig. Torino : the same evangelist whom we have already noted as engaged in the work at Florence. Before many months of 1852 had passed, he was fairly settled in Constantinople and ready to commence operations there.

Favourable as this new field might seem, there were notwithstanding many difficulties to be met with in it ; some of which bore a serious character. The influence of the Jesuits, for instance, had to be reckoned with as a strong opposing force. That order, since its suppression by Clement XIV., had been forced far afield. The events of 1847–48 made its members seek firmer establishment in such widely separate spots as Belgium and Constantinople; and in consequence of the Catholic reaction of 1850, they seem to have occupied the latter place with such vigour that their pretensions and efforts formed a real hindrance to evangelical work among the Italians there. What gave the greatest trouble however was the temper of these Italians themselves. A large proportion of them were political exiles, of whom one cannot think without remembering Ovid at neighbouring Tomi ; for they, like him, languished out their lives and sang their "Tristia" in the deferred and

heartsick hope of return to their beloved Italy. These
men were afraid of attending a Protestant service,
lest by so doing they should come under the unfavourable notice of their Consulate, and so find
additional difficulty in obtaining passports for home.
Sig. Torino did all he could to meet their difficulties and smooth their path, holding little gather-
ings of two or three together, and studying in every
way to avoid attracting the attention of those who
might regard what was being done with disapproval.
Soon however he found that the gospel had a serious
rival in his hearers' hearts, occupied as they were with
the cause of Italian liberty and with republican
schemes. "What is the use," said they, "of coming
to tell us of conversion and of judgment to come?
We have heard that a thousand times. But speak
to us of the social and civilising power of the gospel,
and you will find an echo in all our hearts." A
strange recantation surely this of the Saviour's words,
"Seek ye first the kingdom of God and His righteousness, and all these things shall be added unto
you."

In spite of these discouragements, Sig. Torino
laboured bravely on, holding a regular service attended by some fifteen Italians, and conducting a
school for their children, which had a much more
apparent success. But the time drew near when this
position in the gospel campaign, so wisely chosen
and fortunately occupied, was to acquire a new and
unlooked-for importance. The Crimean War broke

out ; the allies were joined in their expedition by a
number of troops from Sardinia ; Duncan Matheson,
well known as "the Sardinians' friend," came with his
Bibles and Catechisms, and in a moment the Italian
evangelist at Constantinople, who began to think his
labour in vain, found a wide door of usefulness
opened to him in the hospital and the troopships.
Dr. Stewart, when he urged the establishment of this
station at Constantinople, had from the first reckoned
on the reflex influence of work done there upon the
Italians at home ; but he could hardly in his most
sanguine moments have foreseen how largely the
enterprise was to be rewarded. A most favourable
impression of Protestantism was produced in the
minds of the soldiers by the care and kindness which
the evangelists spent upon them ; and, returning to
their own country, these men carried in their knap-
sacks copies of the Scriptures and other religious
works which must have been as lights in many a
dark place where otherwise they could never have
come. What a stroke was it, and what a success, to
turn these troops into an army of Italian colporteurs !

But there was a land lying much nearer Leghorn
than Constantinople that offered an even more
tempting field for the good seed. Piedmont, from
which came most of the troops we have been speaking
of, formed part of the free kingdom of Sardinia, and
presented a much better opportunity for evangelical
work than could be enjoyed under the despotism
which reigned in Tuscany. It was—in its western

valleys—the home of the Waldenses ; and when, in
1848, Sardinia received a liberal constitution, this
charter of national rights was accompanied by an
express edict of emancipation passed in favour of
that ancient Church.   The Waldenses had suffered
bloody persecution and bitter exile in past ages ; and
from the days of their "glorious return" to their
native valleys in 1689, they had lived under the
closest restraint.   Now however they were free, nor
can even the coldest heart read without a thrill of
sympathetic emotion how on that day of triumph and
thanksgiving, when the streets of Turin were crowded
in celebration of the new Constitution, universal
acclaim called the Vaudois to the van, and " Evviva
i Valdesi, Evviva l' Emancipazione !" was the loud
homage of a thousand tongues to the time-worn
banner of the mountaineers as it came proudly on,
floating at the procession's front.   Here then was a
neighbouring land whose constitutional liberty was
invaded by no reaction of tyranny, where Austrian
influence counted for nothing, and where a native
Church, strong in the purity of her principles and
the antiquity of her establishment, was now free and
ready to take the field in the gospel cause.   Everything seemed to point to Piedmont as a place where
much might be done to deliver men from the fetters
of Rome.

Progress was soon made in the direction just
indicated.   Urged by the indefatigable Beckwith, the
Waldenses advanced to Turin ; took possession of

the capital, securing it as a legally recognished parish
of their Church; and, aided by contributions which
flowed in freely from all quarters of the evangelical
world, erected there an imposing sanctuary, which
was opened for Divine worship with great solemnity
in the month of December, 1853. The real importance of this advance is to be measured, not by the
magnificence of the building erected, but by the fact
that, on Christmas Day immediately succeeding, no
less than one hundred converts from Romanism were
there publicly admitted to communion with the
evangelical Church—a truly noble testimony to the
zeal and ability with which during the two preceding
years this mission had been conducted by the Rev
G. P. Meille.

It is most gratifying to note that what took place
in the capital was only a somewhat favourable sample
of the work going on at the same time throughout
Piedmont. At Nice, on the French frontier, a Committee, consisting of many influential persons and including Count Egloffstein, Chamberlain to the King
of Prussia, had begun as early as 1849 to take charge
of the evangelical movement in co-operation with
the London Association. Here again the Jesuits
were busy; but in spite of their opposition, a Bible
Depôt was established in the English Pharmacy,
kept by M. Paulian, and much was done by means
of colportage both in town and district. Two years
later several evangelists were at work in that part of
the Riviera, one of them being that very Betti who

had just been exiled from Tuscany with Count
Guicciardini and his companions. In 1853 the
Waldenses came on the field, and not a moment too
soon, as Darby himself had paid a visit to Nice, and
even succeeded in winning over some of the Evangelical Committee to his peculiar opinions. Sig. B.
Malan was settled as pastor in the town upon a
petition addressed by the Committee to the Table;
and Dr. Stewart, who had a principal hand in promoting this, obtained an annual grant of sixty
pounds from the Glasgow Association as a contribution to his support. The appointment was speedily
justified by its results. Audiences of a hundred
and fifty people began to assemble in the Mission
Church; converts were made, and the colportage
work was pushed along the coast as far as Oneglia.

A still more important advance was that which
secured Genoa as the centre of new operations.
When Admiral Pakenham had to leave Tuscany, he
took up his abode in that town, and continued to
work with zeal and success in the good cause. The
first evangelical meetings were held in a small "upper
room" over the Admiral's lodging on the sixth floor
of a house just outside the arch of the Acquasola.
Finding how important the position was, Pakenham
united his appeal to that which Dr. Stewart had for
some time been making, and both together urged
the Waldenses to come and occupy Genoa as they
had done Turin. An additional encouragement to
this step was afforded by the fact that some of the

Genoese themselves began to make the same request.
Workmen employed at Alessandria spoke to some
members of a trades-union, who had come from
Genoa, of the profit they found in attending the
services of the Vaudois Church at Turin. These
deputies carried back the good report, with the result
that commissioners were sent to Turin asking that
a pastor might be settled among them in Genoa.
It would have been difficult to disregard so many
appeals from so many different quarters, and fortunately the Vaudois Church had the right man at
their command when this favourable moment came.
Sig. Geymonat, since his banishment from Tuscany,
had been working with Sig. Meille at Turin, and,
full of his dearly bought Florentine experience, he
went to make trial of this new field, in the hope that
it might prove as fruitful as it was promising.

A nearer acquaintance with Genoa, however,
brought some discouragements with it. The workmen from whose interest so much had been hoped,
proved, like their fellow-countrymen in Constantinople, earnest in politics rather than in spiritual
matters. Mazzarella, a Neapolitan refugee of liberal
education, of whom great things were expected, hung
back from active participation in the work ; and the
English, who had held out hopes that accommodation might be given Sig. Geymonat, in their church,
refused to grant it for such a purpose. But on the
other hand there was Magrini the engraver, whose
acquaintance we have already made while he was

still in Florence, and who now gave efficient help to
the good work in Genoa while supporting himself by
working at his trade. The evangelical services too
were well attended; and when all allowance was made
for the hindrances which existed, even the Waldenses,
cautious as they were, became convinced that Genoa
offered the opportunity of making a distinct advance
with every prospect of success. Dr. Stewart had
arranged for the supply of adequate funds from
Scotland, and in the autumn of 1852 Sig. Geymonat
was settled as pastor among the Genoese converts.

Results soon followed which amply proved the
wisdom of this step. Many had held back because
the supply of ordinances was hitherto but irregular,
and as soon as this defect was remedied they came
in crowds to the rooms[1] where service was held, and
clamoured for the purchase or erection of a church.
The law, said they, gives us the right of meeting: let
us do so openly, and not in corners like the con-
spirators we are suspected of being; then we shall
shake the city. Sig. Mazzarella even, won by the
success that began to show itself so signally, lent his
valuable if somewhat late and uncertain aid to the
movement. Thus at Turin and Genoa; at Nice too,
and all along the Riviera; not to speak of many
another place, such as Casale or Favale among the

---

[1] The house of Betti, Piazzetta Maddalena, and a hall in the
Casareto Palace, San Giacomo di Carignano, were successively
used for this purpose.

inland villages ; gospel light was spreading with the
fair promise of a coming day of truth and righteousness, when suddenly the sky was overcast and deep
disappointment shadowed like a cloud the hopes that
had been so high.

We have noticed how the Protestant movement
in Tuscany was prejudiced by Plymouthists and
their sectarian spirit. It need not surprise us then to
find the same doctrine spreading to Piedmont and
doing the like ill-service there. Englishwomen indeed they were who introduced these opinions in
Florence ; but had they not found a congenial soil
among the Italian converts, the mischief would not
have been so great. At Constantinople ; at Genoa ;
at Turin ; as well as in Tuscany ; wherever in short
there were Italians inclined to republicanism in politics, a certain number of these showed a distinct
leaning to Independency and even Darbyism in their
ecclesiastical views. " 'Tis the vicious habit of the
Italians," said one who knew them well, " ever to
mingle politics with their religion ; " and added with
pardonable exaggeration : " Those that leave the
Church of Rome must of necessity take their politics
from Mazzini and their religion from Darby ; since
these two are at the opposite poles from the Pope in
the absolute rule he pretends over things secular and
sacred." Without allowing the full force of this
opinion, penned in circumstances which excused if
they did not justify it, we need have no difficulty in
admitting that matters were now in a most unstable

condition as regarded the work of the gospel in Piedmont.   What was the situation—say in the year 1853?
Many refugees—so many that we may almost call
them a crowd—Guicciardini, Mazzarella, Desanctis,
Magrini, Betti, the Albarella ; were associated more
or less closely with the Waldensian Church in her
scheme and work of evangelisation.   It is evident
that only time and circumstance were wanting to
develop and expose in a painful way the deep difference of ideal which divided the men of the South
from those of the North : the one party tending to
revolt against all government, sacred or secular, the
other eager as any to see the progress of Italian
liberty, yet proudly tenacious of their historic unity
and settled Church order.

Let us come however to the actual facts of the
case.   There had been settled for some years in
London a certain Italian political exile called
Ferretti.   He was one of those who proposed the
establishment of an Evangelical Publication Society
in Tuscany, and when this project failed he brought
out the *Eco di Savonarola*, a periodical devoted, as
its name suggests, to the cause of the reformed principles.   Ferretti was a typical example of those who
" mingle politics with their religion " ; for about the
year 1852 he wrote to Sig. Revel, the Waldensian
Moderator, proposing that the Table should support
him in the publication of a newspaper intended to
advocate Vaudois principles along with politics of an
advanced kind.   This offer, it is hardly necessary to

state, was refused ; and from that time dated an
adverse influence, beginning in London, and gaining
strength at Geneva, which had a lamentable success
in separating from the Waldensian Church those
who till then had seemed willing to work harmoniously with her in the evangelisation of Italy.

When once a tendency of this kind sets in, little
difficulty is ever experienced in finding a pretext
which may serve as the justification of schism.   In
the case we are studying, this occurred at Genoa in
connection with an attempt made there to acquire a
church for the use of the converts.   During the
latter months of 1853, a Roman Catholic place of
worship known as the "Gran' Madre di Dio," had
been bought at a cost of £3,000 to accommodate Sig.
Geymonat and his rapidly increasing congregation.
On various accounts this building was soon found
unsuitable, and a site for the erection of a new
church was obtained in the Via Assarotti.   Thus it
was that in the month of August, 1854, arrangements
were made for the re-sale of the "Gran' Madre" to
the Marchese d' Arazzo ; when, like peals of omi-
nous thunder from a clear sky, came two letters
addressed to the Waldensian Table by Dr. Desanctis
and Sig. Mazzarella, in which each of these evangelists resigned his connection with the Church of the
Valleys.

The reasons assigned in justification of this step
were two : first the sale of the "Gran' Madre," which,
be it observed, had not yet been carried out.   This,

said Mazzarella, involves the Church in the guilt of
idolatry ; for *there is no doubt* the Marquis will hand
the building over to Archbishop Charvaz, and then
the abomination of the mass will be set up there as
before.   The second reason, given by Desanctis, was
a less tangible one.   The Waldenses, he said, showed
a sectarian spirit, and were therefore unfit to be God's
instruments in evangelising Italy.   We should have
difficulty in understanding the position of these men,
or the meaning of the reasons they alleged, were it
not that we have already traced this schism to its remote and obscure source in their differing opinions
and jealous dislike of Church authority.

This *coup d'État*—for it merits the name—had
been carefully planned.   It took place at the very
time when the pastors of Turin and Genoa were each
absent from his post : Sig. Geymonat in Geneva,
bringing home his wife, who had gone there on account of the cholera: Sig. Meille lying ill at La Tour.
The situation was a serious one, but prompt measures
were taken to undo the mischief.   The Moderator, on
receipt of Desanctis' letter, hurried to Turin, and
succeeded in prevailing on him to withdraw his resignation, promising that a conference would be held
with him and his friends on the best method of carrying out the work in Italy.   The 15th of September
was fixed as the date of this meeting ; but on the
preceding day the Table received a bulky document
which showed only too plainly how far the mischief
had already gone, and how unwilling those who had

begun this movement were to think of any reconcilia-
tion with the Church they renounced. This paper
contained the formal intimation that an "Italian Evangelical Society" had been formed at Turin, and had
appointed a "Committee of Italian Evangelisation"
to confer with the Waldensian Table on the conduct
of the Italian work. Indeed, when the conference
took place, the Waldensian representatives found that
they were expected to deal not with one but with
two Committees, another having been simultaneously
formed in Genoa.

Unhopeful as affairs appeared, the conference had
this happy result, that Desanctis definitely withdrew
his letter of resignation; and probably time and
patience might have won over Mazzarella and the
others as well, had they not unfortunately received
support and encouragement from without. We have
remarked that London and Geneva—meaning the
Committees in these cities—were responsible for
much of this, and that Nice was not free from the
same charge; but now it seemed as if open war were
on the point of being declared. The cry arose, and
was echoed from these different quarters, that the
Vaudois were unfit to evangelise Italy. They were
no Italians, it was said, but Frenchmen, alien in
tongue and heart from the people of the plains,
rousing opposition instead of attraction wherever
they came. Then indeed the ancient Church of the
valleys found herself in evil case. Episcopalians—
not all indeed, yet many—held aloof with Beckwith

because the Vaudois clung to their Presbyterianism ; Voluntaries looked askance because religion had a civil establishment in the Valleys ; and those in love with Independency and Plymouthism naturally gave their interest to Mazzarella and the men who followed him. English money began to flow in freely to the coffers of the Turin and Genoa Committees ; places of worship and stations of evangelisation, which competed in a vexatious and even scandalous way with those already established, were set up in Genoa, Turin, Alessandria, Pietra Marazzi, and elsewhere ; and this sad division, so prejudicial to the interests of the gospel, was exhibited in face of that Roman Church which, with all her faults, yet presented at least an imposing appearance of unity and strength. Can we wonder that some, on the point of quitting that ancient communion, were scandalised ; that the progress of gospel truth was hindered ; and that one who loved the Church of the Valleys with all her heart, wrote in passionate grief, " The Vaudois cause is lost in Italy " ?

Even the warmest friend of the Waldenses need not hesitate to admit that they had much to learn. God teaches His Church ; but conveys His lessons in the course of experience. Guided by Him, His people learn through their very failures and short-comings the hardly-won wisdom which enables them to fulfil their course, if not perfectly, at least with a gracious measure of efficiency. The Waldenses were free ; but ages of persecution and restraint had left them cautious to a fault : the use of their liberty they had yet to learn. They were conservative as well as cautious, and it seems as if, in their praiseworthy zeal for order, quickened no doubt by the sight of so much that tended in an opposite direction, they hardly realised at first that extraordinary times and opportunities call for the relaxation of ordinary rules. They would not ordain men, even for the mission field in the South, who fell short of the high standard rightly exacted by them in the case of candidates for charges in the Valleys; and evangelists of such quality they could not furnish in numbers adequate to the needs of Piedmont even, far less of Italy as a whole. The determination to accept none but the best is magnificent; we cannot refuse to admire it; but is it war? Would it not have been better to work with what materials lay at hand, than to take up an impracticable position and see these very persons lost to all control by the sad way of schism?

It must also be confessed that there was a want of sympathy between the Waldenses and those who separated from their communion; and that both parties were to blame for this fault. But before we can fairly estimate the extent of Waldensian short-comings in this particular, we must remember what their trials had been. " We have been disappointed," writes one of their pastors, " I might rather say we have had much to suffer from them "; and those for whom the veil has been lifted, and who know the

secret history of the time, will be the last to judge
with severity the somewhat rigid attitude assumed by
these representatives of ecclesiastical order under the
opposition they encountered. The Rev. C. L. Lauria,
an agent of the London Jewish Society, was stationed
at Turin in 1856, and gives an impartial account of
what he witnessed at a meeting held early in that
year between the leaders of the "Società" (as it had
now come to be called) and the Vaudois pastors.
Mr. Lauria went to this meeting with his feelings
engaged against Sig. Meille and his Church by the
evil reports about them which had been widely circulated. What he saw however soon made him take
an exactly opposite view. The meeting took place
in the Vaudois hall at Turin, and the first speech
was delivered by Sig. Malan, who expressed much
pleasure in the hope that it might be possible to
have an "Evangelical Alliance" in Italy ; meaning
that the Waldenses and their brethren of the Società
might work together in evangelising the country.
Mazzarella, and those who with him represented the
Committees, replied that this was impossible. Unwilling to give up all hope of co-operation, the Vaudois pastors (Meille, Malan, Appia, Gay, and Charbonnier) then offered three propositions on which,
in their opinion, a treaty of peace might be based.
First: let the Waldenses and the Società be alike
free to use their utmost efforts in the gospel cause.
Second: in doing this, let each party avoid hindering
the other. Third: let each abide by the form of

Church government which their consciences approve. The representatives of the Società would not however entertain these proposals. The field, they said, was not large enough for both parties; and as for mutual toleration of conscientious differences, they would none of it. Was not a definite Church order enjoined in the New Testament? and with that they endeavoured to draw the pastors into a dispute upon the Sacraments and the Gospel Ministry. To this the Waldenses answered that they had come there not to dispute, but to acknowledge as brethren all who held the essential truths of the common faith, and to devise a *modus vivendi* with them; and proposed that, as this was refused, at least they might unite in prayer before parting. " No!" shouted Magrini, " you can pray by yourselves"; and, taking his hat, he and the other leaders of the Società left the hall in a rage.

The spirit thus displayed augured but ill for the prevalence of peace and charity; and, sad to say, it soon brought forth the bitter fruits of contention in the mission field. Take for instance the typical case of Pietra Marazzi. This village lay in the immediate neighbourhood of Alessandria, where Sig. Gay, the Vaudois evangelist, had been at work for the six months preceding Palm Sunday, 1858. On that day the evangelical service in Alessandria was attended by two men from Pietra Marazzi, who told Sig. Gay that many in their village had begun to read the Bible with interest, and accepted gladly his offer to come and teach them the way of life more perfectly. On the following Sunday he preached at Pietra Marazzi to an audience of a hundred and fifty persons, and made arrangements to continue such services in the future. Before long however two evangelists from the Genoa Committee appeared on the scene ; hired a room in the village ; held conferences with the people, and did not scruple to say "that the Waldenses were a worldly Church, and that theirs was the true one ; that baptism was a superstition, and the ministry a tyranny." Imagine the scandal of such scenes repeated at Alessandria ; at Asti ; at Turin ; at Genoa ; and in fact throughout Piedmont ; and it is easy to understand what the Waldenses had to "suffer" during these years of schism and heart-burning. The temper in which this fiery trial was borne appears in a letter written by Duncan Matheson in 1857. Recording his impressions of the work in Piedmont, he says : "The Vaudois deserve every support. I admire their Christian spirit displayed under every misrepresentation. What tenderness in speaking of the other party here [Turin] and at La Torre ! In Genoa I visited Betti and spoke kindly and in a spirit of love. It is of no use. They have no intention of forming a Church, and so opposite are they in spirit to the Valdesi that it is waste of time to try union. I do not doubt but some of them are true Christians ; and as far as they preach Christ I bid them God-speed. Our path is clear to act as before. It has tried me much ; but

I must say, and say truly, the spirit I have found amongst the Valdesi is different to theirs."

Gallantly as well as charitably did the Church of the valleys bear herself under this severe trial. The Committees of Genoa and Turin had heaped public abuse upon the Vaudois in their periodical, the *Luce Evangelica*, and a retort would have been easy ; but bearing these reproaches quietly, those who suffered them were content to send out a private circular to their friends in Italy and elsewhere, explaining how the Table actually stood with regard to the Società, and detailing the steps that had been taken on either side. At the same time they were careful to "strengthen the things which remained." Sig. Revel set out with Sig. Lantaret on a tour of inspection, and visited the stations at Turin, Genoa, Oneglia, and Nice, giving counsel and encouragement as he went to those scattered labourers who bore the heat of reproach and suspicion as well as the burden of their own proper work in the vineyard of the Lord.

We note with gratitude to God that, in spite of the severe trial to which it was then exposed, the evangelical work of the Vaudois Church in Piedmont gave great encouragement to those concerned in carrying it on. In Genoa, though Mazzarella and others had left, the Sacrament was dispensed, on Christmas Day 1854, to no fewer than one hundred persons. Sig. Gay reported satisfactory progress at Nice, where four night schools had been set up, and two evangelists were busily employed ; while at Oneglia, Bruschi had gathered a promising congregation of some twenty converts. In Turin, many of those who had been carried away at first by the separatist movement began to return to the services held by Sig. Meille; the *Luce Evangelica* ceased to appear; Biava left; and on the 25th of May, 1855, in full Synod, and amid a scene of great emotion, Dr. Desanctis was reconciled to the Church he had renounced, and accepted a theological professorship in the Vaudois college at La Tour. Much remained to give cause for the gravest anxiety; but in the midst of trying and difficult times, grounds of encouragement and hope were thus granted to those who needed them so sorely that they might recover strength for future conflicts and victories.

CHAPTER V.

CLOSING THE RANKS.

"*Regnum coelorum* vïolenza pate
   Da caldo amore, e da viva speranza,
Che vince la divina volontate ;
   Non a guisa che l' uomo all' uom sovranza,
Ma vince Lei perchè vuol' esser vinta ;
   E vinta vince con sua beninanza."
              —*Dante, Paradiso*, xx. 94–99.

THE circumstances recorded at the close of the last chapter were gratifying indeed ; but they supplied no solution for the pressing problem of Italian evangelisation. If any real and permanent advance were to be made, it was plain that such must be founded on a thorough revision of the Waldensian Church constitution. Some thought that much of the difficulty might be met by securing the residence of a Scotch Minister at La Tour, to act as Foreign Secretary of the Vaudois, and conduct their business with other Churches and Societies. It was hoped too that whoever filled this post might do useful work in the college by teaching English there, and by more or less directly opening up to the students the wealth of orthodox theology accessible in that language. This project seems to have been entertained by the Free Church of Scotland's Continental Committee; for in February, 1855, the convener wrote to Dr. Stewart saying they thought he should make arrangements to spend the summer in the valleys, and deliver a course of lectures at La Tour.

Nothing but a thorough-going reform however could meet the need of the times; and we are now to see how this was effected, and what part the Minister of Leghorn took in promoting an all-important change which had the happiest results in bringing about a closer sympathy between the Waldenses and those among whom their missionary operations were conducted.

We may profitably spend a moment here in reviewing the situation as it existed previous to the changes of which we are presently to speak. While the Vaudois Church was still under civil restraint one of her most keenly felt disabilities came with the prohibition which hindered her Synod, or supreme deliberative council, from holding its assembly oftener than once in five years. This made it necessary that there should be some standing Court of Executive to provide for the carrying out of Synodical Acts in the long interval which necessarily elapsed between the holding of one Synod and another. Such a Court the Church constituted in the "Tavola" —a Committee consisting of five members, two clerical and two lay, with another clerical member as Moderator or chairman. This system answered well enough as long as the interests of the Vaudois were bounded by the sixteen parishes of their native valleys; but when emancipation came, and yearly meetings of Synod began to be held; when the burden of Italy and her evangelisation was acknowledged and assumed, then the parable of the new wine in the old bottles was fulfilled, and it was evident that some change of constitution must be made if difficulties were to be surmounted and the grounds of true progress laid.

In this matter of reform the Vaudois were acted on by two opposing influences. One of these had been brought to bear upon them ever since 1837 by their sworn friend and unwearied benefactor, General Beckwith. Himself an Episcopalian both by training and conviction, he saw no hope of rendering the Church he loved more fit for her work but in the way of leading her to copy more closely the Prelatical system of government. There was not a little in the Waldensian Discipline which readily lent itself to such an influence. While the quinquennial period still prevailed, the Synod necessarily retired into the distance, and the Table stood forth with its Moderator in the foreground as for the most part the sole representative of ecclesiastical law and order. Let but this Moderator be elected for life instead of holding office for a term of five years only. Let him be loosed from his parochial cure, and left free to devote his

whole time and energy to the superintendence of the
Church's work in the Valleys and throughout Italy,
and the problem of the Waldenses and their missions
will be successfully solved.   Such was Beckwith's
proposal, and one which he urged with all his influence as long as he saw the least hope of securing
its adoption, believing, as he did, that with it the
future of the Vaudois Church was intimately bound
up.

Fortunately, another spirit leading to other counsels
prevailed in the heart of that Church herself.   The
Vaudois were essentially Presbyterians, democrats
even.   If the Table, as it once existed presented
the appearance of a modified prelacy, it was an
appearance only, and one which arose rather from
the stern pressure of outward circumstance than
from the free development of life within the Church.
Now that this constraint was removed, and Synods
might meet yearly, or as often as should be found
necessary, the spirit of the Vaudois led them to
abridge the powers of the Table rather than to
increase them, and to seek in a direction more native
to the genius of Presbytery that solution of their
difficulties which the future of Italian Missions required.

In this movement they were not left without
encouragement, guidance, and material help.   Dr.
Stewart, whose portrait hangs in the College Hall at
La Tour side by side with those of Dr. Gilly and
General Beckwith, and whose memory is honoured

among the Vaudois as that of one who was not the least of these three great benefactors, never did the Waldensian Church a more signal service than the one he rendered her in this matter of the Constitution and its reform. Scotland is the classic ground of the Presbyterian controversy, and it was fitting that a Scotch Presbyter should advise the Waldenses at this critical time, guiding them in the path which leads with such nicety between the extremes of prelacy on the one hand and anarchy on the other. The establishment of several Free Church Stations on the Riviera had an important influence in the same direction. Genoa was the first of these, the Rev. D. Kay being settled there in 1854. Nice followed the year after, and Cannes in 1857. These charges not only served the religious needs of Scotchmen abroad, but were most useful in keeping before the Vaudois models of Church government and actual examples of the ready way in which the Presbyterian constitution lends itself to the needs of a sound and effective mission work.

But the Waldenses were not to be suffered to fall quietly into Presbyterian hands and Presbyterian ways. One of the Scotch Bishops proposed to visit Turin, and those interested in his mission asked that he should be allowed to hold services in the new Vaudois Church there, with the fond hope that the Waldenses might thus be brought to see the advantages of Episcopalian government and liturgical worship. When private notice of what was doing reached Leghorn, Dr. Stewart was in the act of applying to the Table for the use of the Vaudois Church in Genoa, that the Scotch congregation newly formed there might have a suitable meeting-place ; but he immediately withdrew this request, explaining that he wished the way to be quite clear for the Table to refuse what was asked of them at Turin, and added his own comments upon the real meaning and tendency of what was proposed.   To his great honour be it said that Dr. Gilly, Episcopalian as he was, joined heartily in this defence of the Vaudois. He saw the Primate of England, to whom application seems already to have been made on behalf of the proposed mission ; represented the extreme views of the Bishop who was to go out, and urged with success the impropriety of giving a commission to one who denied the warrant of orders, the efficacy of sacraments, and the title of Church to Presbyterians. We need hardly add that what had been attempted failed, and the Waldenses were left to shape their constitution under an influence more congenial to them than that of High Church Episcopacy.

The direction in which progress was made led, as will readily be conjectured, to the imposing of limitations on the oligarchy so long exercised by the Table. Indeed, the existing state of things was such that its condemnation was involved in its mere exposure. " Five men, each living in a different part of the country, each with his own individual duties, come together at certain intervals to deal with all the affairs of the Church, to whatever branch of her activity they belong—whether missions, works of charity, education, the cure of souls, or correspondence with the home Government and foreign Churches. This tends to destroy the balance and due adjustment of power, since it often renders the function of the Synod a mere name ; though that court is fundamental in Gospel Churches, especially those of the Presbyterian way." Such were the opinions of a Waldensian Professor,[1] and they were shared by many in the Church, who crowded public meetings where these views were expressed, and welcomed them with hearty applause.

Difficulties indeed continued to beset the way of these needed reforms. The party that urged them assumed a somewhat extreme position, asking that the Table should have its powers as a court of commission so restricted as to become a mere formal intermediary between the Synod and certain Committees entrusted with the whole charge of the various departments of Church work. These, it was proposed, should be four in number, and should respectively have the oversight of missions, works of charity, education, and the cure of souls, being exempt from any interference whatever on the part of the Table in carrying out what the Synod entrusted to their care. Little wonder need be felt that reform bearing this revolutionary character met with instant

---

[1] Sig. B. Malan.

and decided opposition both from the members of the existing Table and from others; but it would have been unfortunate indeed had these revolutionary and conservative tendencies been suffered to hinder by their mutual strife the introduction of beneficial changes in the constitution of the Church.

A peace-maker however, and one who at the same time promoted heartily the cause of true progress, was happily at hand in the person of Dr. Stewart. The reforming party had had his sympathy and help all along in their reasonable desire for some change, and their attempt to break up the undue centralisation of power. The Table, on the other hand, and those who supported them, knew that he was unwilling to see that commission of Synod—as in fact it was—stripped of all power over the conduct of affairs in Committees. But there was need of the greatest tact and care in the handling of these negotiations, lest the susceptible feelings of those concerned in them should be wounded. At one time Dr. Stewart had begun to write a circular letter to the members of Synod setting forth his views on the Vaudois constitution; but the fear of seeming to dictate to the ministers of another Church prevented him from pursuing this plan. But at the Synod of May, 1855, he held a meeting of both parties in his lodging at La Tour, which, under his genial presidency, had the happiest effect in bringing about a mutual understanding. At the same time he caused a well-known manual of Church government—"Miller on Presbytery"—to be translated, printed, and circulated among the Vaudois ; and to these steps, so judiciously taken, is due in no small measure the admirable working constitution under which the Waldensian Church now prosecutes her labours in the cause of Christ. A *via media* was found, whereby the Table, relieved of duties beyond its strength, still kept its place as an efficient representative of the Synod, and had committed to it a special charge of home interests ; while the Italian mission field, with all its multifarious needs, was placed under the care of a special Committee, chosen for their sympathy with the work they were called to superintend. Thus a firm foundation was laid for future progress and success.

Nor did any great time elapse before what had been thus done at La Tour showed good results in the mission field. There a new energy speedily showed itself, and was rewarded with an encouraging success. This was notably the case in Genoa ; for in 1856 we find a wonderful activity in connection with the Vaudois station there. The number of services held during the week was greatly increased ; the new church building was being rapidly completed, in spite of the remonstrances of Archbishop Charvaz, who vainly petitioned the king for an interdict ; and a Protestant hospital, where evangelicals were safe from the annoying attentions of Roman Catholic nurses, had been established on the heights above the town. A most encouraging feature of the time also

was the demand for evangelists which came from so
many towns and villages throughout Piedmont; and
it became plain that the Vaudois had not prepared
themselves a moment too soon for entering with new
power into a work which grew in extent and importance every day.   At Novara, at Voghera, at
Courmayeur—to mention only a few of the chief
points—their labours received a hearty welcome;
while Lieutenant Sarzana at Alessandria, and
another soldier-convert stationed with his comrades
at Annecy, joined with marked success in the work
of colportage and Bible-reading.

It is true that Piedmont had not quite fulfilled the
promise it gave of toleration; and we may retrace our
steps to remark some of the checks which the mission
work sustained there from the action of the Roman
clergy and the Government officials.   In 1852, shortly
after he left Tuscany and established himself at
Genoa, Admiral Pakenham undertook a journey to
Spezia for the purpose of seeing what could be done
in the eastern Riviera.   He was accompanied in this
expedition by Dr. Mazzinghi, a Tuscan refugee; and
one day they visited a village called Marola, where
they distributed a number of tracts among the children.   These it afterwards appeared were collected
and publicly burnt in the church; and when Admiral
Pakenham returned next day, he was drawn into
discussion with the priest and two bigoted women
of the place, who soon gave the signal for a general
assault.   The mob gathered and stoned the heretics,

who, when they appealed to the chief of police for protection, were advised to quit the place at once. In a few days Admiral Pakenham was charged with a breach of the peace, and poor Mazzinghi was actually imprisoned for his share in the matter. It is to be noted that the eastern Riviera was by all accounts a district where ignorance and bigotry were unusually gross, and where the people were to an uncommon extent under the influence of the priests. At Marola, for example, the *curato* had provided a warm reception for Pakenham and his companion on their return, by publicly exorcising the devil from a child which the Admiral had been seen to caress the day before, and by telling the people that the Englishman was a powerful necromancer, to whose diabolical arts they owed the loss of several sailors belonging to the place who had died of yellow fever in the Brazils.

In the following year, 1853, no less than four converts were arrested at one time. These were the Cereghini, members of a family residing at the village of Favale near Chiavari. All had become Protestants, and more than one was afterwards distinguished as an earnest labourer in evangelical work. They owed much to the way in which their temporal and spiritual interests were watched over by the Rev. D. Kay, of Genoa, and other sympathising friends, and repaid that care by their constancy and devotion to the good cause. In 1852 one of the Cereghini, a ballad-singer on the streets of Genoa, was employed to sell copies of a tract in which the place and hour of the evangelical service were announced.

Two years afterwards the police made a sudden descent upon the houses of the pastor and evangelist at Nice and Oneglia, and seized a number of Bibles stored there. This unexpected loss was traced to the publication of a letter in the newspapers, in which a heedless friend of the colportage work had told the world too plainly what was being done and who were busy in it. In Piedmont, as in Tuscany, persecution was plainly contrary to the intention of the Government, and should be charged to the high-handed action of individuals, provoked perhaps by some indiscretion on the part of the evangelicals, or compelled by the intolerant clergy of Rome. About the feeling and attitude of these last there could be no doubt, and we may now glance at a scene which illustrates this point with precision. In 1858 Sig. Malan, the Moderator of the Waldensian Table, paid a visit to Alessandria and Pietra Marazzi to inspect the work being carried on there. At the latter place he preached in the square to a most interesting congregation of three hundred people, overlooked, in true "episcopal" style, by the parish priest, who sat in a window of the church to observe what went on. This man had not the courage to oppose the Vaudois preacher in person, but sent the *curato* of a neighbouring parish to silence the enemy, while he remained to view the triumph from a safe distance. What must have been his chagrin to observe that Don Roncato's cries of "blasphemy!" instead of meeting with the approval of the people, excited their indignation to such a point that he was obliged to quit the field? When service was over the crowd, late as it was, followed Sig. Malan and Sig. Gay to their inn, filled the parlour, and stayed in earnest conversation with the pastors till past midnight. Most significant of all and most gratifying were the letters which afterwards appeared in the public prints denouncing the conduct of Don Roncato.[1] These are of value, not only as an exposure of clerical intolerance, but even more as effectually disposing of the assertion only too commonly made in these old days, and occasionally repeated even now, that the Vaudois cannot win a sympathetic hearing for the gospel outside their own valleys.

The Società too had to bear its share of opposition and persecution. Hardly had Magrini begun to work as an evangelist in Genoa when he was watched by the police, who paid him an unexpected visit at three o'clock one morning, and subjected him to interrogation. More serious was an affair which occurred five years afterwards at Alessandria. Mazzarella was at work there with two evangelists, and had made a public statement to the effect that the host after consecration remained bread as it was before. This offended the priests, who complained to the police; and a process was pending against Mazzarella and

---

[1] See Appendix.

his coadjutors in the courts during April, 1858. A
curious scene occurred at the preliminary inquiry.
When Mazzarella was asked his profession, "I am a
servant," he replied. "What did you say?" repeated the official. "A servant," insisted Mazzarella. "Whose servant are you?" "Jesus Christ's!"
In the same way one of the evangelists sought to
baffle his questioner. "Your profession?" "I'm a
minister maccaroni-man!" ("sono Pastore Vermicellaio"). "What do you mean?" "What I have
said—a minister and maker of maccaroni" (Pastor e
Vermicellaio).

Whether they were "provoked to good works" by
the Vaudois success, or taught by the trials and persecutions they had to share with that ancient Church,
certain it is that from this time a movement began in
the Società towards better things. This could hardly
have been otherwise. M. Pilatte, the Pastor of the
French Church at Nice, a man of exceptional ability,
had stated very clearly the case between the Vaudois
and those who left their communion, first in a speech
of great brilliance delivered before the Société Évan-
gélique at Geneva, and again in the Free Assembly at
Edinburgh. The like service was rendered by Dr.
Stewart in an article published by the *Christian Times*
under the title, "Justice to the Waldenses." It would
be too much to suppose that those who gave their
support to the Società were convinced of all that
had been advanced, but of this at any rate there is
evidence, that they were persuaded matters could not

remain as they had hitherto been, and that some kind
of constitution must be adopted by these evangelists
if they were to do the work expected of them, and
retain the sympathy of their friends in Great Britain.
With this view a deputation from the Nice Committee,
consisting of Messrs. Hull, Hudson, and Gordon, set
out to visit the stations in Piedmont; the powerful
influence of Guicciardini was turned in the same
direction ; and as all this pressure from without coincided with the working of a felt need within, it was
not long before a definite attempt to organise themselves into a Church was made by the Società. Not
to mention previous movements in this direction—
there met in Turin during the early months of 1859
what was called the "Synod of all the Evangelical
Churches of Italy." This consisted of eighteen
members: two from Naples, one from Rome, four
from Tuscany, five from Lombardy, and six from
Sardinia. These delegates of the Società declared
their sole article of faith to be "the Bible, the whole
Bible, and nothing but the Bible," but then proceeded with curious inconsistency to spend six days
in debating many of the cardinal points of theology,
such as the doctrine of the Trinity, of original sin,
of the Christian ministry, etc.

The result of this meeting was favourable in more
ways than one. It showed where the men of the
Società stood to their supporters in Great Britain,
and made it plain that they required to be educated
as well as helped with material means, unless their

converts were to fall as far short of a reasonable
orthodoxy as they themselves still did.   On themselves too it was fitted to act most favourably, in
disposing them to think with greater sympathy of
those who wrought by their side in the same great
field of evangelisation.   It is one thing to criticise,
another to construct ; and the Società must have
looked with a kindlier eye upon the Confession of
Waldensian orthodoxy, when they found by actual
experience how necessary a subordinate standard is
to express the sense in which the Church understands
Scripture, and how difficult it was to draw from the
Bible, the supreme rule of faith, an intelligible system
of doctrine in which they were all agreed.

These were the last days before the dawn of Italian
liberty and unity ; and it is most impressive to see
how, under God's guiding hand, those engaged in
evangelising the country were rapidly being prepared
for the vastly increased duties and opportunities
which awaited them in the years to come.   While
in the camp of Victor Emmanuel swords were put
to the grindstone and pieces of ordnance charged ;
while Garibaldi was descending like a thunderbolt on
Sicily, and cleaving a way for his king to the throne
of Rome ; in each division of the gospel army preparation was diligently going on.   God's truth, impressed on the pages of countless volumes, daily
poured from the printers' hands ; hearts were being
taught by experience and drawn together in charity ;
discipline and organisation were closing the ranks

of Christ's army, and preparing IIis soldiers to resist
the enemy with new power; and the way was thus
being made ready for a campaign not the less glorious
that it was spiritual; the result of which should be
to carry the gospel through the length and breadth
of Italy, and even to secure it a seat and an audience
in the very city of the Pope himself. Little did those
who then wrought so diligently know to what great
end their labours were being directed; but we, looking upon the event itself, may well trace the hand of
God in it all; follow His footsteps in the storm and
shock of war—the very God of battles—see Him ride
upon the winds of revolution to His people's aid, and
say with wonder, awe, and praise, " What hath God
wrought ? " " We have seen great things to-day ! "

BOOK II.

THE NEW ORDER.

CHAPTER I.

TRAINING.

"Della profonda congiunzion divina,
　　Ch' io tocco mo', la mente mi sigilla
Piu volte l'evangelica dottrina.
Quest' è 'l principio, quest' è la favilla,
　　Che si dilata in fiamma poi vivace.
E, come stella in cielo, in me scintilla."
　　　　　　　　—*Dante, Paradiso,* xxiv. 142–147.

IT is well known how much the cause of education among the Vaudois owes to the interest taken in it by General Beckwith and Dr. Gilly. Under these pioneers of reform, and during a period extending from 1824 to 1840, almost all the hamlet and parochial schools in the Valleys were rebuilt; and the people were induced to submit to an assessment which raised the schoolmasters' salaries, and thus provided more efficient instruction for the children.

Difficulties of a more serious kind however than ruin and poverty met these philanthropists when they came to deal with the thorny subject of secondary education. Hitherto the "Latin school" had been a peripatetic institution, holding its sessions now in the Val Luserna, and again in the Val San Martino, according to the district from which most of its pupils happened to be drawn. Dr. Gilly wished to found a permanent College at La Tour, and did so in 1835; but the inhabitants of the other valley were so jealous of this institution, seeing in it the withdrawal of their occasional privilege, that it was found necessary to pacify them by building an additional Latin school at Pomaret.

Beckwith and Gilly were unwilling that candidates for the Waldensian ministry should be obliged to seek training at Geneva or Lausanne, instead of obtaining it in their native valleys, and the original plan of Holy Trinity College had embraced a school of theology, as well as the ordinary University curriculum; but circumstances prevented this scheme from being carried out in its entirety until 1855, when the Synod appointed Professors Revel and Geymonat to the theological chairs at La Tour. The arrangement was one which seemed to offer many advantages. It provided useful and congenial work for some of the more talented pastors of the Church, while at the same time it promised to save the students from learning the current scepticism of Switzerland and Germany. On the other hand, as those regarded it whose hearts were set on seeing the Waldenses in the forefront of Italian evangelisation, it was open to the gravest objection. A serious blow had been inflicted on the infant mission at Genoa by the withdrawal of Sig. Geymonat from that place; yet this was the least of the mischief.

It had never been easy to move the Waldenses from home; now the difficulty of doing so was immensely increased. When a student of divinity, instead of seeing the world at Geneva or Lausanne, remained at La Tour till the very moment of his consecration to the pastoral office, he would be less likely than ever to think of any other place than an Alpine parish as the scene of his future life and labour.

Dr. Stewart had reason then to protest, as he did both openly and constantly, against a step which seemed to turn the Church away from the fulfilment of her great mission. But, while protesting, he also sought a remedy for the evil. At first only a partial and temporary cure could be applied. Some of the students—now one, then another, sometimes two at once—were brought to Florence during the vacation and initiated into the mission work that was going on there. Others were supported at the divinity schools of Edinburgh or Belfast during one year of their course; and—most interesting and important of all—some six or eight young converts from Tuscany, Venetia, and Piedmont were enabled, by funds which Scotland supplied, to study for the ministry at La Tour. These infected their companions with a missionary spirit; while at the same time they received themselves an invaluable training for their future work as evangelists. In all these different ways Dr. Stewart endeavoured to provide men of zeal and knowledge thoroughly fitted to serve the cause of missions in Italy.

Five years after the Faculty of Theology was established at La Tour, a grand opportunity occurred to overcome these difficulties once for all; and grandly was it taken advantage of. On the 27th of April, 1859, a travelling carriage containing the Grand Ducal family of Tuscany rolled out of Florence gate and took the road for Bologna, amid the sarcastic farewells of the people, who hastened to demand the protection of Sardinia, and welcomed General Ulloa with enthusiasm when he came among them as the accredited representative of Victor Emmanuel. At once the centre of gravity in Italian affairs was shifted southward to Florence, soon to pass to Rome, its rightful seat ; and, remembering the disabilities and distresses suffered by Tuscan Protestants in bygone days, we can readily believe that the religious world felt this change as sensitively and acted upon it as soon as did the political. Exiles for the cause of the gospel hastened their return from all quarters to the banks of the Arno ; and a year had hardly gone since Florence became free, when the Waldensian Synod unanimously decided that the Theological Faculty of their Church, following the march of the times, should be transferred from La Tour to the capital of Tuscany.

It is not hard to guess whose hand was busy in the arrangement of this important and happy change. The grateful address of the College to Dr. Stewart on the occasion of his jubilee in 1887 speaks with no uncertain voice : " La Scuola di Teologia di Firenze,

non senza vostro impulso ivi trasferita," it says: recording the removal of serious obstacles and the
fulfilment of long-cherished hopes. So remarkable
were the circumstances of this event, and so providential, that they merit our attention for a moment.
When the Synod of 1860 met, Dr. Stewart urged,
as did all the deputies, that the needs of Tuscany,
now free, should be seriously considered by the
Church, and that labourers should be sent there
without delay. Disheartened by the reply, which
was of a most unfavourable kind, he retired to his
lodging to bewail before God in secret the apparent
decline of missionary zeal in the Church he loved.
Suddenly the door opened and a friend—Sheriff
Jamieson—broke in upon his retirement with the
amazing news that by a unanimous vote the Synod
had agreed to transfer the Theological Faculty to
Florence. "This is the Lord's doing!" Dr. Stewart
exclaimed; and acting under a grateful sense of the
Divine interposition, as he himself says, he then
and there resolved to assume the responsibility of
providing the necessary funds for this new establishment.

The money was raised almost at once, and in sums
which make the common liberality of to-day seem
mere trifling; but the occasion was a worthy one,
and the collector's name inspired a well-deserved
confidence. Scotland furnished two contributors who
gave a thousand pounds each, and another who added
five hundred. The Irish Presbyterian Church sent

five hundred pounds, and a thousand more came
from a generous friend of the cause in New York.
Dr. Stewart used these funds to purchase the Palazzo
Salviati, a handsome building in the Oltrarno, which
accommodated the Vaudois congregation and the
Claudian Press, as well as the College Hall and the
Professors' houses.   There then, near the heart of
Old Florence, in rooms which still, by their hangings
of faded silk, remind one of past grandeurs, and of
that Archbishop and Papal Legate who struck his
unsuccessful blow against the tyranny of the Medici,
was fairly established a gospel propaganda, earnest
and many-sided, fresh from the free air of the Alps,
and ready to contend with ardour and perseverance
against the soul-enslaving tyranny of Rome.   The
emancipation of the Vaudois had been formally pronounced more than ten years before ; but now for
the first time it was fully acted on, and one can
readily join in Dr. Stewart's thankfulness when he
found himself permitted to do his friends this signal
service, and at the same time to provide so promising
a means for the good of his beloved Italy.

The course of education thus finally provided was
well adapted to reach the very poorest children, and
to give promising pupils a sound professional training.   Hamlet schools stood in close neighbourhood
with every Waldensian home ; those of the different
parishes formed an intermediate step, which led
easily on to the higher instruction given in the two
grammar schools ; and when, his course of study in

one of these completed, a Waldensian youth aspired
to the discipline of a university, he found it at hand
in the college of La Tour. Thence too, should he
desire to enter the ministry, he could go to the school
of theology at Florence. Thus was established a
system, theoretically perfect, by which pupils might
pass from the first rudiments to the highest results
of scholastic training.

There were practical difficulties in the way however, which pressed with prohibitive force upon the
aspirations of many a talented youth. These arose
from the poverty of the people for whose advantage
this admirable school system existed, but who could
hardly afford to forego the aid of their sons' labour
that they might send them to attend the grammar
school. Yet had this been all, the difficulty would
hardly have existed ; at least, it would not have been
allowed to interfere with the claims of education. A
more serious necessity was that which obliged all
parents, except those who lived near La Tour or
Pomaret, to provide board and lodging for their
children should they send them to the grammar
school. This difficulty was felt with special force
in the Val San Martino, owing to its scattered population ; and many of the people were too poor to
meet it successfully. If advantage was to be generally taken of the instruction provided, money must
be found to support the children of parents who
could not afford to give them this privilege at their
own expense.

Dr. Stewart felt this, and was glad when contributors in Scotland sent him funds which provided bursaries for some twenty pupils during the four years of the grammar-school course commencing in 1860. So much did this new provision add to the popularity of the school at Pomaret, that when two years had passed the concourse of pupils became such that the building erected by General Beckwith was quite insufficient to contain them. Here was a new anxiety, though the cause was one which called for thankfulness. Another school must be built, large enough to provide the necessary accommodation ; and this need became the more urgent when, in 1864, Sig. Comba, the talented and zealous rector of Pomaret, died of fever brought on by overwork in the unhealthy air of a room crowded beyond its proper capacity. While on a visit to Scotland that summer, Dr. Stewart collected a sum of £550; and in the course of twelve months a new and commodious Latin school was ready to receive the pupils who came to attend the winter session of 1865. The feeding of these children was another matter which deserved and received attention, from the important bearing it had upon their health and success in study. The same hand which found money for bursaries and school-building gathered in later years what provided a generous diet of soup and meat for those who had been tempted to starve themselves at the very time and in the very way of life which make substantial nourishment most essential. Pomaret had now reason

to be proud of her grammar school and its thorough
equipment.

When provision was thus made for supplying wants
in connection with secondary education in the valleys, it was felt that something must be done for
those scholars who attended the college at La Tour.
A measure of support had already indeed been
afforded them; for Dr. Gilly obtained a contribution
of £2,000, which was invested for that purpose.
More however was required, and a mortification
executed by Mrs. Campbell of Stonefield, happily
supplied the deficiency. By the wise management
of Dr. Stewart this capital yielded eight bursaries,
one of £19 in rhetoric, another of £21 in philosophy
—each of them tenable for two years; besides six
others of £5 apiece, to be held by as many scholars
during the grammar-school course. The importance
of this bequest is to be measured, not so much by its
monetary value, considerable as it was, and almost
doubly so in a community as poor as that of the
Vaudois, but rather by the stimulus which it applied
to the scholars in their studies. Dr. Stewart had
insisted that a searching examination should be the
means of selecting those on whom the bursaries were
to be bestowed; the lines of this examination he had
himself laid down with the greatest care; and far-
reaching results were at once apparent; for in consequence of the first competition it was found necessary to remodel the teaching given by the masters,
that scholars might be properly prepared to satisfy

the new standard. The Moderator of the Table declared that a great benefit had been conferred upon the college; and the good effects of what was then done have been continued to the present day.

A more exacting, though not less necessary, task lay in the obtaining of bursaries for divinity students in Florence, who had to leave their homes and encounter the cost of living—vastly greater than they were accustomed to—in the then capital of the country. Calculated by a rigid economy, the yearly expenses of each student amounted to £30; and friends of Italy were found willing to support a number of men every year according to this scale. The burden of yearly solicitation however was a heavy one, and on the lamented death of Dr. Revel it occurred to Dr. Stewart that he had now an opportunity of procuring a permanent endowment for the college at Florence like that which Mrs. Campbell's generosity had provided for La Tour. A sum of £1,200 was accordingly obtained by him to form a memorial of Dr. Revel, with the understanding that the interest would be paid to Mrs. Revel during her lifetime, and should thereafter become available for bursaries in the divinity school.

Another difficulty, fortunately unknown in Great Britain, proved a real obstacle to the Italian students, and brought new cares on those who sought their welfare. This was the conscription; and many were those, drawn for the army, who owed to Dr. Stewart the means which enabled them to continue their studies in peace by hiring a substitute to serve in their place.

To value these details at their proper worth, we must regard them in the result they contributed to produce—a result sufficiently grand to reward an hundred-fold even the severe toil and anxious thought which they demanded. The highway of learning was now free. The poorest child, possessed of talents and perseverance, might raise himself to that professional, if not sacred, position which confers the only rank recognised in a democratic country like that of the Waldenses. Or let us rather look at the matter as he did to whom this benefit was mainly due. The need of Italy was a crying one; and here at last the key was found and applied to make a very treasure of Waldensian energy and faculty available for the mission field of the South. "Our humble College," sings the Senatus of Florence in 1887, "counts but few students at any one time; yet proudly boasts herself the mother of sixty-nine ministers of the Word." When the needs of seventeen parishes in the Valleys during the course of twenty years are fully allowed for, there remains a considerable surplus of well-equipped men who must in that time have been prepared and left free to engage in the work of evangelisation. Recording so happy a result we can in a measure understand the joy of that indefatigable friend of Italy, who thus saw his dearest desires, whether for the ancient Church of the Valleys or for the land of his adoption, crowned with a brilliant and lasting success.

CHAPTER II.

THE CAMP.

" Ben si convenne lei lasciar per palma,
    In alcun' cielo, dell' alta vittoria,
    Ch'ei s'acquistò con l' una e l' altra palma ;
    Perch' ella favorò la prima gloria
        Di Giosuè in su la terra Santa,
    Che poco tocca al papa la memoria."
                        —*Dante, Paradiso,* ix. 121–126.

WE are now to pass from the subject of education to that of missions ; to review the field
for which the colleges were training their students,
and to remark the success with which it pleased God
to crown their labours both in Tuscany, at Rome,
and throughout Italy.   In entering on this new
division of our subject we may recall the name of
Desanctis, belonging as he who bore it did, to both
worlds—to that of study and that of action alike.

When we last took note of this honoured servant
of Christ, he stood amid the affecting enthusiasm of
the Synod of 1855, accepting his chair of theology,
and thus calling forth the Church's solemn joy and
inspiring her Te Deum of thanksgiving.   It was in

Florence however, and not at La Tour, that his labours in that faculty commenced ; and thirteen long years elapsed before he actually held the position to which the Church designed him in 1855. Hardly had the Synod of that year closed its sittings, when clouds again gathered, misunderstandings arose ; and Desanctis, resigning the position he had just accepted, left for Genoa, where he began to aid Mazzarella and Betti in conducting the Società's operations there.

Though inclined to Independency, Desanctis was far from sharing the Darbyite views of those with whom he was now associated ; and circumstances arose which showed plainly how much nearer he stood to the Waldenses than to the Società. The story is a curious one, and well merits recital here. Desanctis, when he came to Genoa, left an empty place at Turin ; and Guicciardini, who took a watchful interest in all that concerned the welfare of his party, wished to have Sig. Rossetti, a nephew of the well-known poet of that name, brought over from London to fill this vacancy. There was some difficulty about Rossetti's passport, as he had been a refugee from Naples for political reasons ; but this was got over in an interview which Guicciardini had with Cavour, when that statesman promised to order Rossetti's papers from the Sardinian ambassador in London. Thus no long time elapsed before he was settled in Turin as an evangelist of the Società.

Some six years passed without any sign of

trouble. Desanctis and Mazzarella worked harmoniously at Genoa, and even opened a kind of divinity hall there for the training of evangelists. At the close of that period however the crisis came. An anonymous pamphlet appeared, the title of which—" Principii della Chiesa Romana, della Chiesa Protestante e della Chiesa Cristiana "—is enough to indicate pretty clearly the character of the opinions it advocated. This it seems was from the pen of Rossetti, assisted by Guicciardini and Magrini ; and it was meant as a manifesto which should win the approval of the Società generally ; thus committing that body to the support of a full-blown Plymouthism. The spirit and style of this extraordinary production may be judged of by the following sentence : " From the beginning," says the ingenuous author, " the Waldensians have been the most tenacious and the most tiresome adversaries of the Italian Church, and the Christians of Italy have not suffered from the Papists half what they have endured from the Waldenses."

Desanctis had thought himself one of the leaders of the Società : he now discovered that he was being led ; and in a direction contrary to his convictions. His own conduct towards the Waldenses had been far from blameless ; but he felt that charges so outrageous as those of Rossetti could not be endured, and that the Darbyite doctrine of the book demanded some protest from him. He wrote a strong article in the *Eco della Verità*, a periodical

which he then edited ; and he was reinforced in this
position by an admirable letter sent in circular from
the Nice Committee to all the evangelists whom they
supported in Italy. " We protest," wrote the Committee, "against the misrepresentations and invective
indulged in with regard to the object and present
attitude of the Vaudois missionaries in Italy, honour-
ing as we do those Christian feelings which have im-
pelled them to go and proclaim the gospel in those
portions of their country where, in times past, their
forefathers were persecuted to the death for the truth's
sake. . . . And finally we protest against the manifest endeavour of the author of this most objection-
able book to persuade Christians at large that he can
include in his so-called ' Chiesa Cristiana ' all those
Churches (*i.e.* congregations) over which the Lord has
placed you as overseers, and that you share his sectarian opinions ; whilst, on the contrary, we have the
firmest conviction that neither his views nor his spirit
are participated by many individuals amongst your
Churches, much less by the Churches themselves."

The direct challenge which these words conveyed
was repeated a few weeks afterwards by Dr. Desanctis in an even more emphatic form. He and
Mazzarella, with those who followed them in Genoa,
had joined the Scotch and Vaudois congregations of
that city in observing the week of prayer. So salutary did this evangelical union prove, that it was
proposed to continue holding these joint-meetings
once a month. But such fellowship with the other

Churches was not at all to the taste of Betti; now depôt-keeper for the British and Foreign Bible Society in Genoa, and a pronounced Darbyite. He protested strongly against this alliance, and letters written in the same sense were received from the Plymouth party at Florence. Under this influence, Mazzarella began to waver. Desanctis now felt that his own position must be further cleared, lest he should even seem to sympathise with the Darbyites. His " Declaration," addressed "to the Evangelical Christians of Italy," appeared in March, 1864, along with a tract from his pen entitled, " I Plimmutisti"; and it concluded with these words of direct appeal: " I wait your judgment with confidence, and require you to pronounce it without delay."

Only a few of the " Churches" thus addressed by Desanctis responded to his appeal in the way he hoped for. Among the minority however was a large and influential congregation in Florence ; and as to the others, whatever reasons may have led them to give their tacit approval to Rossetti and his book, after-events showed clearly enough that they had no intention of casting in their lot with the Plymouth party. At Genoa affairs came to a threatening crisis. After considerable delay a meeting was held to decide the burning question of the day. Mazzarella pronounced in favour of Rossetti's views, and concluded his statement with much abuse of Desanctis for what he had published on the subject. The meeting almost unanimously agreed with these opinions; and in consequence of the decision thus unequivocally expressed, Desanctis withdrew from his connection with the congregation : an act in which he was supported by one individual, Sig. Pompeo Rossi. Foolish as this step was from a worldly point of view—for Desanctis had no other means of subsistence than the salary he received from the Società—he was not allowed to suffer for what he had done. Dr. Stewart, with the spirit of the Scottish Disruption still hot at his heart, felt a natural interest in this sacrifice of worldly advantage to religious principle. He published an account of what had taken place where it was likely to meet the eyes of those who cared for the gospel cause in Italy ; and before long Dr. Desanctis was settled in Florence with full and congenial occupation as editor of the *Eco* and *Amico di Casa*, and evening lecturer in the Waldensian Church.

The Florence of these days had become a completely different place, as regards evangelical work, from what it was under the Grand Duke and the old *régime*. Besides the Palazzo Salviati, with its college, its church, and its printing press, the Waldenses had a hall on the other side of the Arno, where weekly services were held by Sig. Geymonat and two assistants—one of them Dr. Revel, President of the Evangelisation Committee. There were also two other places of worship frequented by Italian converts not belonging to the Vaudois communion. One of these, and at this time the more important, was lodged in the ground floor of the Palazzo Bor-

ghese, Via Pelagio. This congregation enjoyed the
ministrations of Sig. Gualtieri, a convert with a strange
history. He had once been the parish priest of San
Donato al Cistio, near Florence ; but making known
his change of faith to Dr. Stewart in 1858, he was
assisted to escape to Genoa. The Nice Committee
afterwards took Gualtieri up, on his declaring a parti-
ality for the Società, and sent him to Florence, where
he acted as the pastor of a congregation consisting
of about two hundred converts. The Darbyites, now
diminished to some sixty persons, formed the fourth
evangelical congregation in Florence, and worshipped
in a hall at the Barriera under the ministry of Sig.
Magrini, whose stipend was provided by Count
Guicciardini. The relative proportion of these two
congregations in Florence, once the very source of
Italian Darbyism and its strongest rallying-point,
affords some ground to think that Plymouth opinions
had not at this time such a hold of the country as
before. Rossetti's pamphlet was probably designed
to reanimate a drooping cause ; and even Magrini's
congregation were so far from approving the accusations it contained, that they bound over their minister
to abstain from abusing the Vaudois in the pulpit : a
species of polemic in which it seems he was too fond
of indulging.

Besides these places of worship, there were evangelical schools where many children received a good
education. One of these had been opened some
years before by the Scotch ministers. It was now

under charge of the Waldenses, directed by a Committee chosen from all the evangelical Churches, and consisted of three classes, attended by a hundred scholars, who were taught in Sabbath school as well as through the week. There was also a school attached to the Wesleyan Mission, which had been begun by Sig. Ferretti, and was now prospering exceedingly under the care of Sig. Bolognini, formerly employed in mission work at Malta and Constantinople. Nor must we forget to notice a boarding-school just opened by the Kaiserswerth Deaconesses. This institution proved most efficient in providing sound Protestant teaching for girls belonging to families who could afford to pay the very moderate fee demanded. To complete our view of evangelical Florence as it was in these days, let us glance at the remarkable work carried on there by Miss Burton. That devoted servant of Christ had begun her labours among Italian navvies employed in the construction of railways in Switzerland. On her removal to Milan and Florence she began to work among the different regiments of Grenadiers stationed in these cities, and thus laid the foundation on which Sig. Cappellini has built his " Chiesa Militare " with such notable success.

In all these diverse agencies, co-operating on the whole so harmoniously and successfully, we see the fruit of seed which was sown amid the tears of sorely tried faith while times of darkness and persecution still lasted. That fruit was naturally more evident and abundant in a city like Florence, where the interest drew to a focus. Yet much that was hopeful presented itself in other places besides the capital—in the retired town of Siena, for example. A convert from Pontedera had got employment there, and used his opportunity well, speaking freely both to his master and his fellow-workmen of what the gospel was doing in his native place. These "words fitly spoken" awakened much interest ; and in the end an invitation was sent to the evangelicals at Pontedera, asking that one of them should come to Siena and expound the new opinions there. Barsali and Fantozzi went on this errand, and had more than one opportunity of preaching the gospel to large audiences composed of considerable employers as well as of workmen. The impression made was such that an immediate demand sprang up for Italian Bibles and other evangelical books.

Nor was it long before an evangelist came to reside at Siena, and fostered by his presence and care the work so well begun in that place. Among the plans suggested by Dr. Stewart to the Edinburgh Italian Committee for providing suitable men to labour as evangelists in Italy was one which proposed that funds should be found for the support of Scotch divinity students willing to give themselves to the Italian field. One such man at any rate offered himself for this work—the late Rev. J. Simpson Kay, who laboured for many years as Waldensian pastor at Palermo. Mr. Kay left Scotland in 1862, and was directed to proceed to Siena ; partly in order that he might acquire Italian in its utmost purity—for Siena is famed in that way—and partly that, as he gained command of the language, he might support and advance the evangelical movement there. On Mr. Kay's settlement at Palermo, which took place when he had been about a year in Italy, the work in Siena was taken up, first by a Waldensian student from the Palazzo Salviati, and then by the Rev. Mr. Moorehead, a zealous young missionary from the United Presbyterian Church of America. Siena is now the seat of a regular Waldensian Mission.

After Florence, Leghorn was perhaps the most important centre of operations in Tuscany. Ever since 1852, when the nucleus of a congregation was formed in that city by the conversion of the servants in the Manse, a little band of native Protestants had been steadily gathering there. Sig. Cocorda, the Waldensian evangelist at Florence, paid occasional visits to the flock at Leghorn ; but in 1859 their numbers had so much increased, and the opportunities which the neighbouring city of Pisa afforded were so great, that application was made to the Table to settle a regular pastor in that district. Sig. Ribetti was sent in answer to this appeal, and under his charge the congregation at Leghorn increased so rapidly that in a few months it was necessary to seek a new and more commodious place of worship.

This success seems to have roused the slumbering

spirit of persecution. The chief of police summoned the proprietor of the house where service was held, and tried to get him to refuse it to the evangelicals. Coppi, an advocate in Leghorn, came to the next service and threatened to raise the mob against the Protestant pastor and his hearers; and a few weeks afterwards a troop of *gendarmes* appeared in the hall, silenced the preacher, and forcibly dispersed the congregation. Recourse was had to Ricasoli, then in power; but he paid little attention to the case until urged to do so by a Scotchman of his acquaintance whom Dr. Stewart had made aware of the facts as he passed through Leghorn. The result was a promise that Sig. Ribetti would be allowed to continue his work, and protected from all molestation.

New difficulties however of a very vexatious kind soon appeared in connection with an effort which was made to provide a decent and commodious church for the Protestants of Leghorn. A suitable property having come into the market, the Vaudois Committee of Evangelisation ventured to buy it at the price of £1,500, on Dr. Stewart's assurance that he would become responsible for the collection of the sum needed. A warehouse which occupied the ground thus acquired was at once taken in hand and altered so as to suit the sacred purpose which it was now to serve; and all was thus in readiness for the decent performance of Divine worship, when suddenly the chief of police sent an interdict debarring the converts from so using their property, since it lay but

three hundred yards from the parish church of SS.
Pietro e Paolo.   Ricasoli, on being again applied to
assured Dr. Revel the interdict would be withdrawn ;
and, in fact, the church was solemnly consecrated on
the 19th June, 1861, in presence of a crowded congregation of four hundred worshippers, among whom
were the Scotch ministers of Leghorn and Florence
in their official robes.

This attempted persecution was little to the credit
of Biscossi, the governor of Leghorn, and the other
authorities of the town.   They kept the ground
they had taken in opposition to the evangelicals to
the very last ; and even dared to issue a summons
against the pastor and the beadle of the Church after
the Government had sent instructions that Protestant
worship was not to be interfered with.   This was
done in the belief that the evangelicals did not know
what Ricasoli had ordered, and might still be intimi-
dated so as to refrain from acting upon the liberty
the Government allowed them.   Saddest of all, it
seems that behind these misguided men who used
their "little, brief authority" so ill, stood the religious
society of St. Vincent de Paul, urging them on to
commit outrages against the law of the land as well
as the charity of the gospel of Christ.

Dr. Stewart wrote to Scotland an account of the
dedication of the Vaudois Mission Church, from
which we may take the following extract, as it tells
his reasons for thinking this event one of the greatest
importance :—" First, It affords a new and great

opening for evangelical work in Leghorn ; second, It indicates the line which Ricasoli—the successor of Cavour—is prepared to take in his administration, and the decision with which he intends to carry out his views ; and third, It is a fresh triumph in the great cause of religious liberty in Italy. With a free constitution and a preached gospel, this noble country and noble people may yet be a praise and glory in the earth." The prediction thus made that the Leghorn Mission was likely to provide new opportunities of successful effort was soon justified by the event. No less than seventy-two converts were added to the membership of the Vaudois Church before Christmas, and a shrewd proof that this progress was substantial appears in the keen opposition which continued to be offered by the Roman Catholic party.

Here we must take account of a sad event which troubled the hearts of the evangelicals sorely. Barsali, who had seemed to be a pillar of the Church at Pontedera, yielded to the threats and blandishments of Cardinal Corsi, and returned to the bosom of the Roman Church. Every means was now used by the clergy of that Church to turn to advantage what had happened. Barsali was brought to the Cathedral of Pisa, where he solemnly recanted his profession of the Protestant faith, and the priests made constant opportunities of keeping him under the eye of the public. His gifts of intellect and utterance were of no mean order—a circumstance which favoured the plans of those who now had him in hand. There was Sig. Ribetti, the new Vaudois missionary in Leghorn, drawing crowds to his conferences and making many converts. Would it not be well to have Barsali challenge him to a public dispute? Nor need there be any fear of the result; for should the Waldensian prove too strong in argument, how easy would it be to raise a cry of blasphemy, at which the police might readily interfere and put an end to the dispute. So thought the priests, and a public challenge was sent to the Waldensian pastor in Barsali's name. The tactics of the enemy however were too well known by this time; and Sig. Ribetti, who understood the measure of fair play he could count on in the circumstances, begged to decline the challenge. Then stood forth Padre Romola, the Superior of the Capuchin Convent in Leghorn, and printed several abusive letters against the Mission Church and its minister. To this new attack Sig. Ribetti, relying on the freedom supposed to belong to the press, replied by means of a pamphlet, which was eagerly bought up by the people. It seems as if the aim of his enemies was to induce him to take such a step; for no sooner had he done so than he was summoned, tried, and condemned by the Pretorial Court of S. Leopoldo to suffer a term of five days' imprisonment, and to pay the costs of the process. An appeal was at once taken from this decision; but meanwhile the Romanists had gained their point: the evangelical minister and his people had been harassed and in-

volved in heavy legal expenses. That it was possible
to institute such a process arose from the anomalous
condition of the law at that time. When the Grand
Duke left, the Constitution had been proclaimed, and
therefore nominally Tuscany was under the same
laws as Sardinia ; but strange to say the Leopoldine
Code, which had taken the place of the " Statuto " of
1848, was allowed to remain in force. This offered
an alternative ground for legal procedure, of which
the priestly party eagerly availed themselves when-
ever they wished to annoy the evangelicals.

In spite of such petty but vexatious persecution the
cause of the gospel at Leghorn continued to flourish
in a very gratifying way. Within fifteen months of
Sig. Ribetti's arrival his congregational roll displayed
the names of no less than one hundred and forty
converts from Popery. In material things too a
substantial progress was made. Before the year 1863
had closed, Dr. Stewart was able to announce the
gift of a handsome service of communion plate, sent
to the Italian congregation by a Glasgow friend, and
to report on his own part that the whole sum ex-
pended in the purchase and alteration of the Church
property had been covered by the subscriptions of
those who responded to his appeal.

We must not forget to notice the Leghorn evangelical schools. This enterprise was commenced in
November, 1861, and those who encouraged it were
fortunate in securing the services of an active
young master full of the enthusiasm of his profession,

who not only taught the children of Sig. Ribetti's congregation by day, but of his own accord held evening classes for the instruction of adults. Four years afterwards the number of scholars in attendance was so increased that several teachers had to be employed. By this time the sound secular training which these classes afforded was ably supplemented in a Sabbath school, superintended by a pious Danish lady—Miss Dalgas—who not only rendered this eminent service, but also taught the children music on Saturdays, and aided Mrs. Stewart in the meeting she held for their mothers, where much was done to secure religious training for the young in their own homes. We must picture to ourselves an attendance of ninety pupils at the day-school: all, with hardly an exception, the children of recent converts or of those who were yet in the Roman Catholic Church ; and a night-school presided over by one of the municipal council, Sig. Remaggi, who was often to be seen playing the part of a teacher, and surrounded by eight or ten working men, whom he was instructing,—for such was the state of things in 1866. A year afterwards the number of scholars was one hundred and sixty-five, divided into four separate schools or classes, and already this promising enterprise had begun to bear fruit of the best kind, for one of the most hopeful scholars was sent by Dr. Stewart to study at La Tour with a view to the ministry, and two others were ready to take the same course as soon as bursaries could be found for them. In

March, 1868, was held the first of those annual bazaars in aid of the Leghorn schools by which Mrs. Stewart has been able to provide, year by year, no small part of the subsidy necessary to support this important work. Leghorn has furnished the mission field with no less than twenty pastors and teachers, almost every one of whom was trained in these evangelical schools. It may safely be said that few agencies have wrought a greater blessing in Italy than this.

Leghorn, important as it was in itself, deserves further notice here as an effective centre of operations from which the gospel was brought to bear upon neighbouring places. One of these was the island of Elba. An interest in the reformed religion had been awakened there by tracts which the Madiai gave to some sailors of the island who happened to be at Nice. Inquirers then came from Elba to visit Sig. Ribetti at Leghorn ; and he arranged to go over and hold occasional services for them. Two years afterwards a Waldensian pastor was placed there in charge of a couple of stations, which could count between them two hundred communicants.

The city of Pisa also, lying as it does but fifteen miles away, felt the full stream of that evangelical influence which had its source in Leghorn. Some five and twenty years before this time Mdlle. Calandrini—a Swiss lady—had taken up her residence there, and held Bible readings in her own rooms. Dr. Tito Chiesi was one of those who became converts by this means. Presently Mdlle. Calandrini

was forbidden by the Government to return to Pisa ;
and then followed the ten years of persecution.   On
the change of government in 1859, it became plain
that there was evangelical life stirring in the town,
and an affecting account exists of the first semi-
public Protestant service held there in the month of
December.   The "upper room," with its little company of four and twenty persons ; Rovillo, the blind
missionary from New York, led in by Gambaccini,
who shared with him the duty of the ministry ; the
simple addresses and fervent prayers on the one
part, the solemn silence and reverent attention on
the other ; all were eloquent with the very spirit of
the gospel.

This interesting work in the Casa Tellini came
almost immediately under the direction of Sig.
Ribetti, who visited Pisa twice a week to attend to
the converts' spiritual interests.   But the needs of
Leghorn soon became too great to allow of this
being continued ; and at the earnest request of Dr.
Stewart and Dr. Chiesi, another Waldensian, Sig.
Salomone, fresh from his studies in Belfast College,
was sent to take charge of the Pisan converts.

For a time all went well, and then Plymouthism,
which seems to have dogged the steps of the Vaudois
in their missions, as Pharisaism did those of St. Paul
in his, made havoc of the Church at Pisa.   Gambaccini set himself against the young pastor, and
wrote to the Darbyites in Florence to deliver Pisa
from the Waldenses.   The room in the Casa Tel-

lini was reserved for the evangelists who came in answer to this appeal; and Sig. Salomone had to find another for himself on the Lung' Arno. Almost all the converts embraced these new opinions: the Vaudois evangelist found his place of meeting deserted, and he was obliged to quit the field.

The Maremma railway, designed to connect Leghorn with Civita Vecchia, was then in course of construction; and the contractors—Mr. Brassey and others—laudably anxious to consult the spiritual interests of their workmen, applied to the Waldensian Committee of Evangelisation for a suitable missionary. This request coincided with the troubles at Pisa; and Sig. Salomone was sent to a more grateful scene of labour in the Maremma. There his opportunities of usefulness were large, as he not only preached the gospel to the men on the line, but got access to the different villages and towns by which it passed; and pushed his labours as far as Orbitello, on the frontier of the Papal States. On the completion of the railway, Sig. Salomone was sent to Modena, and proved himself an able and successful evangelist both there and in the adjacent cities of Bologna and Ferrara.

Meanwhile matters went anything but smoothly at Pisa. On the 24th of March—Palm Sunday—1861, there was a riot which had nearly ended in the destruction of the Casa Tellini and those who worshipped in it. Lorenzo Poggi, a recent convert from Romanism, was in the act of taking his new-born son to be baptised at the evangelical church, when he was met near the Ponte a Mare by a mob armed with sticks, who stopped the carriage, forced him to get out, and made the coachman drive with the child to the Cathedral, where it was baptised according to the Roman rite, and then conveyed to the Foundling Hospital. Not content with this outrage, the crowd now began to cry, " Down with the evangelical church!" and took their way straight to the Casa Tellini, increasing in numbers as they went. There the morning service was over, and some of the congregation had left; but forty-six persons remained, among whom were three Englishwomen and the Hon. Mr. Vernon. With horrid cries of " Death to the Protestants!" the infuriated mob now filled the street and began to hurl stones at the windows, to force the entrance with a crowbar; and, their efforts in that way failing, they climbed the roof and tried to tear off the tiling. For three long hours the desperate assault continued. "Kill them! kill them!" shouted the crowd. "We'll hack them to pieces! We'll set fire to the house!" and there is little doubt they would have carried out their blood-thirsty purpose, had it not been for the courage of an officer of the Royal Carabineers, who placed himself before the door with one or two of his men, and exclaimed, " When you get in, it shall be over my dead body." He also offered to get the English people away safely, if they would come out; but Mr. Vernon gallantly answered that they preferred to share the fate of their fellow-Protestants, whatever that might be. At last, after the most inexcusable delay, the National Guard turned out and dispersed the mob. This outrage seemed to arise from the excited passions of the common people; but contemporary accounts give one to understand that it was instigated by a conservative party, to which Cardinal Corsi and many members of the local nobility belonged. These people deplored the departure of the Grand Duke; detested the newly proclaimed Constitution; and contrived this violent way of interfering with the religious liberty which it guaranteed. They were the more easily able to effect their purpose as the Lenten sermons just preached in the Cathedral by the Frate Ferri had been directed against the, evangelical movement, and had left the minds of the people in an excited state. Nor did these endeavours cease upon the failure of the first attempt by violence. The Cardinal Archbishop issued a pastoral in which the severe drought of 1861 was traced to the work of the Protestant preacher—Sig. Tecchi—in Pisa; and those who were under Corsi's influence withdrew their custom from the unfortunate evangelicals. Thus oppression came in to do that which violence had failed in effecting.

Had nothing but persecution from without befallen the evangelicals in Pisa, their case would have been comparatively an easy one. Plymouthism had a fair field there and every favour; but was soon found wanting. Mrs. Young, a resident in the city, interested herself in the converts; built a church for their use; and, as they had rejected Waldensian ministrations, she arranged with the Nice Committee to send them an evangelist. Sig. Tecchi accordingly was settled in Pisa; but before long troubles arose, and on the evangelist's death, which took place in 1862, grave disorder entered the congregation, as his widow assumed her husband's place, presided in the meetings, and attempted to rule the discipline of the Church. It is needless to tell more of the melancholy story. De Michelis succeeded to the pastorate, and was soon obliged to give way to Perazzi, an ex-priest, to whom Mrs. Young gave the use of the chapel she had built. At last, in 1864, the Waldenses were invited to return; and Sig. Prochet, then at Lucca, recommenced the work which Sig. Salomone had been obliged to leave three years before. It is true that this was not done without opposition. Sig. De Michelis, when dismissed from the chapel, secured a room at the Piaggione, where he retired with those converts who adhered to him. This rival service was still in existence when Sig. Prochet came on the field, and the contention it caused must have seriously embarrassed his first steps towards strengthening the things which remained; but his success was such that he could soon report an audience increased two-fold, and an interest which continued to grow.

"Amid the excitement of Italian movements, and the numerous agencies at work, the Waldensian

Church is the safest and surest to abide by." Thus
wrote the Rev. Mr. Macdougall of Florence in 1862;
and looking at what we have seen at Pisa, we can
only echo his sound opinion, noting with satisfaction
how the Church of the Valleys entered in, both there
and elsewhere, at the open door which was set before
her. From Courmayeur, Aosta, and Como in the
distant North; by Turin and Milan, Genoa and
Bologna, Ferrara and Florence, Lucca, Leghorn and
Elba; to Siena and Perugia in the central provinces;
and even distant Naples and Palermo in the South;
that grand impress of the Vaudois, with its *lux
lucet in tenebris*—its candle lighted under the stars
of night—was now being fulfilled in the labours and
successes of some fifty mission stations.

The opening of Southern Italy to the gospel, however, is a matter too important to be dealt with in a
single sentence. Every one remembers Garibaldi's
daring descent upon Sicily; his triumphant progress
through that island; his landing at Aspromonte;
and the *coup de main* by which he possessed himself
of Naples, and added the kingdom of the two Sicilies
to the dominions of Victor Emmanuel. What happened in Tuscany on its annexation took place also
in the South. Those interested in Italian evangelisation watched Garibaldi's course, following him with
their prayers; and as soon as the kingdom of Naples
was delivered from the tyranny of "Bomba," they
sought to take possession there as they had already
done in Tuscany.

The first evangelist whose name deserves mention here was the Marquis Cresi Vastarini, a convert who had studied at the Oratoire in Geneva, as well as in the Theological Halls of the Free and United Presbyterian Churches of Edinburgh. Dr. Stewart, who took a very helpful interest in his career, sent him to Naples after he had acted for a short time as evangelist in Bologna; and it was in the capital of the South—his native city—that he "made full proof of his ministry" by superintending the depôts for the sale of religious books, and the work of colporteurs; by visiting the sick in hospitals, and conducting mission services among his fellow-townsmen. Thus a substantial foundation was laid for the labours of those who followed.

Some two months after this mission station had been opened, the well-known Gavazzi paid a visit to Naples. His eloquent denunciations of the Papacy excited the greatest enthusiasm, nor was the effect merely a transient one. A Committee of Evangelisation was formed; a hall was rented; and Sig. Cerioni, a converted priest, was engaged to aid Sig. Cresi in the charge of what proved a rapidly increasing congregation.

To consolidate and direct this recent and promising work was the desire of Dr. Stewart, and in seeking to do so he followed the plan found so effectual elsewhere, by getting a station of the Free Church of Scotland established in Naples. Even before Sig. Cresi went there, Dr. Stewart paid a visit to Naples for the purpose of ascertaining the number of Scotch residents, the possibility of obtaining a suitable place for worship, and the like. A year afterwards— on the 15th November, 1861—the Rev. Mr. Buscarlet, now of Lausanne, who had then completed a term of service as assistant pastor at Leghorn, was settled in the newly formed charge at Naples.

In the wake of the Scotch followed the Waldenses. Sig. Appia, who had been working as an evangelist at Palermo, accepted the call to become pastor of the Swiss Church in Naples; and, with the help of an assistant, engaged in the missionary operations which were being carried on there. This work was very largely of an educational character, owing to the dense ignorance which lay upon these Southern peoples. Schools were taught in connection with each of the three congregations we have mentioned; and the generosity of the Countess Steinbock supported another institution for the secondary education of girls. The teaching thus given contributed in no small degree to the success of the Protestant propaganda. Mr. Buscarlet tells how a sharp young Neapolitan questioned him one day on the Reformed doctrine of original sin and baptism; and how the lad used what he learned, baffling his priest who preached baptismal regeneration to him by alleging the case of the penitent thief. One can see that only time and training were wanting to make these southern Italians mighty in the Scriptures and valiant for the truth; and it is interesting to find Mr. Howells,

the well-known novelist of America,[1] bearing independent testimony to the work of the Neapolitan
Protestant schools. "No one can study their operations," he says, "without feeling that success must
attend their efforts, with honour to them, and with
inestimable benefits to the generation which shall
one day help to govern free Italy." Mr. Howells
saw the schools under Mr. Buscarlet's guidance, and
it is to him and his zealous coadjutors that the author
pays this tribute of well-deserved appreciation.

We must not forget to notice the work which was
carried on at Ancona. This seaport on the Adriatic
coast had a temporary importance as the then ter-
minus of the railway which formed part of the over-
land route to India ; and, for other reasons too,
Dr. Stewart had long kept it in view as a station
which might well be occupied in the interests of
Italian evangelisation. When the Ionian Islands
were ceded to the crown of Greece, Dr. Stewart proposed to the Continental Committee of his Church
that the Rev. Mr. Charteris, for many years chaplain
at Corfu, should go to Ancona, where his missionary
experience and knowledge of the languages and life
of the Levant might have been of the greatest service. Circumstances interfered to prevent the accomplishment of this plan ; but Ancona had a large
Jewish population, and in 1861 the Free Church
Committee charged with the interests of Israel were

---

[1] In his " Italian Journeys."

induced to send the Rev. Theodore Meyer as missionary to the Jews in that place.

It cannot be said that Mr. Meyer's labours in
the Ghetto of Ancona were attended with striking
success; but he had much encouragement in acting
as the pastor of the British residents in the town, and
was able to do a great deal for the Italians as well.
A year after this appointment was made, we hear of
a depôt for evangelical books in Ancona; of three
colporteur-evangelists busily spreading the gospel
through Umbria and the Marches; and of a little
assembly of converts gathered by one of these men
at Perugia, among whom a Waldensian pastor was
soon settled.

A strange story is told of this Perugian congregation. It seems that an Italian of the place had so
far fallen away from religion as to turn his back on
it altogether, and to seek the devil instead of God.
Books of magic, when he could find them, became
his bibles; and he desired nothing so much as the
advice of some one who could tell him how to raise
the devil and form a league with him. When in
this frame of mind he happened to enter the Cathedral, where a friar was sounding forth denunciations
of the evangelicals in Perugia. "They are wolves in
sheep's clothing," exclaimed the excited preacher;
"they pretend to be Christians, but in reality *it is
the great devil they serve*, and not God." "What!"
said the astonished hearer to himself, "do these
Protestants indeed worship Satan? then they are the

people for me." Full of this strange belief and stranger hope, "blind" and "led by a way he knew not," if ever man was, he sought the room where the Waldensian pastor gathered and fed his little flock. There he heard what touched his heart, and soon he was rejoicing in Christ. Was there ever, one wonders, a more striking instance of the power God uses to bring good out of evil?

At Ancona too Mr. Meyer had remarkable and unexpected opportunities of preaching the gospel to Italians. Let us follow him on one of his excursions to the southward. Leaving the train at Pescara, he finds a monk waiting him with the warmest welcome. This, it appears, is the Superior of a monastery in the neighbourhood, where Reformed opinions have found an entrance; and he has come with beasts of burden and an attendant lay-brother to carry off the Free Church minister, bag and baggage: so eager is he that the fraternity should have instruction in the faith. The following day witnesses a strange chapter in the history of the brotherhood, when at command of their Superior and in company with three secular priests, one of them a canon of the Cathedral near by, they sit at the feet of a Protestant pastor, and hear the free gospel of salvation echoed by their sounding vaults where have rung for ages past only the responses of the Breviary and the Missal. Mr. Meyer can have had few such *picturesque* opportunities; but occasions constantly presented themselves when this zealous missionary could deliver his message with effect.

The story of Barletta, a town which became famous through Protestant Europe as the scene of a horrid outbreak of fanaticism in 1866, may help to make our impression of this work on the Adriatic coast more vivid. Barletta was then a place of local importance, where, as is still the fashion in these parts, a population of some 20,000 souls was gathered in from the deserted fields of the neighbourhood. Mr. Meyer paid a visit there during one of his journeys, and recorded a most favourable opinion of Barletta as seeming to afford an encouraging field for evangelisation. Many Bibles were in the people's hands; not a few studied the Scriptures eagerly; and at a public assembly—the first of its kind ever held there—presided over by the mayor and the chief of police, Mr. Meyer preached the gospel with every sign of success. Two years afterwards there was a regular evangelical congregation in Barletta, consisting of more than one hundred members, who had the evangelist Giannini as their pastor.

Such a success soon aroused violent opposition on the part of the priests. Choosing their time—St. Joseph's Day—when the churches were unusually crowded, they made a determined attempt to inflame the passions of the people against their Protestant neighbours. This appeal was only too readily answered. A disorderly crowd, headed by Don Ruggiero Postiglione, who had taken a chief part in denouncing the evangelicals from the pulpit, poured along the street, shouting as they went, " Kill the

Protestants!" The little place of worship was surrounded; a determined assault was made; the entire
tenement was given to the flames; and four persons,
two of them evangelicals, the others neighbours who
tried to offer resistance, were dragged to death before
the great crucifix which these barbarians bore on a
processional staff as the standard of their infamous
war. Nine other inhabitants of the town were seriously injured; and Giannini, against whom the assault was specially directed, only escaped with the
greatest difficulty. He took first to the house-roofs;
and then lay hid for some days in a cellar till order
was restored and his safety assured him.

The outrage at Barletta, like that at Pisa, bore
something of a political character. Both were the
results of a conservative reaction in which the aristo-
cracy were then attempting to overturn the establishment of constitutional liberty under the House of
Savoy.

We may well believe that no more conspicuous act
of gallantry was displayed during the whole evangelical campaign than that which appears in the
conduct of Mr. Meyer on this occasion. He was at
Ancona when the outrage took place in Barletta, but
hastened as soon as he heard of it to the seat of
danger. Arrived there, he nobly vindicated the civil
liberty of the gospel by holding a public service in
Barletta on the Sabbath immediately succeeding the
horrid deed of blood. Our feelings tell us that this
service must have been of an unusually affecting

character; and the report of one who was present says that not a single eye was dry. The Government took strong measures against those concerned in this outrage; and a Committee, hastily formed in Florence, collected and disbursed a sum of £400 in aid to the wounded, and compensation to those whose worldly goods had been destroyed. Let us note too that in Barletta, as elsewhere, "the blood of the martyrs" was "the seed of the Church." When Giannini returned to the scene where his labours had suffered so rude an interruption, he was welcomed by crowded assemblies, and encouraged by increased earnestness evident among the people.

In spite of all he was doing at Ancona, Mr. Meyer's position there was a somewhat doubtful one. Here is his own account of it: "Two thousand Jews are, under any circumstances, too small a number for keeping up a mission among them." "If my instructions tied me down to work solely and exclusively among the Jews, I should already have asked the Committee to recall me." The Jewish Committee naturally felt themselves bound to retire from a position which, however important in other respects, did but little for the conversion of Israel; and in 1867 this earnest minister of the Word, who, like St. Paul, had turned to the Gentiles when Israel would have none of his message, was removed to Amsterdam. A Waldensian evangelist immediately filled the vacant place at Ancona; and thus the work Dr. Stewart took so much interest in, and which had been so carefully fostered by him, was continued and even extended.

We must now take account of another and most promising field which was thrown open to those who sought to spread the gospel in Italy. The hated yoke of Austrian dominion, shaken from Lombard and Tuscan shoulders, yet rested on those of Venice ; but in consequence of the short and decisive campaign of 1866, that island State, once the proudest home of liberty, had her ancient traditions revived, and was joined with popular acclaim to the Crown of Italy. Even while hostilities were in progress, the army afforded occasion for evangelical work, which was largely taken advantage of. Professor Appia, of the Waldensian College, organised a corps of *infermieri*, or ambulance assistants, who, with the knowledge and approval of Garibaldi, did wonders for the bodies and souls of the wounded on the bloody field of Bezzecca. Besides these young men, two pastors from the Valleys were regularly enrolled as army chaplains. It is true that as they were posted at Milan and Bologna respectively—far from the scene of actual conflict—and as their appointment had reference merely to the Vaudois soldiers enrolled in the army corps, their opportunities of general usefulness were not so great as had been hoped for. Still, in spite of friars and sisters of mercy, these devoted men got access to the common hospitals ; and often did faces, dull with pain and weariness, grow bright as "the young Protestant priests" went their rounds among the beds. At Bari too, where a large number of Garibaldi's men were gathered, colporteurs and evangelists received a ready welcome and did much for Christ in the crowded camp. But it was in the result of the war, rather than during its progress, that the gospel cause was seen to triumph. When camps were broken up and hospitals closed, then amid the happy people of these nine Venetian provinces, hailing their new-found liberty with tricolors and *evvivas* of joy, the ministers of the Word saw their advantage and entered in.

On the 8th of October, 1866, Dr. Stewart wrote to the convener of the Continental Committee as follows: "I was up lately in Venetia, looking after the first introduction of some of our Bible Society's colporteurs there. I did not go into Venice itself, because the Austrians were putting all sorts of obstructions in the way. But I would like you and Principal Lumsden to consider the great importance of having a Scotch minister settled at Venice, and, if you view the matter favourably, to bring it before the Colonial and Continental Committee. . . . A minister settled there might do much to help forward the Italian evangelisation." This wise advice was speedily acted on. It has not indeed been found possible to establish a permanent station of the Free Church at Venice; for the number of resident Scotch people is very small; but Mr. MacDougall of Florence, who gave supply there during the first

months of freedom, and, very notably, the Rev. A.
B. Campbell of Markinch, who succeeded him in
that duty, were able to realise Dr. Stewart's plan,
and did much in the cause of the gospel at its first
introduction among the Venetians.

"Happily Mr. Turin of Milan arrived ten days ago,
having been enabled to find supply for his pulpit at
home. A large hall is on the point of being secured,
and if Mr. Turin can be released from his work at
Milan, and transferred to Venice, a large extension of
the deeply interesting and most promising movement
here is confidently expected. The Waldenses, whose
agent he is, had a right to enter on the work here
thus early, for not only are there members of all the
evangelical Churches of Italy gathering here (one
from Barletta among the rest), and a goodly band of
earnest Venetian youth attracted to the Bible cause ;
but in the 29th regiment of foot, stationed here for
the winter, there are no fewer than seventy Waldensian soldiers. . . . Besides Venice there are
openings in Verona . . . and in Mantua, from
which an earnest call to Mr. Turin has come, signed
by a large number of searchers after truth." So
wrote Mr. MacDougall on December 14th, and
added on the 21st : "Mr. Turin has been obliged to
leave ; so I go on nightly with the most interesting
meeting I ever saw. Last night twenty men and
some women came forward and signed an address
which one of them had drawn up, begging for a
settled evangelist."

This movement was too successful to escape notice from the Roman clergy, and as in many other cases, petty persecution was the order of the day in Venice. Workmen were refused employment; owners of house property were dealt with to withhold accommodation from the evangelicals; while pulpits resounded on all sides with denunciations of the "heresy" which was spreading so rapidly. Meanwhile the call for an evangelist had been answered. Sig. Comba, the Waldensian pastor at Brescia, was transferred for a time to Venice, where he began to hold meetings nightly with the people ; and so great was the eagerness to hear which these conferences awakened in the Venetians, that Mr. MacDougall wrote on March 18th, 1867 : "It is to be regretted that one or two more Waldensian evangelists could not have been spared to take advantage of the present wonderful desire to hear the Word preached, by opening services in all the four quarters of the city."

The work which was begun in this spirited and hopeful fashion continued in spite of all opposition. If the pulpits pronounced against it, was there not Gavazzi newly come to Venice, and thundering with his mighty voice in its favour ? Sig. Comba was succeeded by Sig. Ribetti of Leghorn, and he by Sig. Torino ; and in this way the immense labours incident to the establishment of the mission were successfully overtaken by a rapid exchange of labourers. Meanwhile Mr. Campbell had arrived to represent the Free Church of Scotland in Venice, and entered at once into the mission work which was going on. He intimated the Italian meetings at the close of his own service, and took " all the visitors he could lay hands on " to see for themselves what was being done. " As the general result of this interest," so he wrote on June 10th, " I am now in a position to say that the funds necessary for the support of the Venetian Mission for the next year are nearly all supplied."

Besides gathering what covered working expenses, Mr. Campbell, seconded by Mr. Colton, the American Consul in Venice, collected a sum of 3,000 francs, with which he paid the rent of a building fit to accommodate the Italian congregation when it met for worship, and to provide rooms for the residence of the pastor and schoolmasters. This palace—for it was indeed such, and recalled, by the splendours of its frescoed hall, the cardinals, senators, and generals of the noble family to which it belonged—stood near the Church of San Giovanni e Paolo, and proved, in the new use now made of it, a grievous offence to the *curato* of the parish : a zealous Dominican monk. Between this man and Sig. Torino ensued a sharp war of pamphlets, ending with a published declaration on the part of the Romanists, to which the recent outrage at Barletta gave point, that they would attack the Protestant place of worship and turn it into a sepulchre for the heretics. So real was the menaced danger that the *Questore* of Venice took alarm, and warned Sig. Torino to act with the greatest prudence that the people might have no excuse for an outbreak of violence. Fortunately the measures taken were effectual, and the threatened attack never took place.

When the mission in Venice was fairly established and provided with a suitable place for conducting Divine worship, it was felt that the services of a permanent pastor must be secured. Sig. Comba, who had already made trial of Venice, accepted this post ; and hardly had he entered on the work when its responsibilities grew so heavy that he asked the Waldensian Committee to send him a colleague. Sig. G. P. Pons came in answer to this request, and two school teachers were also sent that the equipment of the mission might be complete. This may seem a large staff of labourers for so recent an enterprise, but the circumstances were of a nature to require extraordinary efforts. Mr. Colton says : " I wrote you a few days since in regard to the wish of Mr. Comba for a new *locale*, and perhaps for *two* places of worship in other parts of the city. We found one suitable location which I think will answer for the present. . . . Mr. Comba will preach in it at present, and until some one can be found as a colleague to him. We cannot afford to work Mr. Comba to death." It seems that at this time there were no less than four hundred and forty catechumens to be examined with the view of their becoming Church members ; the schools were crowded, and a large outlying population, some on the mainland and some in the lagoons from Torcello to Chioggia, were ready to welcome the preaching of the gospel. As

Mr. Colton said : "The work we have undertaken is of greater proportion than we anticipated ; but I am sure we cannot complain if the Lord has so honoured our efforts and given us such a glorious harvest. I only hope that the work will extend till it takes in the whole population."

"But how," it may be asked, "did the Waldensian Committee of Evangelisation support these various mission stations which it established?" If we except the Roman States, still closed against the entry of a pure gospel, there was now scarcely a wide district of the country anywhere left without at least the neighbouring influence of some centre of truth and life. How was so vast a charge, so considerable a current expense, sustained by the Vaudois Church?

There are those who say that missions should be almost if not altogether self-supporting, and who would argue from the enthusiasm which the gospel excited in Italy, that no difficulty should have been experienced in obtaining from the converts themselves sums of money sufficient to support if not to extend the enterprise. Indeed the Waldensian evangelists kept this possibility in view, and, while restricting their own expenses as far as was consistent with a proper discharge of duty, they were faithful, like St. Paul, in exhorting their hearers to practise the same self-denial that they might be able to contribute to the support of ordinances. But "not many rich were called" in Italy. The converts were for the most part poor, and weighed down by an ever-increasing burden of taxation. They could not even support their own pastors, so far were they from being able to provide a surplus to meet the needs of an extending work.

There may perhaps be a feeling that the stipends of the Waldensian evangelists were excessive, and that the difficulty was therefore an artificial one. Yet the facts give no countenance to such a suggestion. At home in the Valleys, it is true, the pastors could live on an income of some sixty-five or seventy pounds per annum; but throughout Italy, and especially in the towns, where for obvious reasons the missionaries had for the most part their residence, the conditions of life were very different. We have noticed the burden of taxation: this burden oppressed the Waldensian Missions in a twofold way, both leaving the converts little to give, and making comparatively large stipends necessary for the due support of the ministry among them. It was calculated that a schoolmaster must have forty pounds a year if single, or sixty if married; an evangelist sixty to a hundred pounds; a pastor one hundred to one hundred and forty, according to the state of each. Nor can such an estimate be considered excessive when we take into account the demands which these missionaries had to meet. Their congregations were poor, and the religion they professed cut them off from all that charitable succour in sickness which countless confraternities lavished upon their Roman Catholic neighbours. The public hospitals were open to them indeed ; but to enter these was to court that intolerable kind of persecution in which the "sisters of mercy" excelled when they had to deal with Protestants. In short, there was but one way out of the difficulty ; the pastor must be the almoner of his people : a necessity which encroached far upon his already scanty stipend.

Less than the above-named sums then could not be supposed enough to support the missionaries. Yet their number in 1865 was fifty, all told ; from which data—taking eighty pounds as the mean stipend—a simple calculation gives us £4,000 as the least possible annual expenditure by which these missions could be kept at the point they had then reached, without making any provision for extending them. Sig. Prochet stated to the Free Assembly in Edinburgh, that the converts of the Waldensian congregations contributed as much as those of all the other Italian mission agencies put together. We may take it then that they were, at least, not behind their neighbours in the grace of liberality ; but to provide £4,000 a year—nearly £100 from each station—was quite beyond their attainments, if not beyond their power. In what quarter then were Dr. Revel and the Committee of Evangelisation to seek the help they manifestly needed ?

Dr. Stewart, it will be allowed, had done much for the Vaudois. Possessing a thorough acquaintance both with Italian needs and Waldensian faculties, enjoying the full confidence at once of the Synod at

La Tour and of many large-hearted benefactors in
Scotland and throughout the world, he was able, as
we have seen, to meet many most pressing demands
in connection with the buildings and funds necessary
for the training of a fully educated ministry. The
men in fact were ready and eager—so were the fields
—"white unto the harvest"; but no one, however
earnest his good-will, however wide his acquaintance,
or indefatigable his efforts, could hope to meet by his
own personal exertions the constant and ever-growing
demands for stipend : the daily working expenses of
so great an enterprise. Feeling this as he did, Dr.
Stewart was at the same time resolved that, for the
very sake of what he had already been permitted to
accomplish, the Waldensian Missions should not be
given up. Happily for the cause of the gospel in
Italy, this determination led to the discovery of a
basis which has since provided, if not amply, at least
sufficiently, for the support and even the extension of
the Waldensian work in Italy.

It was at the Synod of 1865 that the plan took
shape. The report then presented by the Committee
of Evangelisation showed an increase of agencies at
work, and so far was of a gratifying nature. It also
recorded that by extraordinary efforts money had
been found to meet the debt with which the financial
year was opened. But the state of affairs thus revealed
was so unsatisfactory as regarded the support of these
growing agencies, that it was felt something must be
done without delay to put matters on a better foot-

ing.   Some weeks before, Dr. Stewart, who had early
realised this need, wrote to Dr. Revel as follows :
" There are to be at the Synod two Guthries, Dr. A.
Thomson, Dr. A. McEwen, Mr. William Robertson,
Edinburgh ; besides one or more of the Scotch
ministers in Italy.   There may be, and I hope there
will be, English too.   Now all our three Churches
are represented : Established, Free Church, United
Presbyterian Church.   What would you think of
having a special conference (either at the hotel or in
the church during dinner-hour) with all these for the
purpose of our laying before them the need of more
systematic help ? "   The hope here expressed that
"English too" would be present was not realised; but
Dr. Stewart was able to arrange the conference he
proposed.   It met in the Hôtel L'Ours—in the room
occupied by Dr. Guthrie.   The Scotch ministers in
Italy joined their voices to those of the Vaudois
Committee in urging on the deputies from Scotland
the need of regular and liberal remittances of money
to the amount of at least £4,000 per annum, that the
mission work might go on unembarrassed by those
cares which had hitherto proved such a hindrance.
The deputies were unanimously of opinion that what
was wanted might be obtained if, as the Committee
had proposed, Dr. Revel paid a visit to Scotland and
pled his own cause.   They added the advice that this
deputation should be delayed till November, and that
Dr. Stewart should be sent home to take part in it.

There were many reasons which made it difficult

for the minister of Leghorn to leave his post at the
time desired ; but on the deputation being deferred till
February, 1866, he consented to accompany it ; and
the confidence he inspired, joined with the interest of
Dr. Revel's addresses, and the persuasive eloquence
of Dr. Guthrie, who made one of the three advocates,
secured a triumphant success for the cause of the
Italian Mission. " The facts lie in a nut-shell," wrote
Dr. Stewart, shortly before he consented to plead by
word of mouth. " Since ever constitutional liberty
was given to Piedmont in 1848, I have urged them
(the Vaudois) to leave their valleys and to undertake
the evangelisation of Italy. First I pled alone,
then Hanna joined me ; and when God took him,
MacDougall did. In answer to their declaration that
they were most ready, that they felt the obligation,
that they had the men but not the means, we have
ever said to them : ' The battle against Popery and
the evangelisation of Italy is a common cause ; all
the Churches of Christ are as deeply interested in it
as you ; go on in faith, and they will not allow you to
want ; the funds will be forthcoming.' They have
listened to our invitation ; they have occupied the
ground in a marvellous manner ; but the demands
are daily increasing, while the interest in their work
is decreasing in Britain."

This concise statement was amplified into an effective plea when Dr. Stewart presented the case of
Italy in the speeches he delivered in Scotland. His
lengthened acquaintance with the Vaudois, which

began long before the days of their emancipation in 1848, enabled him to bear valuable testimony to their moral worth and to their unquestioned soundness in the faith. From this ground he argued that they were pre-eminently fit for the work to which God had called them in the mission fields of Italy, reminding his audiences how untrustworthy the Italian character as moulded by the Church of Rome had ever been found by those who designed to employ newly made converts as pastors and evangelists; and that this was particularly and pre-eminently true of those who had been trained for the priesthood. One chief danger of the Italian Protestants, he added, lay in their leaning to Plymouthism; and he urged that since the Waldenses possessed a sound Church government and an educated ministry, they were worthy of all confidence and support in their work for Italy. They were poor, he said, but independent. They would resist any attempt of the Free Church of Scotland to dictate to them, as they had repelled the suggestions of General Beckwith and Dr. Gilly. He was come, he concluded by declaring, not as a Free Church minister, but as a friend of the Vaudois and of Italy, to ask his countrymen whether an enterprise so needful and so nobly begun should be abandoned or restrained because of the poverty of those who conducted it; or whether the necessary sum of £4,000 a year could not be subscribed by Scottish Churchmen for the support and extension of such self-denying labours. The result of this appeal was that local branches of the Waldensian

Aid Committee were formed in some twenty Scottish towns to gather subscriptions and forward them with regularity to the Committee of Evangelisation in Italy. This money amounted in the course of a few months to the handsome sum of £3,000, one-third of which was at once forwarded to Dr. Revel as the firstfruits of Scottish liberality.

When Dr. Stewart appeared at the Synod of 1866, it must have been with feelings closely akin to those of St. Paul on his last visit to Jerusalem, "to bring alms to his nation and offerings." Certain it is that a new courage inspired him and his fellow-workers. Material help had in this case been accompanied with the yet more precious gift of sympathy. The Waldenses, in their remote corner of the land, were linked by golden chains of love to their brethren of the larger evangelical Churches, who now bade them God-speed with every most convincing proof of true interest in the great and arduous work they had undertaken. Nothing could have been more satisfactory or of happier augury than this most practical form of Evangelical Alliance, which certainly afforded cause for the most lively thankfulness to all concerned in the religious future of Italy.

CHAPTER III.

UNION IS STRENGTH.

"O fratel mio, ciascuna è cittadina
    D' una vera città : ma tu vuoi dire,
Che vivesse in Italia, peregrina."
        —*Dante, Purgatorio*, xiii. 94-96.

HAVING seen the mission work of the Waldenses thus firmly established in Italy, and prepared for another great advance, let us turn for a little to those other bodies of evangelicals which still maintained a separate position at the inevitable cost of more or less antagonism and heart-burning.

Taking a general view of their history, we find that, though chequered, it displays on the whole a bright and promising progress. Little by little Plymouth principles yielded to a sounder conception of Church polity. We may be left in some doubt of the precise attainments of these brethren at this period or the other ; but only the dullest sense can fail to see the direction in which they are moving, and the end to which their progress leads—a system of Church doctrine, government, and worship so sufficiently at one with those of the Vaudois Missions as to leave one or other Church blameworthy if an incorporating union do not take place between them. Such a union, when God's good time for it is come, is indeed to be fervently desired by every true friend of Italian evangelisation.

Let us in the meantime trace the lines upon which the progress we speak of has proceeded. We may commence our survey with Florence, partly because detailed accounts of the doings there are abundant ; and also because that capital was a true centre of evangelical life, which can be relied on to exhibit movements typical of those taking place throughout the country.

The step taken towards Church order in 1858 was followed, it seems, by a reaction, under the influence of which a number of those who had lately seceded from the Plymouth party returned to it again. Those that were left persevered for a while ; took a hall and elected deacons : but a fresh schism took place in this remnant, by which the congregation was again dissolved—one party joining the Waldenses, and the other returning to the Plymouth Brethren.

We are not to suppose that those who returned "whence they came out" continued satisfied with their new situation ; for when Gavazzi fell like a wandering star on Florence in 1861, urging with his stentorian tones the cause of order and organisation, a considerable number gathered at that rallying cry and constituted the congregation over which

13

Sig. Gualtieri presided in 1864. This work was carried on under the superintendence and by the help of the Wesleyan Church; and when that body withdrew its mission from Florence, those who had composed Sig. Gualtieri's congregation joined the Chiesa Libera.

It may be well to define the relation of the Waldenses to these different movements. As soon as the bloodless revolution of 1859 set Florence free, Sig. Malan, followed by Sig. Cocorda, entered on that promising field of labour. In 1860, when the School of Theology was transferred from La Tour to Florence, Prof. Geymonat took charge of the work at the request of the Committee of Evangelisation. The services were held in the room then rented for the use of the Scotch congregation, and at first the audience was but small—presenting in this respect a marked contrast to the crowds which poured through the same entry to attend the Plymouth services of Sig. Magrini and Sig. Gualtieri, who then worked together.

Meanwhile the Italians inclined to order were worshipping in a hall on the Corso Vittorio Emmanuele, near the Cascine, and they continued to do so until the latter months of 1860, when, owing to the unsatisfactory conduct of their pastor, this congregation was dissolved. By Christmas—three months after the arrival of the Vaudois in Florence—a large number of those who had belonged to the now disbanded congregation on the Corso came to Sig. Geymonat, and nearly filled the Scotch hall when he preached in it. In spring (1861) the Committee of Evangelisation took a larger place of meeting in Via Vigna Nuova, and there the work was carried on with growing success.

The cause of this attraction is not far to seek. In 1855, after the first great schism in Piedmont, the Waldensian Synod passed a declaratory Act (xxv.) regarding the spirit in which the Church designed to pursue her mission work in Italy. Thus it ran :—

" The Synod, desiring to obviate all misunderstanding regarding the nature of the work of evangelisation carried on by the Vaudois Church, unanimously declares that the sole end of the Vaudois Church in providing for the preaching of the gospel beyond her own bounds is to fulfil the Lord's command, ' Preach the gospel to every creature,' and to lead souls to the knowledge and obedience of Jesus Christ ; and consequently she makes no pretension to impose on them her own form of Church government."

Professor Geymonat, in the work he carried on so zealously in Florence, kept this declared principle of action always in view. He gathered a congregation by preaching the gospel ; he proved from the Word the necessity of Church order ; he expounded and established on scriptural grounds the polity of the Vaudois Church ; and then, calling his converts together when the time was ripe for action, he asked them to determine and adopt according to conscience and God's Word whatever constitution might seem best.

The result may be given in the words of their own letter to Dr. Stewart : a communication which shows the close connection he had with this (as with every other) hopeful work of evangelisation in Italy, and at the same time testifies to the sense these converts had of his efforts on their behalf :—

" Reverend Sir,—The Session of the Evangelical Italian Church of Florence feels it a duty to acquaint you with the fact that the said Church has been constituted, and the Session formed. Those who sign this letter are aware how much you, sir, have done for the evangelisation of Florence, and for the establishment of the College and the Evangelical Church ; they know that if the Waldensian Church has used its utmost zeal to evangelise Italy, you, sir, have done no less to provide the necessary means ; wherefore the Session and Church just constituted, feeling the debt of gratitude they owe to the Vaudois Church, are at the same time sensible they owe no less to you, and would consider themselves wanting in the duty of gratitude did they not officially acquaint you with the formation of their Church. You, sir, were present when our commissioner handed our letter to the Synod of the Waldensian Church ; it is therefore unnecessary to repeat that we have constituted ourselves a Church on the basis of the Word of God, taking for our rule of discipline the Constitution of the Vaudois Church. On this basis

we have assembled in an orderly way, and have
elected our session or consistory, composed of the
six elders who sign their names below, and presided
over by Professor Paul Geymonat as pastor; we
have formed our Deacons' Court, composed of the
six deacons who sign this letter; and we are constituted a Session and Deacons' Court, according to
the forms required by the Constitution. We are
well persuaded that you will receive this notice with
pleasure, and we hope you may be willing to aid the
youthful Church by your counsel. We on our part
shall do our utmost to deserve your patronage.
Florence, 18th June, 1866. (Signed) Riccardo
Pratesi, Diacono. Cappelli,O.R. Lodovico Conti.
Paolo Geymonat, Pastore. L. Desanctis, Anziano.
Bunsen. Antonio Bianchini. G. Appia Pr. Frascini
Gregorio. Federigo Hamilton."

This might seem at first sight a congregation too
Waldensian in its constitution to prove attractive to
those brethren who were groping after a better Church
order than the Plymouth congregations supplied;
but there is evidence to show that some of them
at any rate regarded the matter in another light.
Ferretti, whom we have already mentioned as the
founder of a flourishing school in Florence, and who
had since, like Gualtieri, been taken into the pay of
the Wesleyan Church as an evangelist, speaks as
follows of the new enterprise: " Florence, 15th Sept.,
1866. The Waldensian Church of Florence has
constituted itself into the Evangelical Italian Church,

has renounced the name 'Waldensian,' the use of the Vaudois Liturgy, and the authority of the Reverend Waldensian Table, retaining the Vaudois Constitution for a year only, on trial, to see whether it suit or no. At the year's end, if they find it suitable, they will continue under it, otherwise it will be rejected. The new Church provides its own funds, and has elected a consistory of deacons and elders, and Messrs. Desanctis and Geymonat have offered their services gratuitously as evangelists." No one can fail to see that the writer of these lines meant to speak in a tone of approval; and if this new venture met the views of Ferretti, a typical Florentine convert, it is not too much to suppose that there were many of his kind ready to gather in hope round Geymonat and Desanctis, and support them in the effort they were making to unite the scattered fragments of Italian Protestantism.

The builders of Jerusalem held the trowel in one hand and the sword in the other ; and, like them, the Waldensian leaders were called sharply and soon to the defence of the work in which they were engaged. So promising an enterprise, so attractive a rallying point could not fail to excite the jealousy of those who saw in this progress towards Church order the downfall of their hopes for. Italy. Plymouthism, which seems to have had its strongholds at this time in the congregations of Magrini at Florence and Mazzarella at Genoa, repeated its former mistake and "wrote a book." This production was a pamphlet which current opinion attributed to the pen of an English-woman residing in Pisa. It consisted largely of extracts from the Vaudois Confession of Faith, selected in such a way as, in the opinion of its authoress at any rate, to prove that the doctrines of justification by works and of baptismal regeneration were held by the Waldensian Church.

Dr. Revel and Professor Geymonat had an easy task in the answer they immediately issued from the press. "A Defence of the Evangelical Doctrines of the Waldensian Church"—for such was the title of their reply—was felt to have disposed of "A Letter on the Free Italian Church" and its accusations in a thoroughly satisfactory way; and it is gratifying to find that this unwise attempt, instead of stemming the stream that had begun to flow, only gave a new impetus to the cause of consolidation and union.

The most effective answer however to this attack was one of a practical kind, which it is curious to find came from Pisa: the very town whence the attack itself had proceeded. De Michelis, the evangelist there, had already drawn up a Confession of Faith, and he now invited delegates from all the Free Italian "Churches" to meet in synod at Bologna that they might confer on the question of the creed. This conference took place on the 16th of May, 1865, and was attended by the representatives of twenty-three congregations. Its proceedings were not of a very conclusive character, as the delegates were only instructed to ascertain the mind of their respective congregations on the general question—whether there should be a Confession of Faith or no. There is no doubt however that this conference was looked on as a step to more complete organisation ; for Magrini of Florence and Mazzarella of Genoa—the acknowledged leaders of the Plymouth party—showed their disapprobation of it. The former recorded his dissent from the proceedings: the latter actually retired from the congregation at Genoa because the members resolved to send a commissioner to the conference.

Thus the Free congregations began to come out boldly from the narrow and sectarian position in which the Darbyites would have kept them. This of itself implied an approach to the Waldensian Church, but even explicit proposals of union were not wanting. Happy would it have been for both parties and for the cause of religion in Italy had so desirable a result been actually brought about.

The author of the plan was Gavazzi, a man whose eloquent utterances in defence of religious liberty against the Papacy did much to prepare good ground for the sowing of spiritual seed. He was widely known among the congregations of the brethren, and had the sympathy of all but such as were determined Plymouthists. Nor was it to the members of the Free "Churches" alone that he was a *persona grata*. He had just said handsome things of the Waldenses in a pamphlet he published about this time against Plymouthism, and so decided was the friendliness of his attitude that one who knew him well—the Rev. J. R. MacDougall of Florence—wrote (3rd April, 1868): "I trust we shall yet get him yoked in true fellowship to the Waldensian car."

Full of this hopeful scheme, Gavazzi approached Dr. Desanctis with the request that he would draw up a Confession of Faith to serve as the basis of union. When this was ready it was laid before the Wesleyan missionary in Florence, the Rev. Mr. Piggott, in order to secure his assent and that of the various evangelists—Gualtieri and others—working under his direction. Mr. Piggott drew his pen through the Calvinistic passages. Dr. Desanctis as promptly, when the matter was referred to him, disowned a document he could no longer recognise as his own confession of faith, and thus the matter ended for the time.

We may gather from the history of this fruitless negotiation a shrewd notion of how parties then stood among the Protestants of Italy. On the extreme right there were the Waldenses and those converts who like Desanctis adhered to them. These stood strong in their Calvinistic faith and Presbyterian discipline. The Wesleyans formed the middle party, with Gavazzi and the others who preferred Arminian views. Next came the congregations of the Bologna Convention, not yet decided which part to take, or whether it were desirable to have a Confession of Faith at all. On the extreme left lay the irreconcilable Plymouth party, now so insignificant in numbers and isolated in position as to exercise henceforward little appreciable influence on the Protestant movement.

It is moreover possible to conjecture from this state of affairs what turn events would take. Gavazzi and the middle party, repelled by the representative of rigid Waldensian orthodoxy, drew nearer to the Free congregations. An influence was thus brought to bear on these which rapidly ripened their purpose to achieve a settled faith and discipline. And precisely at this crisis one came to their help who could lead them farther than the point Gavazzi had reached. Mr. MacDougall of Florence took up the cause of the Free Churches in 1869, and began to do for them what Dr. Stewart had so long done for the Waldenses in the furnishing of material help to their struggling congregations.

Signs were soon given that these good influences did not fail of their due effect. In the end of June, 1870, twenty-five deputies of the Free congregations convened in Synod at Milan to vote upon a Confession of Faith. The Synod finally agreed upon eight articles, embracing as principal points—" The perfect and immutable authority of the Bible ; the corruption of human nature through the sin of Adam ; the salvation of the sinner—originating in the free love of God the Father—procured by the sacrifice, resurrection, and intercession of Christ the Son—and communicated by the Holy Spirit ; the sanctification of the Christian by the grace of God ; the Church the Body of Christ composed of regenerated believers ;

the universal priesthood of believers, and a special ministry ; the resurrection."

No doubt the dogmas of this Synod left much to be desired. It will have been perceived, for instance, that they make no mention of the Sacraments : an omission which seems to have been studied ; for there was the greatest diversity of practice among the various congregations with regard to these rites. " Io direi piuttosto," writes Sig. Torino of Milan, in 1865, " che le Chiese Libere rigettano affatto il Battesimo, poiche fino ad ora non ho mai sentito che abbiano battezato una persona qualunque." [1]

Yet what an advance is marked by this Confession, imperfect as it is. The name " Chiesa Libera " too— also adopted at this Synod of Milan—was of the happiest augury. It was not indeed coined at that time, having been recommended to the Società, and adopted by them not long after the schism of 1854, as a protest against the Waldensian creed and ministry, by which they conceived that Church was held in bondage. Nor are we to suppose that because the name was adopted by the Synod of 1870 in the singular number, it was therefore intended as a sign that these Free congregations were now united under Presbyterian Church government. Their relation to each other was one of openly acknowledged independency, and at the Synod which they held at Rome in

[1] " I should rather say that the Free Churches reject Baptism entirely ; for to this day I have never heard of their baptising any one whatever."

1873 "a motion was made, and only lost on a point of order cleverly raised, that the name of '*Union of the Free Christian Churches of Italy*' should be adopted instead of the '*Free Christian Church*'; in order that the independency of the various Churches on one another might be more clearly proclaimed." Nevertheless we may take it that the name adopted at Milan was highly significant. It indicated that a new influence was at work among these congregations, urging them in the direction of closer union and higher organisation. This was the spirit in which the point of order was raised in 1873, and it has been active ever since till of late it found full scope in the negotiations for union with the Waldensian Church.

In 1884 this union, so desirable in many ways, began to be seriously talked of. At the Synod of the Waldensian Church held that year, Sig. Prochet, as convener of the Committee of Evangelisation, submitted a proposal for an incorporating union with the Chiesa Libera. This was favourably entertained, and the Committee were instructed to confer with the representatives of the Chiesa Libera, and to report the result to the Synod. Dr. Stewart, who was unable to be present at La Tour, wrote as follows on the subject : "If the proposed union could command a unanimity of votes with reciprocal concessions on both sides, with brotherly love, and 'in the power of the Spirit,' the result would certainly be to strengthen the cause of Christ in Italy, and to contribute to the glory of God. But to obtain this result, allow me to suggest that you must put your hand to the work, not only with much prayer, but with a prudence and judgment which have not been manifested in the preparatory meetings, in which apparently the dominant feature was an enthusiastic challenge thrown to difficulties. The very nature of the temporal interests of your Church demands such judgment." [1]

This wise advice shows that difficulties were already felt by those who were engaged in carrying out the recommendation of Synod. The Waldensian name it appeared was a stumbling-block to many in the Free congregations, while it was cherished with all the tenacity of a natural and reasonable affection by those, whose ancestors had suffered death itself for the truth which that venerable name represented. In a case like this sentiment approaches the character of duty. But, as Dr. Stewart pointed out, it was no mere sentiment, it was a wise self-interest which advised the preservation of the ancient name. Yet on this rock the union negotiations were once more wrecked.

On the 30th March, 1886, the Waldensian Committee of Evangelisation adopted the following resolution: "The Churches which have arisen out of the mission work intend that the name 'Chiesa

---

[1] In Italy the law recognises only the Church of Rome, the Waldensian Church, and the Jews, as corporations capable as such of holding property.

Evangelica Valdese' shall be retained to represent the Church in its totality before the Government and foreign Churches. But these Mission Congregations, availing themselves of the liberty guaranteed them by the Waldensian Synod of 1855, assume for themselves the name of 'Chiesa Evangelica d' Italia.'" The Synod of the same year decided that the name of the united Church should be "Chiesa Evangelica Valdese," leaving individual congregations free, should they prefer it, to style themselves "Chiesa Evangelica —d' Asti—di Brescia," etc.

It might have been thought that this decision would have met all the difficulties of the case. Both contracting parties were agreed to avail themselves of the name "Valdese" as that in which the joint property should be held. The Waldensian Church did not propose to force her own name upon a single dissenting congregation of the Chiesa Libera. That Church however, in its Synod of May, 1887, decided to reject the article. A report to this effect was received at La Tour in September, and with a cordial expression of the brotherly feeling existing between the Churches, negotiations for their union were— only temporarily let us hope—relinquished.

We should do wrong were we to think of these events as fruitless because they did not issue in an actual incorporating union. The articles unanimously agreed on in February, 1885, by the representatives of the Chiesa Libera as well as by those of the Waldensian Church are highly interesting as giving un-

doubted indications of the progress that had taken
place in the former communion. If we select those
which seem most significant, it appears that the congregations which twenty years before had neither
corporate union with each other nor a formulated
rule of faith were now prepared to give their adhesion
to the Presbyterian form of Church polity, to be represented by the Waldensian Table in their relations
with Government, and to adopt the Vaudois Confession of Faith as the standard of orthodoxy among
their clergy.

Dr. Stewart's prophecy of 1847—"The Italians will
become Presbyterians"—little likely as it seemed,
has thus so far been fulfilled. Professor Geymonat's
insistence on the wise deliverance of 1855 in his
work has been justified. The Chiesa Libera has gone
"from strength to strength," till to-day she stands
at no immeasurable distance from the Waldensian
Church. May we not hope then that a Church which
has made such notable advances will soon enter into
visible corporate union with those who, separated
from her by no essential article of faith or discipline,
seek the same glorious end which she pursues in the
evangelisation of Italy. The historical sense, fore-
casting future events from the past, invites us to
expect this as naturally and necessarily as our interest in the gospel cause engages us to pray for it.

CHAPTER IV.

THE CITADEL.

" Ma Vaticano e l' altre parti elette
Di Roma, che son state cimiterio
Alla milizia che Pietro seguette,
Tosto libere fien dall' adulterio."
                    --*Dante, Paradiso,* ix. 139-142.

THE history of the Chiesa Libera and its relations
with the Waldensian Church has tempted us to
push our survey as far as the events of recent years.
Let us now retrace our steps, and remark some
matters of the highest importance to the progress of
the gospel in Italy.

When, in the seventh decade of the century, Tuscany, Naples, and the Venetian provinces had been
successively added to the Italian Crown, the central
States, constituting the temporal dominion of the
Popes, still remained independent of the National
Government. This position of affairs presented many
elements of instability. It was supported by French
troops, with which the Papal throne was surrounded,
and was guaranteed by the treaty made with

Napoleon III., but the Franco-Prussian war of 1870 cut the Gordian knot with the sword. The troops of France were recalled to fight for their own country. Sedan saw the emperor a prisoner ; and so at last the long-deferred will of the Italian people had its way. On the famous 20th of September the national troops entered Rome, and took possession of the Eternal City as the legitimate capital of their country.

If the Italians had long coveted Rome as the centre and guarantee of their national life, the Protestants among them had waited no less eagerly for the downfall of the Pope's temporal power, that they might preach the gospel both in the Roman States —long closed against them—and in the capital itself. When the great opportunity actually came, it was taken advantage of at once. Those who established their theological school at Florence with such splendid audacity followed with like persistence the further triumph of their country's arms, and planted the standard of the cross in the very centre of national life and power.

The first Italian Protestant service in the Eternal City took place in the Hôtel de l'Univers on the 9th of October, 1870, and the honour of holding it belongs to Sig. Prochet, Dr. Revel's successor in the convenership of the Evangelisation Committee. "I am just returned," writes the Rev. J. B. Will, "from the first Waldensian service in Rome. Cav. Jervis, who is still here, kindly offered the use of his room

14

in the Hôtel Univers, which is capable of holding at
least fifty persons.   There were only fifteen present,
but I hope that this is the commencement of a work
which will grow, and that in Rome we shall yet see
one of the most flourishing stations.   There was
something most touching in hearing the first chapter
of St. Paul's Epistle to the Romans read, and in
Mr. Prochet's discourse from the words, 'I am not
ashamed of the gospel of Christ.'"   At a second
service held in the evening of the same day, eighteen
persons were present, including four soldiers from the
garrison.

The Waldensians, when they entered Rome, found
it already occupied by friends from whom they received much help.   Eminent among these was the
minister of the Free Church congregation there.   As
early as 1859—not to speak of former efforts—the
Rev. Mr. Trail, of Boyndie, began to hold occasional
services for Scotch residents and visitors.   The result
was of such an encouraging nature that Dr. Stewart
wrote (Dec. 5th, 1859) to the convener of the Continental Committee, urging that a suitable man should
be sent out without delay to occupy this most important station.   Dr. William Laughton, of Greenock,
accepted the appointment for the following winter,
and settled himself in the upper storey of a building
above the great flight of steps which lead to the
Piazza di Spagna.

Both the time and the place demanded the greatest
caution.   Dr. Laughton made a thorough study of

Rome and its inhabitants, native as well as foreign; but kept himself so retired by day as to be accessible only to those who brought him introductions. It was found that though Cardinal Antonelli would give no direct sanction to a Presbyterian service, he would not interfere with what might be done quietly in that way in a private house. Acting on this tacit understanding, Dr. Laughton accordingly preached in his own rooms—18, Piazza Trinita dei Monti—during eleven weeks of the Roman season. There was no singing at these services, and the congregation dispersed one by one, for fear of attracting attention; yet in spite of these precautions, which some thought ridiculous, the audiences were large, showing that a gratifying interest attached to the new venture.

This useful and encouraging work was kept up in succeeding seasons by the Rev. W. Fraser, of Gourock, and the Rev. J. E. Carlile. In 1864 Dr. J. Lewis was appointed, and continued to serve the station for the next ten years. For a time the congregation worshipped in a hall situated in the Via Pontefici, then, in the year when Rome became free, a more suitable place of worship was found in a building outside the Porta del Popolo, bought for the Free Church of Scotland. This continued to be the home of the congregation till 1885, when their new church in the Via Venti Settembre was opened by Dr. Gray, the present pastor.

We have seen how the Waldensian Mission work was supported in other towns of Italy where Free

Church stations existed, and need not wonder to find that Rome offered no exception to this rule. There it was a popular cause which invited and received such help. Sig. Prochet's services as a minister of the gospel were so much appreciated by the Romans that almost at once there arose the necessity for a larger place of worship and the co-operation of another evangelist. The hall in the Via Pontefici was accordingly secured, and Sig. Meille, who had been working at Florence, came to Sig. Prochet's aid in Rome.

In spite of these advantages there was much to hinder the evangelists and to call out the sympathy of their friends. Clerical influence was still strong enough in the city of the Pope to drive Sig. Ribetti, Sig. Prochet's successor, from one hired hall to another. Such a state of affairs could not exist without inflicting the most serious damage on the new enterprise. Even had no interference been attempted, this way of conducting Divine service in places of a semi-private character had something in it which repelled the Romans instead of attracting them : especially people of the upper classes, of whom a certain number—some of them even belonging to the ranks of the nobility—had begun to attend the Waldensian Mission.

The solution of such difficulties could only be found in acquiring permanent possession of a suitable church, and to this pressing need the Committee of Evangelisation set their minds with the view of supplying it as soon as possible. The task however was no easy one. Rome was now the capital of Italy ; her population had vastly increased, and the value of the property within the walls risen so much, that it was calculated not less than £6,000 would be required to purchase a building fit for the purposes of the Waldensian Mission. Even this apparently liberal estimate fell short by many thousands of the sum actually required.

Where were the funds so urgently needed to be obtained? Naturally would the Waldenses have turned in their perplexity to that tried friend of theirs who had already obtained for them the money which settled their college so handsomely in Florence. But such an application was unnecessary. Dr. Stewart had of himself assumed the burden of this new effort, and was taking steps to render the establishment of the Waldenses in Rome an accomplished fact. He reminded his friends in Scotland that Dr. Revel, for whose memorial bursary they had just been subscribing, had, as the last official act of his life, put the mission in Rome on a permanent footing by the appointment of a regular pastor, and invited them to honour that eminent servant of Christ by a new and more visible monument, which might, as the home of the Waldensian Mission at Rome, further in an eminent way the interests of the gospel in Italy.

The sum of £6,000 first aimed at, was raised in the course of a few months. Mr. Lenox, of New York, who had shown a like munificence already in the case of Florence, headed the list of contributions with £1,000 ; and in October, 1873, so much had been subscribed that Dr. Stewart could purchase the Palazzo Scultheis, at the corner of the Corso and Via Caravita, for the sum of £9,900, and had still £1,500 in hand to meet the expenses of transforming the building into church and schools.

Still the contributions kept coming in, till they amounted to something like £15,000. This surplus suggested a new plan of operations. Certain shops on the ground floor of the Palazzo Scultheis were held on leases—some not expiring till 1882—which prevented the Committee from effecting the necessary alterations on their property until nearly ten years had elapsed. But no farther off than the adjoining street stood the Oratory of the Caravita, which, like a number of other churches, had just been confiscated by the Italian Government. It was generally understood at the time that the buildings thus dealt with would be sold to the highest bidder, and Dr. Stewart proposed to employ the surplus of £4,000 which remained in his hands by purchasing the Caravita for the Waldenses. Had it been possible to carry out this plan, the Protestant Mission would have entered into possession of a building with a strange history. The Caravita had belonged to the Jesuits. It was connected with the Collegio Romano by an arch across the street, and formed the focus of those constant "Missions" by which the society sought to bring

the whole of Rome within its net. Desanctis, in his
" Roma Papale," tells a curious story of the Caravita.
One evening a man entered this place of worship
and contrived by the dexterous use of a couple of
sponges to absorb all the holy water, substituting for
it the contents of a bottle of ink. Proceeding to the
neighbouring Caffè Veneziano, this ingenious spirit
recounted his stratagem, and bade the public await
the result. As soon as service in the Caravita was
over, many of the bigots who had attended it came
to the celebrated caffè, and, acting on their instructions, began to enter into the freest conversation with
those who sat beside them, designing to report all
the liberal talk they heard to the Reverend Jesuit
Fathers. On this occasion however, betrayed by the
black marks they bore on finger and forehead, they
were discovered and openly shamed.

When the Caravita was confiscated, it was assigned
to the Home Secretary's department; and though
Dr. Stewart and Dr. Lantaret saw that official and
tried to persuade him to sell the church, he found it
would make so convenient a library for his archives,
that nothing would induce him to part with it. A
hall was accordingly taken in the Via dell' Umiltà :
the officials of the Waldensian Mission were lodged
in the upper floors of the Palazzo Sculthcis ; and Dr.
Stewart watched his opportunity to secure, either the
Caravita itself on a change of-ministry, or some other
suitable building.

In the end it was found better to build than to

purchase. During 1879 a favourable site in the new Via Nazionale came into the market. The surplus in Dr. Stewart's hands, increased by a mortgage on the Palazzo Scultheis, proved sufficient to buy this ground and to erect on it a handsome church capable of seating four hundred people.

One might have supposed that, with the acquisition of a site and the commencement of building operations, the difficulties of the Waldensian Mission would have disappeared. But one of a peculiarly vexatious kind was yet to be encountered. The Carmelites had a church closely adjoining the Waldensian ground. This fraternity, naturally anxious to prevent the erection of what they considered a "heretical temple," availed themselves of a law forbidding any structure to be raised within nine feet of a public building, and applied for an interdict against the Waldenses. This was granted by the Court, and the Committee of Evangelisation had no resource but to wait as patiently as they could the result of an appeal which had been taken to the Court of Cassation.

At last, in 1882, the appeal was sustained, and an arrangement was entered into by the parties to the suit which left the Waldenses free to build as they wished. On Sabbath, 25th November, 1883, the church was dedicated to the worship of God. The bright sunshine of an Italian winter fell on crowded pews through three memorial windows, bearing the honoured names of Revel, Desanctis, and Stewart.

Solemnly was the Bible brought in, and placed on the desk, with an impressive prayer of consecration. Then Sig. Prochet, who, thirteen years before, had been the pioneer of this mission, and of evangelical work in Rome, ascended the pulpit and announced once more, though now in very different circumstances, the appropriate text : " I am not ashamed of the gospel of Christ."

How strange is the page of history which this event opens to us! At the head of it stands the name of St. Paul himself, who in his chains ministered the word of God to them of Cæsar's household, and sealed the truth with his blood. On this follows the ancient record of those witnesses who protested in early ages against the growing corruptions of a Church now become Papal, and who for the fearless part they played were driven to the mountains of the North, and forced to dwell "in dens and caves of the earth." Still noting the onward march of time, we find the footsteps of God going before His people and preparing their way. All unwittingly " the kingdoms of the world become," by reason of their enforced service, " the kingdoms of our God and of His Christ." Gradually the waters of captivity are rolled back and dry land appears. By successive advances, from Torre to Turin, from Turin to Florence, and from Florence to Rome, the old ground, apparently lost for ever, is recovered from the hands of the enemy ; and the Waldenses, in this the representatives of Divine truth, Catholic and triumphant in the Churches of the Reformation, are seen seated at last in what for ages had been the apparently impregnable stronghold of Roman error and superstition.

What a power lies in the gospel of Christ! When we see a Scottish Churchman like Dr. Stewart spending his life for Italy : urging, inspiring, enabling the ancient Protestant Church of that country to "wait on the Lord and keep His way, till her righteousness was brought forth as the light and her judgment as the noon-day," it is not of man we muse, nor of any body of men, however venerable, devoted, or successful. We see "the power of God" triumphing in him and in them, and we trust that power shall yet prevail even more visibly and completely, to the salvation of Italy and of the world.

CHAPTER V.

PIONEERS.

" Non vi si pensa quanto sangue costa
    Seminarla nel mondo, e quanto piace
Chi umilmente con essa s'accosta."
                —*Dante, Paradiso*, xxix. 91–93.

IN earlier chapters of this book we have already
taken notice of the part played by the press in
the evangelical movement ; but it is as well we
should now devote our attention more expressly to
the consideration of what was, and is, one of the
most important gospel agencies at work in Italy.
The place of honour here belongs of right to the
British and Foreign Bible Society.   Lieut. Graydon,
the Society's agent in Switzerland, had been eagerly
watching for an opportunity to cross the Alps ; and
in 1849, when the Constitution ruled affairs in Piedmont, a way seemed to be opened for that advance.
It is true that the censorship of the press was left
in the hands of the bishops, without whose leave
nothing could be published of a religious kind ;
but Lieut. Graydon observed very acutely that, while
the spirit of the law no doubt regarded all books

whatsoever, the letter made mention merely of those printed within the country. Resolved at any rate to put the matter to the proof, he ordered some Bibles to be sent from London to Turin, and attended in person at the custom-house to see what would be done with them. The officials seemed puzzled, as one case of Bibles after another was opened before them. They had their suspicions of such merchandise, yet hardly thought the books would have been dispatched unless the sender had made sure they were free to enter the country. At last some one had a happy thought. There were the Waldenses, who had liberty to use such books. No doubt then, the Bibles were meant for them : and without more ado the whole consignment was passed. In a few days these books were being openly sold in the streets of Turin. The court preacher indeed cursed them from his pulpit, but, in consequence of this, those who sold the Bibles had visits from several persons of high rank, anxious to obtain copies of that book which was " everywhere spoken against."

Meanwhile Bibles were finding their way into Italy from the South, *via* Malta and Sicily, Naples and Leghorn — a good work in which the Rev. J. Lowndes was the principal agent—and soon the way was opened for a much more daring effort. These were the days when the Pope and the Grand Duke met at Gaeta. In the absence of these personages from their respective capitals, it was resolved to try the bold experiment of printing Bibles on Italian soil. Editions of the New Testament were accordingly issued from the press at Florence, Pisa, and Rome. One of these—that printed in Pisa—was successfully distributed, but the two others were confiscated. As to the Florentine one, the Grand Duke laid hands on it as soon as he came back from Gaeta, seizing not only the copies found at the printing-office, but also a number which lay in the house of Admiral Pakenham. This was a serious loss to the Bible Society, whose the books were ; and Admiral Pakenham, as we know, was banished from Tuscany for the part he played in the matter. Then came the days of the Madiai, when it was found necessary to adopt a regular system of smuggling, that foreign Bibles might be put into Italian hands. All this we have already dwelt upon in another connection, but it is well we should record here some of the results which followed these persistent efforts to circulate the Word of God.

In speaking of the persecuting times, we noticed the escape of a friar from the S. Spirito Convent in Florence. His story is fitted to show the native power of God's Word, and, as such, it merits recital here. In 1851 Padre Verona, for such was his name, had his interest in the gospel awakened by the conversation of some friends who had become Bible-readers. He accordingly purchased a Bible and a few evangelical tracts, which served to give him some idea of the way of truth. Presently the season of

Lent came round, and his Superior sent him to
preach a course of sermons at the remote village of
Castel Piano, near Siena. His position was now a
difficult one. Though persuaded of the errors of
Rome, he was not as yet prepared to quit that
communion altogether ; and, accordingly, by way of
compromise, he resolved to preach at Castel Piano
indeed, but to preach the gospel there as freely as
possible. During the earlier days of his ministry all
went smoothly enough, till at last the time came
when, if he would not break the order commonly
observed in these courses of sermons, he must plead
with the people to spend their money in purchasing
masses for the souls in purgatory. This he did,
though the shoe pinched sorely, but how did a sword
pierce his soul when, afterwards, seated in the con-
fessional, he heard a widow say that she had been
so moved by his eloquence as to sell her poor faggot
—the only thing she had in the house—to buy, as
she supposed, a term of rest for her husband's soul !
Verona then felt the falseness of his position intolerable, and resolved at all costs to quit the Church of
Rome.

Returning to Florence, he wrote two letters : one
to tell his brother, the Superior, what he meant to
do ; the other to give an account of the money and
affairs of which, as bursar, he had charge. These
letters, together with a sum of five pauls due to his
servant, he left on the table of his cell, and locking
the door behind him, he quietly departed. Mean-

while the news of this intended escape had been
brought to Leghorn by the kind solicitude of Sig.
Bolognini, who travelled thither with the purpose of
arranging a place of refuge for the fugitive in that
city. Mr. Thomas Bruce, one of Dr. Stewart's elders,
opened his hospitable doors to Padre Verona, as he
did to many another Italian Protestant in danger;
but, on his first arrival, the ex-friar thought for a
moment that he had fallen into a trap. The clerical
beaver of a priest who was engaged as tutor in the
house proved, as it hung in the hall, the innocent
cause of a terror quickly dispelled. Verona was now
among friends. His habit was soon exchanged for
a suit of less compromising cut, which had been kept
ready for him ever since his escape was expected,
and in a few hours he started again for the North.
By a fortunate chance, an Englishman—Mr. Mansel
—was just on the point of leaving Leghorn for home.
He willingly put Padre Verona's name on his passport as that of his servant, and even altered his route,
that the fugitive might reach safe ground as soon
as possible. Arrived without mishap at Genoa,
Padre Verona proceeded to Switzerland, where he
learned the truth fully. He was afterwards employed
for some time as a missionary to his fellow-countrymen in Syria, and, returning thence, died, not long
afterwards, at Turin, well spoken of for his faith and
good works. Can we wonder if, in spite of bigoted
Romanists and unbelieving Protestants, those who
trusted the power of God's Word redoubled their zeal

and their efforts to scatter the seed of life broadcast over Italy?

Even more striking in its results was the case of the Gregori family. These were people in humble life, belonging originally to Bagni di Lucca. Thence they removed, about the year 1852, to Leghorn, where the father died. Gregori had followed the occupation of a courier, and this way of life providentially brought him into the service of an Englishman, who gave him an Italian Testament as a parting present. On his sick-bed—for he had a protracted illness—this book became dear to him; and when failing sight forced him to give up using his own eyes upon it, he made his little daughter read it aloud for his comfort. No other book was like it, he said, or could give him the same help— surely the speech of one who died a true, though hidden disciple of Christ.

More, however, was to follow. The young girl, who had learned to read and to love the Bible at the bedside of her dying father, kept up this good habit when he was gone. At the time of Gregori's death, his daughter and the rest of the family were still in attendance on mass and the other offices of the Roman Catholic Church; but in a little they were placed in circumstances more favourable to the development of the Scripture knowledge they possessed. The widow Gregori was taken into the Scotch Manse as a servant, and her children naturally came much about the house where she worked. In this way the daughter was brought under the instruction of the Rev. G. Wisely—now of Malta, but in 1853 Dr. Stewart's assistant at Leghorn. She began to feel how far the doctrine of the priests was from agreeing with what she read in her beloved Testament, and in the end, not only this inquirer, but the whole family were converted to the evangelical faith.

Giovacchino Gregori—the son—was sent to school by Dr. Stewart, and showed such good parts that he was accepted as a candidate for the ministry of the Waldensian Church. Mr. Burns, of Bloomhill, generously furnished the means for his support while he studied at La Tour, and, after passing through the usual curriculum, he acted as evangelist at Lucca and in the island of Elba. In 1865 Gregori was settled as Waldensian pastor in Naples, and died two years afterwards at Catania, "full of faith and of good works." Truly, if one in a thousand of the Bibles so widely distributed was blessed to such a result, those who sowed them in the fields of Italy might well feel that the harvest was an abundant recompense for their labours!

When the days of persecution, during which these events occurred, had passed away, those engaged in circulating the Scriptures redoubled their efforts for the enlightenment of Italy. The Grand Duke had not been two months gone from Florence when Lieut. Graydon sent a number of Bibles to that place. At first the customs threw some difficulties in the

15

way, but before long the new-found rights of the Italian people were declared to include free trade in the Word of God—a welcome change which contributed much to the development of Italian colportage.

In 1860 Lieut. Graydon was succeeded by Mr. Bruce, of Leghorn, who had for ten years past been principally concerned in bringing Bibles to Tuscany. The late agent had sent Bibles to Palermo, in the track of Garibaldi and his famous expedition; and as soon as Mr. Bruce received the appointment, he went to Naples, that he might superintend the introduction of the Book there. As usual, the custom-house made difficulties, and much precious time was lost in trying to persuade the officials to part with the suspicious goods. At last these initial obstacles were surmounted. On a frail cart, creaking and swaying under its precious burden, the cases were brought down the Strada del Gigante, and lodged in the coach-house of the Hôtel de Russie, where they remained till their contents could be got into circulation among the people. Several colporteurs were soon at work, and, strange to say, they had encouragement from not a few of the clergy, who became purchasers of Bibles. As for the Garibaldini, it was quite a common thing to see one of these red-shirts standing by the evangelical book-stall, ready to recommend the Scriptures to all comers, or, should need be, to protect the colporteur from abuse or violence. In the very Toledo, a main thoroughfare of Naples, which has its name from that

Spanish Viceroy who first made Italy acquainted
with the hated terror of the " Holy Office," a lad,
laden with a tray of Bibles, might be heard, as he
made the street ring, crying, " Il Libro! Il Libro!"
Such are the strange revenges time brings, and such
the encouragements God sends to those who wait
on Him while working in His cause.

In 1860 — a year of great developments — the
National Bible Society of Scotland took the field,
and appointed Dr. Stewart their agent for Italy.
Acting in this capacity, he employed the Claudian
Press at Turin to print a large-type edition of
Diodati's New Testament for the Society. This
printing establishment, named after Claude, the
evangelical bishop of Turin in the ninth century,
did, and still does, so much good service as a
missionary agency, that we may well devote a little
attention to its history.

The "Società dei Trattati Religiosi per l' Italia"
(Italian Religious Tract Society) was founded by
the Waldenses in 1855. The central Committee in
Turin consisted of three members—Rev. Sig. Meille,
Sig. Peyrot, and Sig. Malan — and of as many
assessors—Dr. Revel, Rev. Sig. Bert, and Rev. Sig.
Malan, with Rev. Sig. Pilatte, of Nice, as honorary
secretary. "In the first instance," wrote the Rev. G.
P. Meille, "we have opened on behalf of the Society
a religious book depôt, where those who care for this
kind of literature may find all sorts of evangelical
publications. A central Committee, sitting in Turin,

manages the affairs of the Society. Sub-committees will be established in different towns, for the purpose of promoting the sale of books, and of collecting money to carry on the work. One or two presses with founts of type are what we want. Thus we could at the same time print our books and the *Buona Novella*, and also give important work to some of our own people. May I beg to recommend both these projects, which are but parts of the same enterprise, to your Christian interest."

The liberality of two members of the Irish Presbyterian Church — the Misses Lyster of Dublin — answered this appeal by providing funds for the purchase of a press and type, and for five years employment was thus given to some eight or nine Italian Protestants in printing the *Good News*, a periodical devoted to the cause of Waldensian Missions, as well as a host of other evangelical publications. Not a few of the books issued by the " Italian Evangelical Publication Society " were sent to Turin to be printed by the " Northmen," as Dr. Stewart and Mr. Hanna used to style the Waldenses in their "little language."

Early in 1862 the scene of these operations was transferred to Florence. Mr. Henderson of Park, Mr. Macfie of Liverpool, and other friends of the cause furnished a new roller press and a fount of type, and the printing establishment was set up in a spacious annexe of the Palazzo Salviati. One can fancy with what satisfaction Mr. Hanna would have seen this hopeful development of the work in which he was so much interested. His lamented death, which took place in 1857, removed from earthly concerns one of the most able and indefatigable of Italian missionaries, and it was left for his successor in the pastorate of the Scotch Church—the Rev. Mr. MacDougall—to act as secretary to the Claudian Press Committee.

Two years after the press commenced work in Florence, such progress had been made that the Committee could publish a catalogue containing the titles of some two hundred publications then on sale in the various evangelical depôts throughout Italy. At this time no less than three periodicals appeared regularly from the same source. One was a weekly newspaper —the *Eco della Verita*—edited by Dr. Revel, and, from July, 1864, by Dr. Desanctis. Another was a magazine for children—the *Scuola della Domenica* (afterwards *L'Amico dei Fanciulli*)—which had even then a circulation of 4,000 copies. The third periodical—*Letture di Famiglia*, a kind of Italian *Leisure Hour*—was newly begun by the Rev. D. Kay, Free Church minister of Genoa, and did good service in bringing the truth to Italian homes under an attractive form.

The Claudian Press catalogue was itself widely circulated in the bookselling world of Italy. Orders came in from many towns where no evangelical depôt existed, and the common channels of trade thus began to convey the water of life.

When two years more had passed, the work was become of such importance as to demand the services of a secretary and treasurer who could devote his whole time to the task. The Rev. J. B. Will, hitherto Dr. Stewart's private secretary, received the appointment, and entered on his new duties in the early days of July, 1866. He continued to superintend the work of the Claudian Press for twenty-three years, till his death, on the 31st of July, 1889, deprived the evangelical cause in Italy of one of its most zealous and successful labourers. During all this time most of the Protestant literature which saw light on Italian soil passed through Mr. Will's hands, and he also bore, as treasurer, the heavy reponsibility—often to be met only by drawing on his private resources—of procuring from one quarter or another the money necessary to keep the press at work. He now rests from his labours, and the great day will declare how much he did for the spiritual welfare of his adopted country.

Free to use the ordinary press of the country, and furnished besides with a printing establishment all their own, the Protestants of Italy would have been to blame had they not taken full advantage of their opportunities. We are not surprised then to find that succeeding years saw the *Amico di Casa*, the *Amico del Soldato*, the *Strenna dei Fanciulli*, and the *Rivista Cristiana*, added one by one to the list of periodicals already in circulation, and designed to meet the wants of various classes in the community.

All this store of good books would have been little better than so much lumber in the camp, had it not been for the corps of colporteurs, who, valiant for the truth, went forth to the battle of the books. Not to mention those employed by the Nice Committee and the various native Churches, Waldensian and other, the British and Foreign Bible Society had the names of some thirty on its roll; while Dr. Stewart, as agent for the National Bible Society of Scotland, superintended the operations of twenty or more who were engaged in the same work. Then the pedlars who offered to an ignorant and superstitious peasantry Dream Books, Legends of the Saints, or, it might be, some volume yet more distinctly degrading, were met successfully on their own ground; and the Home Almanac, the Children's Prize, if not a Bible or a Testament, passed readily from the hands of the colporteur to those of his customers.

Let us hear the story of one of these little books, and how God made it mighty in a dark corner of the land. Early in the year 1867—it was on one of the days of the week of prayer—Sig. Gregori, the Vaudois pastor at Naples, found three peasants awaiting his return from church. These were men from a remote village in the hills beyond Benevento, called Fragneto L'Abate, and they were come to ask instruction about the Lord's Supper, desiring if possible to have the pastor celebrate that ordinance with them. Sig. Gregori asked how they had been led to this step, and in reply they disclosed an interesting history. A copy of the *Amico di Casa* had found its way to Fragneto, where it was diligently read and pondered. The texts of Scripture with which its pages were filled made a deep impression on the readers, and excited their desires to possess the Word of God in a complete form. This too after some delay they succeeded in getting, with the result that four families became convinced Protestants without any other influence than that of the mere Word of God. Their belief in the mass, in auricular confession, in Mariolatry, the worship of saints, and in purgatory, disappeared successively before the power of the truth ; and when the pastor visited them in their village, he felt justified in dispensing the Communion to nine persons, one of whom was the lawyer of the place. " So mightily grew the Word of God and prevailed."

We might speak of the zeal with which this trade in the truth was pressed when Rome fell into the hands of Victor Emmanuel—how colporteurs entered the Eternal City along with the Italian troops, and depôts were opened there for the sale of the Scriptures. We might dwell upon the efforts made in the same cause at Naples, in connection with the Maritime Exhibition of 1871, or we might record the rise and progress of the Italian Bible Society, a movement from within the country which was hailed with the warmest congratulations by those who desired the religious welfare of Italy. But in closing this brief record we may rather advert to an enterprise which stands altogether by itself; as the fruit of much patient and successful labour, and the crown of a life well spent in the service of Christ.

In 1862 Dr. Stewart commenced to write his invaluable Commentary on the Gospels. The evangelists of Italy had no means of acquiring libraries, and even had money been at their disposal for such a purpose, the books they needed did not exist in a form accessible to their reading. To gather and combine the best results of British and German scholarship and piety; to issue the work at a price which might bring it within the reach of the humblest student of God's Word in the land: such was the author's purpose. In 1865 he wrote: "I consider this one of the most important missionary efforts. . . . I am working at it sixteen hours a day." In spite of this extraordinary application, so much of the author's time was taken up with his great correspondence and constant work on committees, in addition to his pastoral duties in Leghorn, that four years elapsed ere the first sheets of his commentary began to issue from the press.

Hardly had the first Gospel been published when a striking testimony was given to the justness of the author's judgment in regarding his labours as an important missionary work. Dr. Bottacini, of Mirano in the district of Venice, an able and accomplished lawyer, bought a copy of the Commentary, and became, by the blessing of God on what he read, a professed

Protestant.   There is evidence in Dr. Stewart's letter-book of the eagerness with which this convert antici-pated the appearance of each successive volume of the Commentary ; and one who admitted him to the Scotch Manse in Leghorn when he made his first visit there, tells how he entered Dr. Stewart's study with the fervent words : " At last I have the great joy of beholding him to whom under God I owe my conversion," and how it seemed as if his gratitude could never find sufficient expression.   One such instance of the benefits which his work brought forth was enough to reward the author for many an hour of weary toil.

Encouraged by this manifest token for good, and by the warm welcome his pages received from evan-gelical workers everywhere throughout Italy, Dr. Stewart toiled on; often encroaching on the hours of rest in order to make more rapid progress.   His St. Mark appeared in 1874, St. Luke in 1880, and the manuscript of St. John was ready for the printers before the month of March, 1887, when the author's jubilee was celebrated by an interesting gathering of delegates representing the various societies with which he was connected.

History dwells on the death of the Venerable Bede, telling us how that solemn summons found him in the cloister of Jarrow busily writing a fair gloss on the Gospels.   " Master," said Wilberch, " there is but one sentence wanting."   " Write quickly," Bede replied.   " Now it is finished," answered Wilberch.

"*Ita, consummatum est.* Thou hast spoken very truth, for the end is indeed come," said the aged saint. "Lift me up; for I would look toward the place where I have been wont to pray, and once more call upon the Father." "Glory be to the Father and to the Son and to the Holy Ghost," sang Bede, as they held him in their arms, and with the hymn of praise his spirit passed into the glory of which he spake.

Even such a grace of beauty and completeness rested on the last days of this other worker in the same great cause, who shared with the Venerable Bede the *perfervidum ingenium septentrionis,* and who by the Southern as he by the Northern sea spent his latest strength in translating and enforcing the words of his beloved Lord. While the last sheets of his St. John were passing through the press under the loving care of Mr. Will and Sig. Meille, Dr. Stewart gently "fell asleep" with the holy words of the Communion Service on his lips : a comforting token to those who watched by his sick-bed of that heavenly union with Christ after which his whole life was one long aspiration, and with which he is now satisfied.

Who can doubt that the God whose grace thus links the nineteenth century to the eighth—with Whom one day is as a thousand years and a thousand years as one day—will assuredly accomplish in His own time the complete evangelisation of Italy and of the world ?

APPENDIX.

I.

TRANSLATION OF SERMON PREACHED BY DR. STEWART AT THE OPENING OF THE SCOTCH CHURCH, LEGHORN. *See p.* 20.

IL CULTO CHE CRISTO RICHIEDE NELLA SUA CHIESA.

Al Concistoro ed ai Membri della Congregazione, questa Predica fatta all' apertura della Chiesa Presbiteriana Scozzese in Livorno, ed ora stampata a loro richiesta è dedicata dall' affettuosissimo loro Pastore ed Amico.

" *Gesù le disse, Donna, credimi che l' ora viene, che voi non adorerete il Padre nè in questo Monte, nè in Gerusalemme. . . . Ma l' ora viene, e già al presente è, che i veri adoratori adoreranno il Padre in ispirito, e verità: perciocchè anche il Padre domanda tali che l' adorino.*"—S. Giovanni cap. iv, vv. 21 e 23.

L' odio scambievole de' Giudei co' Samaritani è di proverbiale notorietà. Nè una parte sola sfogava quell' odio, nè solo un' altra parte era di quelli sfoghi la vittima : altrimenti le simpatie nostre sarebbero tutte per coloro che avessero ingiustamente e senza vendicarsi sofferto : gareggiarono pur troppo costoro tutti nel più intenso rancore, ed ogni nuova vendetta veniva con acerbe rappresaglie contraccambiata. Il Vangelo stesso ne dà prove.—Perchè i discepoli giudei, avvicinandosi ad un villaggio samaritano, se ne veggono chiudere in faccia le porte, chiedono che sopra gli offensori sia fatto cadere il fuoco celeste ; ed allo stanco viandante che siede presso il pozzo di Giacobbe in Sichar, la inospitale donna Samaritana nega un "bicchier d' acqua fredda" unicamente perchè egli appartiene alla nazione da lei abborrita.

Ma come mai andò colà il Salvatore? Perchè mai si espose

egli a cotale insultante rifiuto? Un motivo naturale ne vien
detto nel racconto medesimo : "andando in Galilea, doveva
Egli passare dalla Samaria" (verso 4); ma per una mente
illuminata dallo Spirito di Dio v' era un' altra ragione evidente
e valevole quanto la prima. L' incontro del Salvatore e di
quella povera donna Samaritana al pozzo di Giacobbe non era
un caso fortuito : un' anima doveva esser salvata, e Gesù il
Salvatore andò quivi; una lezione che sarebbe estesa a tutta la
vera Chiesa del Dio vivente fino agli ultimi tempi della sua
esistenza, doveva allora venire partecipata, ed il "Maestro
venuto da Dio" andò quivi ad imprimerla negli animi colla sua
incontrastabile autorità, perchè "Egli è capo sopra ogni cosa
alla Chiesa" (Efesi, i. 22). Questa lezione riguardava la natura
del culto che Dio gradisce.

Ma quelli che Cristo converte ed insegna col suo Spirito
hanno bisogno "di insegnamento dopo insegnamento, di linea
dopo linea," prima che giungano alla piena intelligenza della
verità. Il cieco di Betsaida (Marco, viii. 24), a cui Gesù unse
gli occhi, nel suo primo sperimento della vista aveva percezioni
confuse ;—ei vedeva, è vero, ma vedeva imperfettissimamente,
"Io veggo," disse "camminar gli uomini che paiono alberi ;"
e solo quando ritornò al Salvatore, e che questi di nuovo gli
mise le mani sopra gli occhi, fu intieramente ristabilito, "e
vedeva tutti chiaramente." Questo cieco di Betsaida, è un tipo
di tutti i ciechi spirituali che Gesù Cristo illumina, e di cui
sveglia la coscienza colle operazioni del suo Spirito. Pochi,
nessuno forse, al momento della sua conversione, è cosi illuminato, così spiritualmente ammaestrato da dare a Cristo tutta la
gloria della sua salute, e da essere affatto spogliato di se stesso.
Che significa infatti il linguaggio del peccatore riscosso e turbato
di cui parla il profeta Michea ? Non è il linguaggio dei propri
meriti, del propri sacrifizi ? (Cap. vi. ver. 6, 7.) "Con che verrò
io davanti al Signore ? con che m' inchinerò io all' Iddio altissimo? gli verrò io davanti con olocausti, con vitelli d' un anno ?
Il Signore avrà egli a grado le migliaia de' montoni, le decine
delle migliaia delle bestie della valle grasse ? darò io il mio
primogenito per lo mio misfatto? il frutto del mio ventre per
lo peccato dell' anima mia ?" Che significa il linguaggio di

Saulo prostrato innanzi al Salvatore nella via di Damasco? Che significa il linguaggio del Carceriere di Filippi, quando saltò dentro tutto tremante, e cadde a' piedi di Paolo e Sila? Che significa la prima domanda di questa donna Samaritana appena condotta a riconoscere Cristo come Profeta, se non la tendenza a fondare la sua salvezza sui propri sforzi, le proprie fatiche, i propri sacrifizi, e non sulla sola base Biblica,—la Giustizia di Cristo? In tutti questi casi, nel caso pure di ogni uomo salutarmente chiamato da Dio, svaniscono queste erronee viste in presenza dell' insegnamento, e della luce della Spirito Santo, come sta scritto, "la luce si leva nelle tenebre a quelli che son dritti" (Sal. 112. 4).

Ma la Donna Samaritana, come la vediamo nel verso antecedente, è il tipo di una numerosa classe di Cristiani di nome, sul carattere dei quali io vorrei chiamare specialmente la vostra attenzione, per l' esame di voi stessi. Quando fu condotta a riconoscere Cristo come Profeta, il suo primo ed ardente grido non è quello del Pubblicano nel tempio : "O Dio, sii placato inverso me peccatore" (Luca, 18. 13); si attiene stretta alle forme esterne del culto,—semplici accidenti della religione,— e vorrebbe volentieri occuparne la propria attenzione, e quella del Salvatore. Essa non chiedeva già : Come sarò io liberata dall' ira avvenire? Come sarò accetta a Dio? Ma, qual è la superiorità comparativa del culto Ebreo sul Monte Moria, o del culto Samaritano sul Monte Garezim? Si possono trovar molti nel mondo intorno a noi che professano d' essere Cristiani, e la cui religione non consiste che in queste forme esterne, le quali momentaneamente occuparono l' attenzione della nostra Samaritana. Costoro compresi da qualche pensiero per la loro salute, dai rimordimenti della coscenza, o dalle ordinarie operazioni dello spirito, hanno cercato intorno a se qualche rifugio, e invece di ricoverarsi presso Cristo, e di non voler essere paghi d' altro che di lui, hanno scambiato il mezzo col fine, hanno lasciata la sostanza correndo dietro all' ombra, e sono divenuti tanto meticolosi zelatori delle forme e dei doveri esterni,—"tanto noncuranti delle cose più importanti della legge, nella loro ansietà per la decima della menta, dell' aneto, e del comino," quanto fu mai sempre il Fariseo, o lo Scriba sotto la legge cerimoniale. Le forme esterne sono, senza dubbio, necessarie per reggere il culto di Dio, ma guai a quelli, o chiese o individui, che se ne occupano esclusivamente, e la cui religione consiste "in vecchiezza di lettera, e non in novità di spirito" (Rom. vii. 6). A questi il Salvatore parla con chiarezza non dubbia nel nostro testo : "Donna, credimi," etc.

Per trattare distesamente queste parole, io mi propongo, colla benedizione del Signore, di rivolgere la vostra attenzione su questi due argomenti.

I.—*I punti di diversità e di rassomiglianza tra il culto Samaritano e il culto Ebreo.*

II.—*Il culto che Cristo richiede nella sua Chiesa.*

I.—In primo luogo consideriamo i punti di diversità, e di rassomiglianza tra il culto Samaritano, e il culto Ebreo ; e

1° *La loro diversità.* Il culto tributato dal Giudeo all' Altissimo aveva la sua origine in Dio. Piacque a Lui di rivelare a Mosè nel deserto, il modo con cui voleva esser adorato dal suo popolo Israele. Diede loro un tabernacolo fatto secondo il modello mostrato a Mosè sul Monte,—stabilì per loro sacrifizi di varie specie, feste, digiuni, e diverse oblazioni, da osservarsi rigorosamente in Israele ; e tutto questo, sebben formale nella sua natura, era però spirituale nella sua tendenza ; e ben inteso mirava a guidare gli adoratori suoi ad un più nobile sacrifizio, ed a più eccellenti promesse. Che i veri Israeliti intendessero perfettamente come il culto esterno e tipico imposto loro adombrava un servizio spirituale, il quale solo potrebbe rendere il primo accetto al Signore, chiaramente apparisce dal linguaggio di Salomone alla dedica del tempio : "Ma pur veramente abiterà Iddio con gli uomini in su la terra ? Ecco i cieli, ed i cieli de' cieli non ti possono comprendere : quanto meno la casa, la quale io ho edificata" (II Croniche vi. 18) ;—e più chiaramente ancora dal linguaggio di David (Salmo li. 16, 17) : "Perciocchè tu non prendi piacere in sacrifizio ; altrimente, io l' avrei offerto : tu non gradisci olocausto. I sacrifizii di Dio sono lo spirito rotto : O Dio, tu non isprezzi il cuor rotto e contrito." Se occorresse più ampia prova, noi la troveremmo nel fatto, che al tempo della nascita del Salvatore, nel pieno godimento delle ordinanze giudaiche, vi erano

però uomini devoti i quali a far compita la loro gioia, "atten-
devano la consolazione d' Israele." Appena ebbe il vecchio
Simeone abbracciato il Bambino Gesù, che benedisse Iddio
dicendo : "Ora, Signore, ne mandi il tuo Servitore in pace,
secondo la tua parola ; poscia che gli occhi miei hanno veduta
la tua salute : luce da illuminare le genti, e la gloria del tuo
popolo Israel " (Luca, ii. 29, ec.) Il culto dei Giudei era dunque
divino nella sua origine,—accennava ad un Salvatore avvenire,
—adombrava tipicamente lo spargimento del suo sangue, e
tutte le sostanziali dottrine della salute ;—quindi dice Gesù in
questo stesso passo, "noi adoriamo ciò che conosciamo, con-
ciosiacosachè la salute sia della parte dei Giudei."

Opponiamo a questa la religione di Samaria. Dal momento
che le dieci tribù d' Israel costituirono un regno a parte, il
peccato di Geroboam cominciò a portare i suoi amari frutti, e
la sua idolatria non cessò che colla loro finale captività. La
loro istoria ci somministra un terribile esempio della tendenza
del peccato a riprodurre e perpetuare se stesso : e per tutto
il tempo che rimarrà la parola di Dio, ci vi sta in faccia al
mondo sotto il tremendo aspetto di un seduttore tinto del
sangue delle anime per mille generazioni. "Geroboam figliuolo
di Nebat, *che avea fatto peccare Israel !*" La storia del culto
di Samaria fin dalla captività delle dieci tribù ci è data nel II
Re (xvii. 24). Il re d'Assiria popolò le desolate contrade con
colonie di nazioni pagane trasportate dal di là di Babilonia, e
ognuna portò seco i suoi idoli, costituendo, in tal modo, una
specie di Panteismo nelle città d' Israel. "Perchè non riverivano il Signore," dice l'istorico Sacro, "il Signore mandò
contro loro de' leoni, i quali uccidevano molti di loro ;" e questo
fu attribuito alla loro ignoranza delle leggi del Dio del paese,
perciò il Re d'Assiria rimandò uno dei loro sacerdoti ad istruire
il popolo. Questo non fe' cessare l' idolatria fra loro, solo valse
ad innestare il Paganesimo sul tronco d' un corrotto Giudaismo.
"Così quelle genti riverivano il Signore ed insieme servivano
alle loro sculture. I lor figliuoli anch' essi, ed i figliuoli de' lor
figliuoli fanno, infino ad oggi, come fecero i lor padri " (Ver. 41).
Ritornati che furono i Giudei dalla captività, gli abitanti di
Samaria proposero loro di confondere i due culti, e di unirsi per

edificare il Tempio ; e pel rifiuto avutone, divennero i loro mortali nemici. Manasse Sommo Pontefice Giudeo, avendo sposata la figlia di Samballat Governatore Pagano di Samaria, fu spogliato del sacerdozio da Nehemia, onde egli edificò un tempio rivale sul monte Gerizim,—ne divenne il Sommo Pontefice, e contribuì in tal modo a perpetuare l' odio tra le due nazioni.

Tale, o fratelli, era la religione di Samaria ;—umana nella sua origine, tendeva ad abbrutire, sconvolgendo ogni idea di bene e di male col mescolar in disperata confusione il vero e il falso, il culto del Dio vivente col culto degl' idoli. Non ci maravigliamo dunque, che il nostro Signore, con breve sentenza, condanni questo culto di Samaria come sterile, senza consolazioni, ed incapace di riforma : "Voi adorate ciò che non conoscete." Qual vantaggio adunque aveva il Giudeo ? Molto, in ogni maniera ! Egli conosceva che 'l' oggetto del suo culto era il sommo Gehova, il signore di tutte le cose,—conosceva che il modo di adorarlo, era quello da Dio rivelato, mentre i Samaritani adoravano un Dio ignoto ! Ma qual responsabilità pesava sul Giudeo ? Grande e grave in verità !—Quella stessa che pesava sopra Betsaida, Chorazin, e Capernaum, paragonati a Tiro, Sidon, Sodoma e Gomorra ;—quella stessa che pesa ora sopra di noi, paragonati ai Pagani ; che pesa sopra quelli a cui è stato dato molto, e da cui molto sarà richiesto.

2° Consideriamo ora il punto di rassomiglianza tra il culto Ebreo, ed il Samaritano. Essa consiste nel formalismo dei due. Dalla stessa natura del culto Samaritano, come noi ve l' abbiamo descritto, egli è evidente che deve esser stato formale affatto. Nella stessa natura delle cose, è impossibile di offrire un servizio spirituale ad un oggetto di rame, di legno, o di pietra, opera della mano degli uomini ; egli è poi evidentissimo che quelli i quali si appagavano d' inchinarsi davanti ai tabernacoli degli idoli, non tributavano un servizio più elevato, nè più spirituale, quando si prostravano all'altare di Dio. Era sempre un freddo e morto formalismo ; e la sola questione in esso ravvivatrice, era quella appunto che accendeva le loro pessime passioni, e i loro più intolleranti pregiudizi, " se (cioè) sopra quel monte, o a Gerusalemme convenisse adorare." Il culto Giudaico rassomigliava al Samaritano in questo, che sebben d'istituzione divina, egli era essenzialmente formale. È ben vero ch' egli era perfetto nel suo genere, perchè era quale Iddio lo credè più adatto allo stato delle cose in quel tempo, e preparatorio di un culto più puro che doveva seguire ; ma doveva esser temporario. Ascoltate l'Apostolo Paolo quando dice (Ebrei, ix. 9, 10) : "Il primo Tabernacolo, nel quale s' offeriscono offerte e sacrifizi, che non possono appieno purificare, quanto è alla coscienza, colui che fa il servigio divino : essendo cose che consistono solo in cibi, e bevande, ed in vari lavamenti, ed ordinamenti carnali ; imposte fino al tempo della correzione." Ed il culto giudaico sempre più divenne formalista, quando ai giorni del Salvatore la gran massa degli adoratori era carnale nel suo intendimento, e le più grette minuzie esaltava come cose della massima importanza,—quando colle tradizioni dei Padri annientava la legge ;—quando riedificava le tombe dei profeti uccisi dai suoi avi, e intanto perseguitava esso pure giusti ; in somma quando "nettava il di fuori della coppa e del piatto, e dentro quelli erano pieni di rapina e di intemperanza" (S. Matt. xxiii. 25). Nel rispondere alla domanda della Samaritana, il Salvatore antepone espressamente il culto di Gerusalemme a quello di Garizim. Ma nello stesso tempo solennemente dichiara l' abrogazione dei due per dar luogo al suo culto spirituale. "Donna, credimi che l' ora viene, che voi non adorerete il Padre, nè in questo monte, nè in Gerusalemme. Ma l' ora viene, e già al presente è, che i veri adoratori adoreranno il Padre in ispirito e verità : perciocchè anche il Padre domanda tali che l' adorino."

II.—Io passo in secondo luogo a considerare il culto che Cristo richiede nella sua chiesa. Egli è universale, spirituale, e sincero.

1° Il culto che Cristo richiede nella sua chiesa è *universale di sua natura*. La religione dei Giudei aveva necessariamente un carattere di grettezza e di esclusismo, perchè era destinata alla loro sola nazione, e costituita in modo da preservarli dalla idolatria e malvagità delle nazioni circostanti ; ma la dispensazione iniziata dal Signore doveva abbracciare,—e fermamente noi crediamo dalla parola di Dio, che nel tempo debito abbraccerà—tutti i regni del mondo, "Ogni nazione e tribù, e lingua, e popolo" (Apoc. xiv. 6). E perciò naturalmente crediamo che la religione da essa inculcata dovrà adattarsi al genio ed all' indole di ogni nazione per cui è destinata,—che dovrà essere libera da tutto quello che è puramente locale ;—dovrà formare, in somma, un vincolo d' unione per tutti quei che l' abbracciano, "sia Giudeo, sia Gentile, barbaro, Scita, schiavo o libero ;"— quantunque diversi siano i loro individuali caratteri ; quantunque opposti i loro nazionali pregiudizi. L' esperienza non conferma ella pienamente la nostra aspettativa ? Se noi siamo veramente figli di Dio, qualunque siano le nostre individuali particolarità, le nostre nazionali antipatie, non è egli vero che noi abbiamo un vincolo d' unione ?—non è egli vero che abbiamo "un unico signore, una fede, un battesimo, un Dio unico, e Padre di tutti, il quale è sopra tutte le cose, fra tutte le cose, ed in tutti voi" (Efesi, iv. 5, 6). Non è egli vero, che più ci accostiamo alla semplicità della scrittura, maggiore sarà il numero di quelli che riconoscono il nostro culto, e più stretta la nostra comunione " con tutti coloro, i quali in qualunque luogo invocano il nome di Gesù Cristo signor di loro e di noi" (1 Cor. i. 2).

Il culto di Cristo è universale nella sua natura, ed in conseguenza condanna *uno spirito gretto e settario*. Egli non vuole che teniamo per nostri nemici, e non come discepoli del comune Maestro, quei che da noi differiscono soltanto nelle forme esterne della religione, per quanto però ritengano le grandi ed essenziali verità della parola di Dio. Egli non vuole che guardiamo con freddezza e sospetto, quelli la cui fede è ferma, e la vita santa, per la sola ragione che non vogliono schierarsi sotto la bandiera da noi inalberata, o che coscienziosamente adottano forme esterne che noi coscienziosamente pure disapproviamo. Un contegno così pregiudicato e anticristiano il Salvatore l' ha espressamente e chiaramente condannato. Questa grettezza di spirito ben presto si mostrò fra i discepoli di Gesù. " Maestro" disse Giovanni in una certa occasione "noi abbiam veduto uno che cacciava i demoni nel tuo nome, e glielo abbiam divietato ; perciocchè egli non ti seguita con noi." Ma che disse il Signore ? approvò egli la condotta dei discepoli ? Gesù gli disse : " Non gliel divietate : perciocchè chi non è contr' a noi è per noi " (S. Luca ix. 49).

Il culto di Cristo è universale, e in conseguenza *non è limitato a luoghi particolari.* Sotto la dispensazione del Vecchio Testamento, speciali località erano determinate in cui tutte le tribù d' Israele dovrebbero adorare. Il Signore elesse un luogo particolare per collocarvi il suo nome, e un culto offertogli in qualunque altro luogo era da Dio rigettato. Da prima, Iddio collocò il suo nome in Silo ; ma più tardi troviamo che dice nel Salmo cxxx. 13 : "Il Signore ha eletta Sion, egli l' ha gradita per sua stanza, dicendo : Questo è il mio riposo in perpetuo ; qui abiterò ; perciocchè questo è il luogo che io ho desiderato." In questo luogo dovevano tutti i maschi d' Israele comparire tre volte l' anno a presentarsi innanzi al Signore. Ma sotto la dispensazione di Cristo, il suo culto non è limitato a nessun luogo, a nessuna parte della terra. Ei non è ristretto a tempj fabbricati dalle mani degli uomini ; non ha bisogno di splendidi edifizi, di cattedrali consecrate per farlo accetto agli occhi suoi ! Ha in se una semplicità, una larghezza, una facilità d' accesso a Dio, che pienamente corrisponde "a quella libertà, della quale Cristo ha francato il suo popolo" (Gal. v. 1). "Dovunque" dice egli, "due o tre son raunati nel nome mio, quivi sono io, nel mezzo di loro" (S. Matt. xviii. 20). Io non intendo già affermare, che non sia necessario e conveniente inalzare, per quanto è possibile, appositi edifizi pel culto di Dio ; nè che dobbiamo viver nel lusso, mentre destiniamo per "luogo ordinario dell' orazione" qualche meschino sito, il cui freddo e misero aspetto male ci dispone al retto adempimento del nostro dovere ; perchè io vedo il Profeta Haggeo fare pungente rimprovero a quelli che così usavano nel suo tempo : "È egli ben tempo per voi d' abitar nelle vostre case intavolate, mentre questa casa resta diserta ?" Io non intendo insinuare che fosse cosa convenevole, e decente in oggi, come nei primi giorni del Cristianesimo era necessario, "di continuare a rompere il pane di casa in casa"[1] (Atti, ii. 46). Ma questo io affermo, che il culto accetto al Signore non è limitato alle pareti sacre ; ma, che sia "nella stanza alta," sia in una oscura e lurida prigione, sia in un granaio, o in una chiesa, sia in una landa ignuda, o in mezzo a

---

[1] Cioè di fare la Santa Comunione.

bufera di neve sopra sterile monte "il Signore è presso di tutti quelli che l' invocano in verità" (Salmo cxlv. 18). Infatti fu impedita nella Pentecoste, l' effusione dello spirito, perchè i discepoli erano radunati nella stanza alta? Fu il culto di Dio impedito, o la conversione del carceriere resa impossibile, perchè Paolo e Sila erano serrati in ceppi a Filippi? Furono le rivelazioni di Dio impedite, perchè Giovanni trascinava le catene di schiavo, e stentava nelle miniere di Patmo? Il culto offerto a Dio dai nostri Padri perseguitati in Iscozia, dai protestanti di Francia nelle Cevenne, dai Valdesi di Piemonte nelle loro alpine rocche in mezzo ad inaudite crudeltà, fu esso meno accetto a Dio perchè risuonava "dalle spelonche, e dalle grotte della terra?" No, fratelli! Egli è lo spirito, non il luogo che fa il culto accetto al cospetto del Signore. "Così ha detto il Signore: il cielo è il mio trono, e la terra è lo scannello de' miei piedi: dove è la Casa che voi m' edifichereste? e dove è il luogo del mio riposo? La mia mano ha fatte tutte queste cose, dice il Signore: a chi dunque riguarderò io? all' afflitto, ed al contrito di spirito, ed a colui che trema alla mia parola" (Isaia, xlvi. 1, 2).

2° Il culto che Cristo richiede nella sua chiesa è *spirituale*. Egli è così in opposizione ad ogni culto formalista, sia nel modo, sia nella sostanza. La legge ceremoniale degli Ebrei, che consisteva in forme, è chiamata espressamente da San Paolo "deboli e poveri elementi." "Ed ora" dice ai Galati, "avendo conosciuto Iddio; anzi piuttosto essendo stati da Dio conosciuti, come vi rivolgete di nuovo a deboli e poveri elementi, a' quali tornando addietro volete di nuovo servire?" (Gal. iv. 9.) Tenaci sforzi furono fatti dai convertiti Ebrei per imporre queste vane forme ai fratelli Gentili, finchè al Sinodo di Gerusalemme fu finalmente e solennemente deciso dagli Apostoli radunati di non imporre loro tale giogo. Che non possa esistere una chiesa visibile senza qualche forma di culto, la cosa è per se stessa evidente; ma la forme stabilite nel nuovo Testamento sono semplicissime;—la lettura della Bibbia, la predicazione del Vangelo, l' esercizio della preghiera, e l' osservanza spirituale e salutare dei Sacramenti,—queste sono le ceremonie lasciate da Cristo alla sua chiesa! Ogni altra viene dall' uomo; ed egli

è noto nella storia della chiesa di Cristo, che quanto più fedel-
mente le varie comunioni Cristiane conservarono la semplicità
del Vangelo, tanto più spirituale fu il loro culto ; e che anzi
più esse deviarono, e moltiplicarono le forme, più rapidamente
degenerò la loro spiritualità, finchè come l' antica chiesa di
Sardi, "avevano nome di vivere, e pur erano morte" (Apoc.
iii. 1). In fatti quelli che patrocinano la moltiplicità delle
forme, lo fanno nell' idea che possono giovare alla devozione di
molti ; ma la devozione fondata sopra di esse solamente, non è
spirituale ma carnale, e il cuor dell' uomo è già tanto carnale
nel migliore suo stato ch' egli corre il rischio di naufragare,
fidando in queste vane forme, non nella Rocca dei secoli.

Ma il culto di Cristo è spirituale in opposizione ad ogni culto
formalista *nella sostanza.* Può esservi perfetta semplicità senza
spiritualità di culto. Io vi prego di rammentarvelo, fratelli
miei ! Perchè sia spirituale il culto, deve il cuore esservi im-
pegnato—un cuore illuminato, riscaldato, animato dallo Spirito
di Cristo. Non basta poter dire : "Signore, Signore, non
abbiamo noi profetizzato in nome tuo, ed in nome tuo cacciati
demoni, e fatte in nome tuo molte potenti operazioni?" perchè
il Signore potrà dire nonostante : "Io non vi conobbi giammai :
dipartitevi da me voi tutti operatori d' iniquità" (S. Matt. vii.
22, 23). Non basta che noi ci uniamo al canto delle lodi, dobbiamo inalzare i nostri cuori in rendimenti di grazie ; non basta
che le labbra si aprano alla preghiera, perchè lo spirito, nostro
aiuto, ricerca le petizioni dal cuore; non basta che noi sentiamo
coll' orecchio esterno, perchè l' impressione così ricevuta deve
penetrare nel cuore. Oh quanti ogni domenica tributarono al
Signore nella sua casa il culto più regolare, senza che i loro cuori
fossero minimamente affetti nè commossi da questi loro eser-
cizi di religione ! Quanti rifuggirebbero con orrore del pensiero
di trascurar per i loro bambini l' ordinanza del Battesimo, che
non mai pensarono ad ammaestrarli nel timor del Signore !
Quanti che siedono regolarmente alla mensa della Comunione,
i quali non mai si sforzano nè pregano per l' adempimento delle
solenni risoluzioni che vi formarono ! Quel culto solo è spirituale ed accetto, il quale viene dal cuore, ed i cui frutti sono
evidenti nella vita e nella conversazione giornaliera. "Iddio è

uno Spirito: per ciò conviene che coloro che l' adorano, l' adorino in ispirito e verità."

3° Il culto che Cristo richiede nella sua chiesa è *sincero.* Egli è opposto a ogni ipocrisia. Intendiamo parlare d' un culto conforme alla conoscenza della verità, come sta scritto : " Colui che s' accosta a Dio, dee credere ch' egli è premiatore a coloro che lo ricercano " (Ebrei, xi. 6). Egli deve essere affatto puro d' ogni frode. Questa mancanza di sincerità tristamente caratterizzava il culto de Giudei del tempo di Cristo. Noi lo vediamo ripetutamente denunziare la maledizione contro l' ipocrisia di quelli che ne erano i sostenitori : " Guai a voi scribi e Farisei ipocriti, voi fate lunghe orazioni con ipocrita maschera ; voi fate la vostra elemosina nel cospetto degli uomini, per esser da loro riguardati ; voi date la decima della menta, dell' aneto, e del comino, e lasciate le cose più gravi della legge, il giudizio, e la misericordia, e la fede." Comparire innanzi a Dio nell' attitudine di un adoratore, mentre i nostri pensieri sono fissi sopra gli interessi terreni, mentre il nostro cuore è dato ai fugaci piaceri del mondo, mentre noi viviamo apertamente nel peccato, o calpestiamo la legge di Dio, compiacendoci in uno spirito d' invidia o d' odio,— questa è una vera menzogna difatto,—egli è un pretendere di dare i' intiero prezzo, mentre come Anania ne riteniamo indietro una parte. Quanto acerbamente Iddio si lagna di una tale ipocrisia nel suo antico popolo per la bocca del profeta Ezechiel (xxxiii. 31) : " E vengono a te, come per maniera di raunanza di popolo ; e siede davanti a te come il mio popolo, ed ascolta le tue parole, ma non le mette ad effetto : perciocchè colla sua bocca vi mostra molto amore, ma il cuor suo va dietro alla sua avarizia." E di Isaia ancora (i. 12) : " Quando voi venite per comparir nel mio cospetto, chi ha richiesto questo di man vostra, che voi calchiate i miei cortili ? Non continuate più di portare offerte da nulla : i profumi mi son cosa abbominevole ; quant' è alle calendi, a' sabati, al bandir raunanze, io non posso parlare iniquità, e festa solenne insieme." Ah ! diletti Fratelli ! quante volte non può il grande Scrutatore dei cuori rivolgere a noi cotesto linguaggio ? Quante volte non ha egli osservata la doppiezza dei nostri cuori negli atti di religione, e l' assenza di quell' umiltà, di quella contrizione, di quell' amore che soli possono fare a lui accetti i nostri servigi ! Sforziamoci d' adorare Iddio in ispirito ed in verità. Rammentiamoci che abbiamo da trattare coll' omnisciente Gehovah, e sebben noi possiamo deludere gli uomini colle esterne apparenze, " Iddio non si può beffare." La sua domanda molto ragionevole è questa : " figlio mio, dammi il tuo cuore," perchè dal cuore proviene ogni bene, come ogni male nella vita dell' uomo. Se il vostro culto è così spirituale e sincero, Cristo vi chiama veri adoratori, e dichiara inoltre che il vostro celeste Padre "domanda tali che l'adorino." " Perciocchè così ha detto l' alto e eccelso ch' abita l' eternità, e il cui nome è il Santo, io abito in luogo alto e santo, e col contrito ed umile di spirito, per vivificar lo spirito degli umili, e per vivificare il cuor dei contriti " (Isaia, lxii. 15).

In conclusione, diletti Fratelli, noi siamo solennemente chiamati in questo giorno, a seguir l' esempio di Samuele, di porre la nostra pietra di rimembranza, e di chiamarla Ebenezer, cioè " Fin qui il Signore ci ha soccorsi " (1 Sam. viii. 12). Noi fummo impegnati in una grand' opera, preparando, secondo le forme semplici dei nostri avi presbiteriani, un luogo di culto al nostro Dio in terra straniera. Noi possiamo vedere la benigna mano del nostro Signore in varie manifestazioni della sua grazia, da che siamo raccolti in congregazione Cristiana, ed ora, in questo stesso giorno, "colla buona mano del nostro Dio sopra di noi" sono state appagate le brame dei nostri cuori, e " la pietra del capo è stata tratta fuori con rimbombanti acclamazioni ! Grazia, grazia ad essa " (Zacaria, iv. 7). Uniamoci adunque solennemente, dando con Davide tutta lode, tutta gloria a Dio. " Non a noi, Signore, non a noi, anzi al tuo nome dà gloria per la tua benignità e verità " (Salmo cxv. 1). Voglia il Signore concedere che questa Casa sia un Bethel, la vera porta dei Cieli per molte anime fra noi. Voglia il Signore concederci il compimento della sua promessa, "In qualunque luogo ove io farò ricordare il mio nome, io verrò a te, e ti benedirò." Conceda il Signore che il culto offertogli in questo Santuario sia spirituale e sincero, e che il gretto ed astioso bigottismo che vede di mal occhio quanto da lui differisce, non mai alberghi in nessuno dei nostri petti. In fine conceda il Signore che non solo questa Casa edificata al suo nome, ed ora solennemente dedicata al suo culto, serva per molti anni alla divozione dei nostri compatriotti, dando loro " di cantare i cantici del Signore in terra straniera ; " ma che lo stesso glorioso Vangelo possa fra breve esser predicato con semplicità e serietà in tutte le Chiese di queste contrade ; e che si compia per questi popoli la dichiarazione solenne fatta dal Signore alla donna di Samaria or sono diciotto secoli, " Donna, credimi, l' ora viene che i veri adoratori adoreranno il Padre in ispirito e verità, perciocchè anche il Padre domanda tali che l' adorino."

II.

Extract from a letter dated 27th September, 1849, and written by Dr. Stewart to Miss Loudon, the Secretary of the Glasgow Ladies' Association.

". . . And now for the state of things here. You know how I fretted at being kept so long in Britain begging money at a time when an extraordinary door of usefulness was opened up for me in this land. I had not been here two months ere that door was closed by the entrance of the Austrians, and the re-establishment of the Grand Ducal Government upon retrograde principles. I fear I was much disposed to say with Jacob at the time, 'All these things are against me,' but I have since learned a lesson which makes me much ashamed of my own impatience, and which shows me that God has been kinder to me, and to our Mission here, and has had more care over it than I would have had for myself. The proof of this is that this day week I had a letter from the ' Delegato Straordinario ' appointed by Government to direct affairs in Leghorn, to appear before him. On doing so he told me that complaints had been made against the Scotch Church, and me, at Florence for proselytising, and he wished to have some information from me. He first inquired whether we have received a written permission from the Grand Duke himself for the erection of our Church? To which Mr. R. Henderson and I answered that we had not, as it was not considered necessary since we had the approbation and consent of Corsini, the Governor of Leghorn, the

Grand Duke's representative, and of the Commissary of Police. The second inquiry was about the Italian sermons which had been preached in our Church. To this we answered that the persons whom I had invited to preach were Brethren who happened to be passing by, and who addressed my congregation ; that these sermons had not been regularly kept up, and that there was no one employed to preach regularly. On which he told us that we might preach in English as much as we liked, but that we were to understand that it was positively forbidden to preach in Italian. The third accusation was that I had been distributing heretical books, and one was named in particular, ' L' Amico del Peccatore.' I was able however to assure him with a safe conscience that the charge was utterly untrue ; that I never had been in possession of that book, and that I had made it a rule never to distribute books to the Italians. And he seemed satisfied with the investigation, though there is no telling with these people whether we may not hear more of it. I found it necessary to lay down the rule I have just mentioned for the sake of my congregation when I first came here, and I have kept to it, the necessity of which now appears. But herein also the Lord's goodness to us has also appeared in frustrating all my wishes. My anxiety to get back was chiefly that I might get my friend, M. Malan, a Waldensian pastor, who resided all last winter at Florence, to preach in Italian every Sabbath, which he would have done ; and with the liberty existing last year and the beginning of this it is hard to say if I should have been prudent enough to stick to my rule about distributing books. I was detained so long in Britain that I had only M. Malan's services for two Sabbaths before the Austrians came in, and that has been made by the priests here matter of complaint against us. I have learned from various quarters that they are excessively enraged at the opening of a Scotch Presbyterian Church, for it appears they know well enough the difference between the Episcopal and Presbyterian as working Churches. . . ."

III.

LETTER FROM THE REV. DR. STEWART TO THE REV. MR. HANNA.

Leghorn, 12th Feb., 1851.

MY DEAR MR. HANNA,—

*   *   *   *   *   *

I had a visit from our friend C. at Pisa to-day.   He tells me he was in Florence last Sunday ; I don't know whether you saw him.   Have you heard of an immense number of "incorruptible seeds,"—"sweeter than honey from the comb,"—having been landed in the Maremma ; which they want to sell for a perennial crop ?   Ask G. about them, or Bet., as the information came from him.   G. was offered a thousand at three p. each. Of course he could not take such a supply; it is too costly for his purse : but it seems impossible to allow them to be taken away again from a soil so well adapted for the growth of them as Tuscany is, and when there has been so much demand for them.   I hear the offer is only a tenth part of the stock.   Now I think our friends in Ed—gh would like to have some of these, and as you have money of theirs in your hands that you could not better lay it out than in buying a considerable stock of these " incorruptible seeds " on their account.   There is no risk of loss, as the sale of them again will cover the outlay ; and of course they will be delivered before paid for.   Will you consult M. G. C. and the others—if you can get hold of them—and see if they would approve of the speculation on behalf of our absent friends ?   If so, I think you might go the length of an outlay of £20.   That would produce 266.   C. says that G. spoke of getting 300, and you should write to P. at Genoa and get him to give the £30 he was to get, as it is the best speculation he could possibly make, and a famous revenge besides.   Think about this, see if it be true, and take steps to buy.   I think you must understand the kind of seed I refer to, and I don't think it necessary to write more explicitly on the subject.   I shall see the Swiss doctor about it, and I am sure as a member of the firm he will approve my suggestion, as the outlay will be a profitable employment of funds that would otherwise be lying idle, and which can only be used as an advance to be repaid again, besides you will always have £10 balance in hand for any emergency. I have no news to give you from this quarter, and I have had no letters from home of late, so that I am much in the dark. How goes on your essay, and how the "doing into Italian" from the English? Excuse my haste and

Believe me, my dear Mr. Hanna,

Yours very truly,

ROBERT W. STEWART.

LETTER FROM THE REV. MR. HANNA TO THE REV. DR. STEWART.

Florence, Feb. 21st, 1851.

MY DEAR DR. STEWART,—

I had heard of the Grossetto seeds, and was quite disposed to invest. In short we have no difficulty in taking a thousand, if they are sent. Mr. Maquay, G., Miss Senhouse, Miss Grant, Miss Taylor, and I, form a joint-stock company *in re*, so that there cannot be much difficulty. None have however arrived here as yet, and we do not know well what to think of such an extraordinary affair. I hope however there can be no mistake, as B. is quite convinced on the subject.

I should so like to have a talk with you about many things, as our position is a somewhat peculiar one just now. The *Times* account was followed up by an article in the *Globe* by Father Prout, and after this a second article in the *Globe* gave the more recent facts, exactly as they were sent. The *Record* introduced the statement from the *Times*: the *Examiner* commented on them. Had the *Witness* anything on the subject? P. wrote to the *Christian Times* asking an article on the new facts, and we think of having them all "done" here, and collected into a missive such as we usually ply in "the cause." If the *Witness* has anything editorial on the subject, we should incorporate it also.

G. has been at length called up before our friends the Delegates, whom he posed, puzzled, and perplexed. So you see things are getting ahead. One of our friends in whose house the reunions were held has been warned, and it is not prudent to meet any longer *chez lui;* but the interest is enormously increasing, and in truth M. thinks he must for a time retire from personal appearance in "conventicles," and prepare a systematic "Instruction" each fortnight, and organize a system by which it may be circulated to the amount of one thousand copies at once and gratis, the expense of preparation being borne by a contribution from the parties for whom it is prepared. In truth this mode seems essential now, and likely to be the most useful now, as any personal labour where there is such risk cannot overtake all that is to be done. An "Instruction" published fortnightly would serve in part the purpose of a service. I think the Prayers must be brought out in this way, forming part of the Instruction, as we both think they would have much greater effect. If right they can afterwards be printed separately. I am quite willing to assist him in the fortnightly preparation of the Instruction, in which we may bring forward the substance of the truth—on Redemption, the Priesthood of Christ, Faith, The Church, etc. In fact this will serve a double purpose, and it seems the only way open now.

M. thinks "The Mother's Catechism" must now be printed [giving the references merely without the passages *in extenso*], as there is a growing desire to instruct their children among the parents. The "Westminster" is too profound for the instructors in the first instance. Just let the expense of printing go to the general account; we shall not lack funds if we are but allowed to go on, as friends here are more and more interested. Mr. Lenox gave me last night an hundred francesconi; but it is for a special object in which he is interested. It is however one of our plans, and hence I took it gladly, and if that object be already secured by funds from another quarter, I take charge of appropriating it to more general purposes, and satisfying Mr. Lenox on the subject. Exclusive of Captain P.'s 1000 lire, I have thus about £67 on hands. Captain P. is willing to aid in the Grossetto seed affair to any reasonable amount.

I wrote to you lately inclosing a list of pamphlets which

I wished Mr. Miller to bring out. Was it in time for that gentleman?

I have heard nothing from Mr. Henderson of the parcel Bet. sent down to him for Genoa. I wrote to him when it was sent. It had not reached Genoa when P. wrote. If you see Mr. H. on Sunday, would you kindly ask about this?

I have only secured four evenings from seven or eight o'clock for my article, but have it fairly begun, and about the fourth written.

Believe me,

My dear Dr. Stewart,

Very sincerely yours,

R. M. H.

IV.

LIST OF CASES OF PERSECUTION IN TUSCANY.

This list was drawn up by Dr. Stewart and circulated privately among the members of the various Italian Associations in Scotland. From it Sheriff Cleghorn prepared his Memorial to Government.

I cannot undertake to give a perfect list of all the persecutions, on account of religious opinions, which have obtained for the Tuscan Government such unenviable notoriety; but the following are the best known :—

1. The reaction of 1849 had no sooner restored the Grand Ducal authority, than the persecution of the small evangelical party in Florence began. On the 18th of May, 1849, about 3,000 copies of Martini's version of the New Testament, printed by Giovanni Benelli, were seized by the police. For printing this edition of Martini, the Court of First Instance condemned Giovanni Benelli to pay a fine of 50 scudi and costs; and the entire edition was sequestrated. This sentence was afterwards reversed in part, by the Supreme Court of Cassation, in the month of March, 1850; but the circulation of the New Testament, without note or comment, was declared to be illegal, and the books were locked up by the police, and afterwards burned near the Arno.

17

2. In the same year, 1850, Captain Pakenham, R.N., was banished from Tuscany on the general charge of attempts at proselytism. I merely indicate the cases, without entering into details. Captain Pakenham was banished in the month of February, 1850.

3. Mons. Paul Geymonat, Waldensian Preacher, was arrested at a *re-union* in the month of March, 1851, imprisoned for a short time, and sent out of Tuscany chained to a felon.

4. Mons. Bart. Malan, Vaudois Pastor, who had been officiating for nearly nine months as Italian Preacher to the Swiss Congregation, which is partly composed of Grisons, speaking the Italian language, was in the same month sent out of Tuscany, and the Italian service was interrupted. The police had previously stationed themselves at the doors of the church to take down the names of the Tuscans who attended, and about one hundred Florentines were cited before the police courts, and forbidden to enter the church again, on pain of imprisonment.

5. On the 7th of May, 1851, Count Piero Guicciardini, Cesare Magrini, Angiolo Guarducci, Carlo Solaini, Sabatino Borsieri, Giuseppe Guerra, and Fedele Betti, were arrested in the house of the said Betti, and a few days afterwards condemned to six months' imprisonment. The sentence was afterwards commuted to exile from Tuscany. The crime consisted in sitting round a table, and reading the 15th chapter of St. John's Gospel, in the version of Diodati. The sentence was pronounced by the Council of Prefecture of Florence, on the 16th of May, and only twenty-four hours were allowed to prepare for departure from the Tuscan territory. The sentence was based on an Edict issued by the Grand Duke on the 25th of April of the same year.

6. On the 17th of August, 1851, the police made a perquisition in the house of Francesco Madiai, where they found two copies of Diodati's version of the Bible. At the same time they arrested Francesco Madiai, Mr. Arthur Walker, Francesco Manelli, and Alessandro Fantoni, and conducted them at once to prison. Mr. Walker was released on the representation of the British Minister, but, on the day following (18th August),

Rosa, wife of Francesco Madiai, was arrested and imprisoned. Francesco Manelli and Alessandro Fantoni were condemned, after eight days' imprisonment, to exile from Tuscany, on the charge of being accomplices of the Madiai, who stood accused of impiety by means of proselytism. The two Madiai remained in prison till the 27th of June, 1852, when they were condemned by sentence of the Royal Court of Florence—the one to 58 months of forced labour in the fortress at Volterra, the other to 45 months of "reclusion" in the House of Correction at Lucca. The Madiai were finally released when their case had been taken up by all the Protestant States of Europe.

7. At the same time, Pasquale Cassacci, who had been imprisoned on a charge of holding heretical opinions, and teaching them to his family, was liberated on his denial of the evangelical doctrines.

8. On the night of the 16th November, 1851, the house of Damiano Bolognini was searched by the police, and several copies of D'Aubigne's History of the Reformation, and of Count Guicciardini's Confession and Narrative, discovered. Bolognini having heard this in his absence at the time from his own house, saved himself by flight, and went into voluntary exile. He has since been employed as teacher in the College at Malta.

9. About the same time, search was made for Angelo Calamandrei, suspected of circulating evangelical tracts at the instance of parties concerned in the Protestant Propaganda. Calamandrei, having remained several days in hiding, succeeded in escaping from Tuscany.

10. Towards the close of the same year, 1851, Stefano Benelli of Florence was arrested on suspicion of being concerned in the Protestant movement. A number of Protestant books, tracts, and Bibles having been found in a room belonging to him, but used by other parties, Benelli was condemned to three months' imprisonment by the Council of Prefecture, and the books were seized by the police.

11. On the 20th of January, 1852, Daniele Mazzinghi and Gaetano Carini were arrested on suspicion of having encouraged an invalid to refuse the sacrament at the hands of a priest.

Carini, not a Tuscan by birth, was banished from the Grand Duchy; and Mazzinghi was condemned to six months' imprisonment in the fortress at Volterra, whither he was conducted in chains; but in a short time the sentence was commuted into exile from Tuscany.

12. In the month of November, 1852, the police made a perquisition in the house of Angiolo Guarducci, formerly compromised in the arrest of Count Guicciardini. A Bible and a few tracts having been found, Guarducci was arrested, and imprisoned in the House of Correction in Florence, where he was kept for about ten months. As nothing could be proved against him, he was not brought to trial; but simply kept in prison on suspicion. Finally, he obtained permission to leave Tuscany, and went into exile.

13. In the month of January, 1853, Carlo Carrana of Florence was condemned to two years' imprisonment in the House of Correction of Florence, for holding opinions contrary to the religion of the State, and also on suspicion of sympathising with political parties opposed to the Government.

14. In the month of August, 1853, there was a perquisition in the house of Natale Lippi, baker, of Florence; and several copies of Diodati's version of the Bible and a few religious tracts having been found in the house, Lippi, along with his son-in-law, and Alessandro Barli, also of Florence, was arrested and imprisoned. After fifteen days, Lippi's two companions were released; but he himself was condemned by the Council of Prefecture to three months' imprisonment, on the ground that he had been overheard by his neighbours reading the Bible in his own house; and that sundry persons had been present for the purpose of hearing him read.

15. Giovanni Ruggero, of San Piero in Baquo, was arrested in the month of April, I believe, and afterwards conducted to the public prison in Florence. After eight months' imprisonment, he was tried and acquitted: the Royal Court of Florence, before which he was tried, holding, however, that the long imprisonment already suffered before the trial was well deserved, as the accused had spoken in private conversation against confession, and the worship of the Virgin.

16. In the month of November, 1853, Pietro Baldi and Michele Manzuoli of Sesto were arrested and thrown into prison, on the charge of impiety by means of proselytism. They were condemned by the Royal Court of Florence to ten months' imprisonment in the House of Correction, besides undergoing imprisonment for three months before their trial.

17. Giovanni Gimignani, of Leghorn, trunk-maker. In the spring of 1853, he was accused to the Government of being guilty of propagandism, by reading the Word of God and other Protestant books to his wife and only son, a lad of fifteen years of age. A woman living on the same landing with him acted as spy—listened at the door to hear what was read—and made this known to the priest at confession. Though confession is given under the *solemn promise of secrecy*, this promise can be broken at pleasure, and it was so in this instance (as also in case No. 7, where the wife's confession was communicated by the priest to Government), the priest immediately laying a complaint against Gimignani with the Delegate of Police. The latter instituted a "process" against him immediately; and as Gimignani feared they would compel his son to take the communion in the Romish Church, he was obliged to fly with his family to Genoa. Since then he has got his son sent off to New York, and has returned himself to Leghorn; and a friend who has some influence has so managed it that he is not now disturbed.

18. In the month of October, 1854, Eusebio Massei of Pontedera was arrested, and condemned by the Prefecture at Pisa to a year's imprisonment at Imbrogiana, for having expressed opinions contrary to the Romish Church, and for having spoken disrespectfully of the Supreme Pontiff and the priests of the Roman Catholic religion.

19. On the 25th of March, 1855, Domenico Cecchetti of Florence was arrested, and condemned to a year's imprisonment at Imbrogiana, for having failed to instruct his children in the Roman Catholic religion; and also for holding Protestant opinions, and reading the Bible with his family. After nearly four months of imprisonment, on the representation of the British Minister the sentence was commuted into exile.

20. About the month of May, 1855, Giovanni Ruggero, of San Piero in Baquo, was found in a grove with a friend reading the Bible. Ruggero having been compromised in a former trial (as already stated) was at once arrested, and along with his friend cast into prison, where both the one and the other at present await their trial.

21. In the month of September, 1855, an "economical" process was begun at Pisa against sundry persons in Pontedera accused of holding evangelical opinions. No fewer than sixteen individuals were implicated ; but as the process has been suspended through the interference, as it is believed, of the British Minister, I shall not mention names.

The following more recent information has been received as to this case :—

We had every reason to hope that the process against Scipione Barsali and fifteen other Pontederesi was at an end. This turns out a mistake. It is true Lord Normanby interfered, and the Ministry promised him there should be no more of it ; but that was just, as I feared, to throw him off his guard. The following letter from Barsali, received on last Saturday afternoon (*2nd Feb.*, 1856), will show that the case goes on :—

"SIR,—The Tuscan Government has not by any means ceased its operations against us. The process against us was remitted by this Delegation (Pontedera) to the Prefecture of Pisa ; and there it appears that the *economic* authority has been found incompetent, and the case has been placed in the hands of the Procuratore Regio. Every day some Pontederesi are called before that Tribunal, and are interrogated regarding our religious conduct. If they examine into my mode of living as well for the past as the present, I have nothing to fear on that score. But considering the subjects who are called up for examination on our affair, there is much to fear. Much as I wish that things may go well, it appears to me a thing inevitable that some of us must go to prison, and I for certain will not be one of those excluded. . . .

(Signed)　　" SCIPIONE BARSALI."

Thus you perceive, in answer to the Government, the case of persecution at Pontedera has not ceased, as we hoped had been the case through the good offices of Lord Normanby ; but it is still going on as actively as ever under the auspices of Corsi, the Cardinal-Archbishop of Pisa, who has openly expressed his determination to put these poor Protestants down. There are from what we can learn fifteen or sixteen of these poor Pontederesi *now under prosecution* for Protestantism.

I have not alluded to such cases as that of Miss Cunningham, imprisoned at Lucca in 1853 ; nor to many cases of voluntary expatriation for conscience-sake ; nor yet to many cases of *private* persecution.

At the beginning of Lent, a fortnight ago, the Grand Duke, in exhorting the parish priests of Florence to hunt out heresy, announced that his Government had positive information that there were *ten thousand Protestants in Tuscany.*

1. On the 6th of August, 1855, a child of Giovanni Buonfiglioli, *Cacciatore* of the Cavaliere Danti, died in Florence. Application was made to the Prior of San Sermindo, near the Porta Romana, to have the child buried. The Prior refused to bury the body, as the parents held Protestant opinions. The Delegate of Santo Spirito, to whom application was next made, told the father that as the Prior would not take charge of the burial, he must look to the removal of the dead child himself. Buonfiglioli had the body then removed to the Protestant burying-ground, outside the Porta Pinti, and on the morning of the 7th August, M. Colomb, the Swiss Pastor at Florence, went to the Delegate of Santo Spirito, to declare, that though the family was wholly unknown to him, he was ready to bury the child, as a duty, not only of Christianity, but of humanity, provided the Delegate gave him a declaration that the Romish Church refused to bury it, and gave him authority.

The Delegate gave no definite answer, but sent for Buonfiglioli and reproved him severely for not supplicating the Prior to do the service. Buonfiglioli then went to the Prior, whom he found in a state of indescribable rage. The Prior ordered him out of the house in words which I shall not repeat, but the maledictory phrases in common use here were the most abundant. The Prior, however, sent that same evening to the Protestant burying-ground, and had the body conducted to the Mortuary Asylum of Florence for interment. The next day Buonfiglioli was dismissed from the service of his master, with whom he had been for twenty-one years, and who had no fault to find with him, except in this—that he was obnoxious to the priests.

2. The second case was that of Francesco Balestrieri, carver and gilder, who died of cholera in the end of August, 1855. The curate of Ognissanti (the parish church) would not bury the body without submitting the case to the Archbishop of Florence, as Balestrieri had refused the Romish sacraments, saying that he looked to Jesus alone for his salvation. The curate, Padre Bernardino Risaliti, having submitted the case to the Cardinal-Archbishop of Florence, F. Minucci, refused, in a formal declaration, to have anything to do with the burial, as Balestrieri had expressed Protestant opinons, and refused the sacraments. The Prefect of the district then ordered the body to be removed to the common cemetery at Trespiano, as cholera was then raging in Florence,—but *that it should be deposited above ground* till further orders. These orders, whatever they may have been, were never communicated to the friends of the deceased, who had occupied themselves about the funeral, and as there were many cases of interment each day at that time, they do not yet know what was done with the body.

V.

LETTER FROM SCIPIONE BARSALI TO DR. STEWART, WITH EXTRACTS FROM CARDINAL CORSI'S INSTRUCTIONS TO HIS CLERGY.

REVERENDO SIGNORE,—

Mi renderò importuno con le frequenti mie lettere: ma la sua bontà vorrà tollerare la mia importunità e compatirmi.

Fino dal primo del presente mese, ricevei una lettera da Firenze, firmata Leopaldi Fabroni, con la quale mi si annun-

ziava essere l' T. stata colà, ed avere parlato relativamente
ai nostri affari religiosi, ed avere fatto a quei fratelli il
medesimo progetto che ha fatto a me, l' ultima volta che ebbi
l' onore di parlarle. Da quella lettera rilevo che quella Chiesa
è irregolata, ed accettasse il progetto dall' T. propostogli, cioè
che qualcuno ci rappresenti presso il governo Toscano ; ed abbi
a una certa responsabilità col medesimo e la stessa condotta
tanto morale che politica, parendo esser questa l' unica strada
per ottenere d' esser tollerati nell' esercizio del nostro culto
religioso. A me sembra che l' accettazione di questo Rappresentante non ostivi alcun modo alla Libertà Evangelica e ciò
mi è sempre sembrato : credo anzi di più : credo che ogni,
anche piccola frazione della Chiesa universale del Cristo, debbe
avere una Costituzione conforme alle prescrizioni della Parola
Divina e leggendosi un Consiglio dirigente, composto di
Anziani, avendo un Conduttore e l'astore che lo presiede, poichè
io credo che il nostro Dio, sia Dio dell' ordine, e non del
disordine, nè può dirsi ordinata una Società quando i membri
che la compongono non riconoscono un' amministrazione visibile
degli statuti che sono obbligati ad osservare. Sempre intesi
però che ogni membro componente questa Società è in tutto
uguale a coloro che prescelti sono a formare il Corpo del
Consiglio dirigente, non esistendo tra i Capi nessuna precedenza,
e che Iddio non ha riguardo alla qualità delle persone, ma
siccome non possiamo negare la differenza dei doni ; colui che
è dotato di quel dono requisito per quel dato ufficio, sia scelto a
quell' ufficio, e consideri quel dono non come esclusiva proprietà, ma come proprietà della Chiesa in generale, e lo impieghi
a vantaggio della medesima.

Un individuo scelto a rappresentare le diverse frazioni della
Chiesa, dimorante in diversi Paesi della Toscana presenterebbe
a prima vista l' idea di un Vescovo Metropolitano, sul modello
dei vescovi della Chiesa Romana, ma io intendo ed ho fatto intendere ai miei fratelli di Pontedera, che questo individuo non
deve esercitare sopra di noi veruna autorità ecclesiastica, che
ecceda le prerogative di qualunque altro Pastore, ma che sia
rivestito del mandato di Rappresentante e gl' effetti dell' ordina-
mento civile : poichè non è supponibile che un Governo voglia

tollerare una Società separata dal resto della famiglia che compone lo Stato, senza che vi sia un Capo che la rappresenti onde conoscere la costituzione, le morti, malviventi, le nascite, ecc : e ciò è il retto andamento della politica amministrazione, poichè, tali incombenze, in Toscana specialmente, sono state affidate agli ecclesiastici. I miei confratelli adunque, convinti di ciò mi hanno incaricato di scrivere la presente, onde pregare V.S. che tanta cura si prende della Chiesa di Cristo, a fare tutte quelle pratiche opportune, con la maggior sollecitudine possibile onde potere venire al momento di vedere stabilita la religiosa Constituzione. Una Società che conta il numero di cinquanta individui, circa, sente il bisogno d'essere organizzata, ed è quello che è impossibile il potere proseguire nello stato attuale.

Noi abitiamo un piccolo Paese, ove la nostra condotta non può sfuggire agli sguardi dei curiosi, e quello che è peggio, ai dardi dei maligni : ogni nostro posto è spiato, e ogni nostra azione è accuratamente osservata. Già vi è un processo sopra le nostre spalle—tutto in noi è delitto—anche il silenzio ! Si accrescono gl'imbarazzi. Il 19, 20, 21, 22, del prossimo mese d'Aprile, viene a fare la visita sinodale a Pontedera, Sua Eminenza, il Cardinale, Arcivescovo di Pisa, ed in questa circonstanza dassi la cresima ai giovinetti. Questa visita ha tutto il carattere di una inquisizione, e non può apportare a noi, altro che guai. Ho potuto avere il libretto d' istruzioni, mandato al Parroco di Pontedera, dall' Arcivescovo, e forse mi è stato dato come un avviso preliminare ; dal contenente del medesimo chiaramente si arguisce, che non potremo sollevarci alle ricerche di sua Eminenza. Le rimetto alcuni paragrafi del Capo primo delle istruzioni predette, ond' Ella conosca che non potremo evitare un interrogatorio del Cardinale. Come contenersi in tale emergente ? Il nostro dovere è di confessare la nostra fede. Chiunque mi avrà rinnegato davanti agli uomini, lo rinnegherò davanti al Padre mio, che è nei Cieli. Ma questa nostra confessione non servirà ella ad avvalorare le deposizioni dei nostri testimoni nel vigente processo ? Il braccio della *Giustizia* pende minaccioso sul nostro capo, come la spada di Damocle : dovremo sfidarlo ? dovremo sacrificar noi e i nostro poveri

figli? Caro Signore, saprete a prova, di qual sempre sia
l' amore di Padre! Sappiamo bene che Iddio impone dei
grandi sacrifizi, ma credo altresì che non si debba andare incontro ai medesimi quando vi possono essere strade per evitarli.
Quando vi perseguiteranno in una citta, fuggite in un' altra.

E ben vero che leggi Toscane non puniscono l' opinione, ma
puniscono e severamente la propaganda dell' opinione riprovata.
Quando in una Paese composta di una sola Parrocchia vi
trovano una quantità di persone che confessano una fede non
conforme a quella dello Stato; e che ritengono dalle comuni
pratiche religiose; che conversano frequentemente tra loro;
sarà forse impossibile impresa a chi vi ha interesse, di per-
cuotere la propaganda, e farne cadere la pretesa colpa sopra
colui che reputano più necessario di sacrificarlo alle loro
vedute? Non sarà considerato come opposizione al libero
esercizio della loro religiosa amministrazione, se non manderemo i nostri figli a ricevere la cresima, e ad istruirsi nelle
loro dottrine, e quindi cavare anche da questo un motivo per la
nostra condanna? e se li manderemo, non sarà impossibile cos-
tringere quei giovinetti, oramai imbevuti delle massime paterne,
ad adoprare la maschera dell' ipocrita, e noi Padri, non avremo
parte a così sacrilega immolazione? In vero la nostra posizione è scabrosa, e duopo abbiamo di consigli, onde poterci
regolare con quella semplicità e prudenza che il Nostro Maestro
ci raccomanda, nel codice suo divino. Da molto tempo io
prevedeva questi ed altri imbarazzi. Ne ho parlato anche con
i componenti la Chiesa di Firenze, e non sono stato ascoltato.
Adesso è giunto il tempo per noi di non potere proseguire senza
un rimedio, e questo altro essere non può che il dare una forma
alla Chiesa, poichè sarà più agevole ottenere una tolleranza
dal Governo, organizzati, che disorganizzati. Il Governo più
difficilmente agirà contro un numero ragguardevole di sudditi
che si confessano apertamente legati da una medesima fede,
che contro uno o due presi alla spicciolata.

L' Europa mentre fa plauso alla cessazione della persecu-
zione religiosa in Turchia, fremerebbe, non vi ha dubbio, se
sapessi perseguitati un numero non indifferente di sudditi, per
motivi religiosi, nel centro della nostra bella Penisola, emporeo

d' arti e di Civiltà.   Or dunque è necessario tutti uniti organiz-
zarci, manifestarci chiaramente, e chiedere il *diritto* che nisun
uomo puo torre all' altro uomo—la libertà di coscienza.   Alla
vostra saggezza, noi tutti gli Evangelici di Pontedera, ci
riportiamo O Signore, ond' Ella, faccia quanto fa duopo per
la nostra organizzazione, per quindi ottenere, per mezzo dei
rispettabili Vostri conoscenti, dal Governo Toscano, la tolleranza dell' Evangelico Culto.

Pontedera, 10 Marzo, 1856.

D. S. V., Revd° Servo Um°.

SCIPIONE BARSALI.

ESTRATTO DAL LIBRO D' ISTRUZIONI TRASMESSE D' ALLAR-
CIVESCOVO DI PISA AL PARROCO DI PONTEDERA, PER
LA VISITA SINODALE DA FARSI NEL PROSSIMO APRILE
1856.

CAPO PRIMO.

Par. 1° Ammonisca il Popolo della prossima visita spiegan-
dogli le cagioni e gli effetti, istruendolo dell' obligazione per
sua parte.

2° Con ogni efficacia e sollecitudine esorti ed induca il
medesimo suo Popolo a prepararsi alla Confessione, colle dovute
disposizioni per ricevere nel giorno della sua visita la santa
Communione, dall' Eminentissimo Arcivescovo.

3° Esorti il Popolo a non partire durante il tempo della visita
per potere esporre al proprio Pastore, quanto occorre per
togliere i disordini, e procurarne il bene, per ascoltar le sue
esortazioni, e rispondere alle sue interrogazioni.

4° Con ispecialissima diligenza ogni Parroco faccia lo stato
dell' anime per esibirlo all' arrivo dell' Arcivescovo.   Questo si
faccia famiglia per famiglia, con la distinzione delle strade e
delle contrade, acciocchè si sappiano i luoghi delle loro abita-
zioni . . .   Si faccia altresì un' altra nota di coloro che non
seguono i rudimenti della fede, necessari per la salute, e dei
quali il Parroco non si e potuto moralmente assicurare che li
sappiano ; e questo, ad effetto, possano istruirsi. . . . Ci
faranno in oltre un esatto rapporto in iscritto (è da notarsi che
terremo riserbato) degli inconvenienti e scandali più gravi che

resistono ai Parrocchi, specialmente per cio che riguarda le conoscenze in fatto di disonestà, di bestemmie, *di dottrine erronee e pericolose, di trasgressioni al precetto Pasquale, di inosservanza delle Feste,* di gravi discordie ed inimicizie tra Parrocchiani.

6° Sia preparato ogni Parroco alle interrogazioni che gli farà l' Eminentiss° Arciv° con lo stato dell' anime alla mano intorno alla qualità delle sue Pecorelle, che dee conoscere ad una ad una, temendo il rigoroso giudizio dell' Eterno Pontefice G. Cristo, se ignora il carattere, la vita ed i bisogni dei suoi Parrocchiani, o se per rispetto umano, o per altro fine contrario al suo carattere, non si fa un dovere di manifestargli apertamente i disordini della sua Parrocchia.

Il Libretto è diviso in 3 capi che conterranno 50 paragrafi ciascuno ; tutti per la maggior parte sul tuono dei soprascritti. Potremo noi passare inosservati ? Il tempo di manifestarsi è giunto per noi ! Sdegneranno gli altri Fratelli di concorrere alla nostra salvazione ? o dividere con noi il pericolo ? Non è più tempo di pregare colla sentinella all' uscio di casa, per non essere scoperti dalla vigilanza della Polizzia.

VI.

BROADSIDE IN THE PIEDMONTESE DIALECT. THIS WAS CIR-CULATED BY THE ROMAN CATHOLIC CLERGY TO ROUSE THE COUNTRY AGAINST THE WALDENSIAN MISSIONARIES.

AVVERTIMENTO

Ai Cattolici Cristiani a non lasciarsi sedurre dai protestanti, ma di star franchi e fermi nella Religione in cui sono nati, cioè nella Religione Cattolica, Apostolica e Romana, la quale è l' unica, sola e vera lasciata da Gesù Cristo, e le porte dell' inferno, non avranno forza di atterrarle. S. Matteo, Capo XVI. 18, 19.

> Mi v' avviso tutti quanti
> Non lasciæve lusingâ
> Da sti quattro protestanti
> Che ve sœrcan d' ingannâ

A vedili in apparenza
Ve pan gente du Segnû
Ma poi dopo son avari
Come Giudda traditû
Quando parlo di protestanti
Non m' intendo de parlâ
Sorve a quelli meschinetti
Che se son lasciæ ingannâ
Ma m' intendo de combatte
Solo quelli capuriuin
Che passaggian per l' Italia
A ingannâ i povei meschin.
A sentili a predica
Ve pan santi d' indavei
Ma toccæghe a seu bottega
Che poi dopo ghe vediei
Vegnan li coa sacra bibbia
Che pan angeli du Sè
Ma in ristretto nu fan pe atro
Che per invidia de mestê.
Sotto u manto da scrittua
Ghan un fin ingannatû
Vegnan chi a dâ addosso ai prævi
Per vegnî poi prævi lû
Son vegnui anche chi a Zena
Pe ciantâ a seu religion
Ma fra-mezo ai sen ministri
Ghe za nata a divixion.
Questa gente figgi cai
Son nocivi a Societæ
Perchè mettan a discordia
In fra-mezo au figgio e au puæ
Perchè u puæ e veu sta cattolico
E se u figgio u nu veu sta.
E de li ne vegnan guerre
Che nu peuan mai ciù quetâ
In te quelle povie case
Ghe succede tanto mä

Se peu dilo francamente
Che u diau u ghe fa u ferrä
Quella bella e santa paxe
Che regnava in quelle case
U Segnò ô l' ha tolto via
Per caxion dell' erexia.
Questi quattro protestanti
  Lu son proprio ingannatui
  Che de sette sacramenti
  Non osservan manco duî
  Lu negan l' cujo santo
  Negan a confermazion
  Negan l' ordine e ô matrimonio
  Negan anche a confescion.
Lu nô veuan fa penitenza
  Non ammettan ô zazun
  E. di ponti da scrittua
  Non osservan manco un,
  L' osservanza da quaresima
  Non ne fan nisciun dovei
  E au venerdi e au sabbo
  Mangian carne a ciu non puei.
Lô dixian maa du Papa
  Dixian maa da confescion
  E ô seu scopo non è atro
  Che distrugge a religion
  Lu non pregan a Madonna
  E negan a seu verginitè
  E da Santa Madre Gexia
  Son za tutti condannæ
A Gexia di cattolici
  A le li ben apparâ
  Ma in ta giexia protestante
  Nu g' han manco d' Artâ
  Lu non tegnan manco a Croxie
  Dove l' è morto ô salvatô
  E non veuan manco vedde
  Un immagine dô Segnô.

Gesù Cristo coi seu apostoli
   Quando favan l' orazion
   S' inchinavan proprio in terra
   Propriamente in zenoggion
   Ma invece i protestanti
   Quando fan e seu orazioin
   Se ne stan la belli driti
   Che pan tanti campanin.
In ta Gexia protestante
   Non se vedde apparemento
   Ma in te case di ministri
   Ghe adornou d' ou e d' argento
   Lu in cangio d' adornase
   Una casa pe-ô Segnô
   Lu s' adornan i salotti
   Che coscì sei godan lô.
I ministri protestanti
   G' han e stanze addamaschæ
   E g' han tanti poveretti
   Che son li tutti strassæ
   Loro vivan in gran lusso
   Van vestii de panno fin
   E se-a marcian in carozza
   Che pan tanti milorduin.
De vedili li all' esterno
   Ve pan pin de religion
   Ma poi doppo nell' interno
   Han ô cheu come un prion
   Se per sorte un poveretto
   U va a serca i dinæ d' un pan
   Lu ghe dixian che le ozioso
   E ô matrattan comme un can.
Lô g'han tanti poveretti
   E sei veddan li a patî
   E langueuii ne-a miseia
   Ma nô-i sercan de soccorì
   O se pure a qualche amigo
   Lô ghe fan qualche favô

Lô ghe dan de quella roba
Che non serve ciù per lù.
E coscì fan a limoxima
Come quella de Cain
E in faccia a Gesù Cristo
A nu va manco un quattrin
Queste cose che ve diggo
E son tutte gran veitæ
Perchè mi con i protestanti
Queste cose l' ho provæ
Amiæ hen che ghe fra lô.
Serti tali Inquisitoi
Che han scosso u dolce Giugo
Per puei megio fa l' ozioso
Questo non pe iddio dô Çe
Ma per puei pigiä mugiê
E a vedili ve pan santi
Poi son marzi intolieranti.
Ve credei che questa gente
Vegnan chi per fa dô ben
Vegnan chi a mette a discordia
In framezo ai buin cristien
E fin tanto che in Italia
Ghe saia sti flamazioin
In Fra-mezo de famigge
Ghe saiâ sempre de quistioin.
In fra-mezo ai protestanti
U ghe regna l' ambizion
E fra-mezo a lu ministri
U ghe sempre a disunion
Ma in cangio fra i cattolici
Li ghe regna l' unitæ
E ghe regna a santa paxe
In fra-mezo a Societæ
Perchè a fede di cattolici
A le stæta ben fondâ
Le lasciâ da Gesù Cristo
Che nisciun a peu atterrâ

18

E se nòi staiemo fermi
Ne-a cattolica religion
Stemmo serti e ben segûi
Che andiemo in salvazion.
Mi v' avviso puæ e muæ
A guardâ i vostri figgin
E tegnî li ben distante
Da sti quattro flamazioin
E procurè de daghe a tutti
Un-a Santa educazion
E insegnaghe a sta costanti
A-a Cattolici religion.
Questa gente amixi cai
Veuan portane a confosion
E fa si che nell' Italia
Nu ghe segge ciu d' union
F non basta grandi guerre
Rinovæ anche fra fræ
E nisciun tranquillamente
Porriá vive in societæ
Se navviemo i euggi a tempo
E se lasciemo incapussâ
Quando saiemo in ta rè
Nô porrieino ciú scapâ ;
Che da-e guære religiose
Noî tegnimolo a moria
Su é eu pagine doro
Che conta ne possa storia
Miserabile l' Italia
Se divisa in ciù frasìon
Pei partii religiosi
Diventemmo i ciu meschin
U nu ghe ciu breve strada
Per fa mille religioin
Che coa Bibbia protestante
Stampâ senza annotazioin.

VII.

TWO ARTICLES FROM "IL RISCATTO." THIS NEWSPAPER WAS PUBLISHED AT ALESSANDRIA, AND ITS ISSUES FOR JUNE, 1858, CONTAINED SOME CORRESPONDENCE RELATIVE TO WHAT TOOK PLACE AT PIETRA MARAZZI.

CARISSIMO CHICHIBIO,

Pietra Marazzi, 10 giugno 1858.

Mi spiace di dovervi comunicare una cattiva notizia. I preti dei nostri paesi sono tutti pieni di rabbia e di fiele : e con questi calori non istupirei che fossero colti da idrofobia. Sapete il perchè? Sono quei benedetti o·maledetti ministri protestanti, che già da qualche tempo si installarono a Pietra Marazzi e vanno sempre più guadagnando terreno : lo vedete, Chichibio, il pericolo? . . . È inutile che vi dica, che i nostri preti non risparmiano le critiche, le·calunnie, le declamazioni, le minacce di pene spirituali e contro i ministri del protestantismo e contro coloro che vanno· a sentirli. Ma tutti indarno. Le nostre popolazioni li vedono volentieri ed accorrono in folla alle loro religiose conferenze.

Domenica scorsa è stato un giorno solenne : e l' uditorio fu più numeroso del solito per la presenza del pastore capo valdese sig. MALAN, il quale fece la· sua predica : la camera delle conferenze, il cortile e la strada pubblica erano piene zeppe di persone venute anche dai paesi circonvicini. Fra gli uditori si trovava pure il parroco di Montecastello don Roncati, attirato, credo, più dal dispetto, che dalla curiosità. Difatti nel mentre il sig. MALAN stava commentando la bibbia, il don Roncati uscì improvvisamente in grandi schiamazzi, gridando : CHE TUTTI COLORO I QUALI SI TROVAVANO IN QUEL LUOGO ERANO SCOMUNICATI E DANNATI ALL' INFERNO (lui eccettuato s' intende ! !) : CHE LA PRESENZA DEI PROTESTANTI ALLA PIETRA E TUTTA QUELLA FOLLA ERA UN' ONTA, UNA VERGOGNA PER QUEI PAESI : CHE I MINISTRI VALDESI NON ISPACCIAVANO CHE FROTTOLE : di poi, volgendosi ad essi chiedeva : DA CHI AVEVANO AVUTO IL MANDATO D'ISTRUIRE E DI CATECHIZZARE,

SE DA CRISTO O DA SATANA : ed altre simili improntitudini e castronerie.

Le vociferazioni del don Roncati costrinsero il pastore valdese a sospendere le sue lezioni : il quale avanzatosi sulla soglia e senza punto turbarsi, fece grazioso invito al parroco di entrare nella camera, ove avrebbe avuto libera la parola per esporre tutte quelle osservazioni che avrebbe creduto a proposito. Ma il Roncati non ne volle sapere, scusandosi col dire : che i canoni ecclesiastici gli vietano rigorosamente ogni discussione coi miscredenti, sotto pena di perdere la messa : e con ciò non accettava la sfida. Ma fosse almeno stato tranquillo : niente affatto. Egli continuò in esclamazioni e vociferazioni indistinte, per cui il pastore valdese non potendo più farsi intendere, dovette chiudere la seduta. In tal modo il parroco di Montecastello può vantarsi di aver fatto tacere, di avere INSACCATO, come egli usa esprimersi, il sig. MALAN, con grande consolazione di don Lora che stava ascoltando dalla finestra della vicina chiesa.

Ma il don Roncati non avendo accettata la sfida, incorse nelle fischiate di tutta quella gente, la quale poco mancò non gli desse anche qualche lezione palpabile. Intanto, chiediamo noi, quale dritto aveva il prete di condannare così pubblicamente la condotta di tutta una popolazione, che nella sua conscienza credeva di poter sentire le lezioni dei protestanti ? Era quello il luogo ? Oltre di ciò, qual diritto aveva il don Roncati di disturbare quella pacifica riunione ? Noi consigliamo il Roncati, e ciò per suo meglio, a non più ripetere simili scandali e a non più fare di queste scene, perchè, se mai disgraziatamente scappasse ad un popolano qualche pugno . . . egli dovrebbe sapere, che in simili casi i pugni sono . . . come le ciriegie : e per quanto il nostro parroco abbia buone spalle e buona schiena, la sua posizione non sarebbe tuttavia niente affatto invidiabile.

Una grave imprudenza adunque commise il parroco di Montecastello. Egli o non doveva presentarsi : oppure entrando nell' arringo, non doveva limitarsi agli schiamazzi che nulla provano, tranne che la forza dei polmoni, ma mostrarsi uomo dotto e fornito di buone e solide ragioni. Ma il don Roncati non è mai stato un uomo di scienza. Egli ha piuttosto buoni muscoli che un buon cervello : e perciò, se si fosse trattato d' un duello a pugni coi ministri valdesi, era sicuro di uscirne con tutti gli onori della vittoria.

Ora poi si dice che il don Roncati in compagnia di don Lora (che è la causa prima di tutti i guai presenti e futuri) muova mari e monti, sia presso l' intendente, che coll' avvocato fiscale, per trovar modo di espellere i protestanti dalla Pietra, accusandoli di massime anticattoliche !!! Come se i ministri valdesi dovessero insegnare altra cosa che la loro religione. L' agitazione e il tramestio di questi preti fanno veramente compassione !! Diremo di più, essi fanno un grave torto alla nostra religione. Non è dessa fondata sopra una PIETRA INCROLLABILE? Non sono i preti convinti della verità di quella massima: PORTAE INFERI NON PRÆVALEBUNT ADVERSUS ECCLESIAM? Dunque a che ricorrere ai modi sguaiati, alle calunnie, ai processi, alla forza per proteggere una religione, che si può così bene e assai più efficacemente difendere con modi dolci e con buone e solide ragioni?

Le menzogne poi e le calunnie sono armi cattive e che per lo più si rivolgono contro quegli stessi che le usano. I nostri preti sogliono rappresentare i protestanti come gente corrotta, piena di ogni sorta di vizi: ed i loro ministri siccome maestri di impostura, di immoralità e di disordine. Or bene, i popolani accorrendo alle loro adunanze religiose, vedono raccomandato e inculcato il disinteresse, la carità, l' amore, la fratellanza reciproca, la pietà, il rispetto ai genitori, alla proprietà ed in una parola ogni virtuosa pratica, mentre viene riprovato qualunque atto cattivo: e ne argomentano, che i protestanti non sono nè possono essere gente così perversa come spacciano i preti. Venendo poi alle qualità personali dei ministri protestanti, li trovano manierosi, dolci, affabili, cortesi, alieni da tutto ciò che v' ha di intollerante e di astioso: mentre osservano invece che i preti cattolici generalmente parlando sono di tempra ben diversa. La conclusione di tutto ciò non può essere pertanto favorevole nè ai ministri cattolici nè a quella religione così malamente da essi rappresentata.

Ecco perchè il protestantismo trova appoggio e favore presso le nostre popolazioni: e a quest' ora avrebbe preso proporzioni ben più vaste ed anche soppiantato affatto il cattolicismo romano, se non si opponesse un' altra specie di religione che è in voga ai nostri giorni, voglio dire l' INDIFFERENTISMO. La condotta riprovevole del clero in generale e le massime d' intolleranza liberticide ed antinazionali de esso accarezzate, devono necessariamente condurre ad una tale conseguenza. Il cattolicismo romano fin che si vuol far servire di puntello al dispotismo ed all' oppressione straniera non sarà mai il benvenuto: e finirà coll' essere ripudiato intieramente, col generalizzarsi del sentimento di libertà e d' indipendenza. ROSMINI, GIOBERTI ed altri valentuomini affezionati al cattolicismo cercarono di scongiurare il pericolo dando buoni consigli al papi ed ai preti. Ma questi scrittori illustri e benemeriti della civiltà e di una condotta esemplare vennero in compenso dei loro sforzi condannati e scommunicati dal papa: e la loro memoria è tuttodì infamata dai preti armoniosi, siccome d'uomini corrotti e perversi. E poi si grida, che il protestantismo fa progressi!! E si vorrebbe che si desse addosso ai protestanti a onore e gloria dell' infallibilità e santità papalina ed a sostegno di uomini che hanno uccisi ed arsi vivi MILIONI di persone per semplici delitti di religione: e che, se potessero, lo farebbero ancora oggidì instaurando i roghi e l' inquisizione!!!

Pietra Maruzzi, 25 *giugno* 1858.

La lotta tra il parroco e la popolazione ferve tuttora e si teme non abbia a finir bene. Le persone più influenti fanno tutti gli sforzi per impedire disordini e contenere la moltitudine nei limiti della legalità. Gli stessi Valdesi, diciamolo pure ad onore del vero e a rischio di essere tacciati di PARZIALITÀ da qualche giornale alessandrino, si adoperano in questo senso a rendere diremo così bene per male. Finora i savi e pacifici consigli sono bene accolti e speriama lo saranno per l' avvenire. Difatti, venne disteso un ricorso all' intendente ed al vicario, sottoscritto da più di novanta individui, i quali chiedono l' allontanamento dell' inviso arciprete. L' intiero paese adunque prese parte alla sottoscrizione, a meno di cinque o sei persone dipendenti dal parroco o per interessi o per ragione di mestiere.

Finora la supplica non ebbe ancora alcun risultato. Le autorità a cui venne indirizzata non presero alcun temperamento : che anzi non diedero neanco risposta ai petenti. Così va fatto ! ! ! Si sa di più, che il vicario communicò il ricorso allo stesso don Lora, il quale lo tenne per una settimana ed ebbe così agio di vedere il nome di tutti i sottoscritti. Ora i cagnotti del parroco si danno attorno presso molte persone, per indurle a ritirare o disdire la propria firma : e a dichiarare persino d' essere state ingannate dai raccoglitori delle firme, i quali avrebbero loro dato ad intendere, che la supplica era diretta contro i Valdesi e non contro il parroco.

Il contegno dell' arciprete e compagni è tutt' altro che conciliativo. Egli minaccia nientemeno che la GALERA a tutti coloro che sottoscrissero contro di lui : si vanta poi di essere irremovibile e mostrasi disposto a scommettere : che nessuna autorità potrà mai privarlo di una parrocchia, che egli vinse al concorso, sudando quattro camicie per risolvere i più astrusi quesiti teologali. Si dice poi : che tutta la fiducia e sicurezza del parroco poggia sulla protezione dell' ex-ministro Rattazzi, a cui è stato raccomandato da madama C. d' Oviglio, parente all' ex-ministro. Pare impossibile, che il Rattazzi voglia assumersi la difesa d' una causa così cattiva : e che egli, uomo democratico e che deve perciò rendere omaggio alla volontà popolare, non si penta di sostenere ed imporre a tutto un paese un uomo giustamente odiato.

Il partito arcipretino confida pure nelle prossime elezioni municipali : e già fin d' ora si agita per farle riescire favorevoli al minacciato e pericolante pastore. Si spera pure, sempre colla protezione dell' ex-ministro Rattazzi, di far cadere la nomina del sindaco sulla persona d' un illiterato cagnotto sfegatato dell' arciprete : e siccome questo cagnotto che è solo contro tutto il paese mostra già fin d' ora una gran voglia di mordere, non avvi alcun dubbio che in brevissimo tempo sarebbe cacciato dallo stallo sindacale, a meno che non si voglia ricorrere alla forza armata per tenere in piedi e sindaco e parroco, nella stessa guisa che ed austriaci e francesi sostengono la baracca papalina.

Il più grande agitatore del nostro paese ed in favore del

parroco è il prete don C . . . ex-cappellano del cimitero. È un uomo irrequieto che suscita lo spirito di partito e le ire popolari. Ha un gran bisogno di essere dimenticato : tuttavia fa di tutto per far parlare di sè. Or bene, sarà soddisfatto : lo terrò d'occhio nelle prossime elezioni, per quindi mandarvi alcuni cenni sulla sua vita che è alquanto edificante.

Un giornale d' Alessandria, l' OPERAIO, mi accusa (benchè con modi gentili) di PARZIALITA' verso i Protestanti, per la lettera stampata nel num. 70 di questo giornale. Posso assicurare l' OPERAIO, che io parlai e parlo colla massima spassionatezza. Potrei con più ragione ritorcere l' accusa contro di esso, incolpandolo di PARZIALITA' a danno dei Valdesi e a benefizio dell' intolleranza. A dire il vero, l' articolo dell' OPERAIO puzza di sacrestia lontano un miglio : e lascia vedere apertamente l' intenzione di sostenere e perpetuare, se fosse possibile, gli abusi ed i privilegi della casta sacerdotale. Difatti, il buon giornale non vuole altra bibbia che quella che porta il VISTO DEL VESCOVO : cerca d' interpretare lo statuto nel senso più ristretto per la libertà, invocando, per quanto riguarda il culto delle religioni dissidenti, le LEGGI GOVERNA- TIVE dei tempi passati d' infausta memoria, le quali quando esistessero, non si dovrebbero mai ricordare da un giornale liberale che per promuoverne l' intera distruzione : senonchè a fronte dell' articolo dello statuto che guarentisce la libertà di associazione, le antiche leggi governative debbono scomparire, lasciando ai Valdesi e ai non Valdesi la facoltà di discutere le loro cose religiose nel modo che a loro garba.

Un bel tratto d' intolleranza ci porge l' OPERAIO quando vuole, che I PADRONI DI CASA NEGLI AFFITTAMENTI AI VALDESI IMPONGANO LORO CONDIZIONI PROIBITIVE : non senza approvare, e questo è ciò che fa più torto all' OPERAIO, anche gli atti di violenza, rallegrandosi : CHE IN VALLE DI S. BARTOLOMEO ALCUNI ASSENNATI UOMINI SIANSI ADOPERATI COLL' APPOGGIO DELL' AUTORITÀ LOCALE PERCHÈ FOSSE RIVOCATO L'AFFITTAMENTO E DI PIU' LI OBBLIGARONO ALLO SFRATTO : ma bravo, signor OPERAIO, sono questi gli esempi di carità e di tolleranza civile e religiosa che porgete agli Alessandrini? Prima si invocano contro i dissidenti in materia religiosa le barbare leggi del medio evo : e se queste urtassero collo STATUTO e non si potessero più rivangare senza offendere la coscienza pubblica e la civiltà . . . una mano di birichini è presto trovata e poi . . . una bella grandine di sassi lanciati contro i Protestanti basta per soddisfare al pio desiderio. Forse lo scrittore dell' OPERAIO non avrà una tale intenzione : ma posso assicurarlo che molti preti interpretano i suoi consigli e si studiano di metterli in pratica in questo modo. E difatti sappia che alcuni preti e cattolici PURO SANGUE fecero di tutto (e ne parlarono anche con me) per indurre la popolazione della Pietra a prendere i Valdesi a SASSATE : senza considerare che gli abitanti della Pietra, non vedendo nei Valdesi quei diavoli e anticristi loro rappresentati dai preti e d' altronde essendo alieni dagli atti di violenza, avrebbero fatto e farebbero pagar cara una tale imprudenza.

A fronte di queste massime, non c'è da stupire se l' OPERAIO intende la libertà di coscienza a suo modo. LA PENSI COME VUOLE, dice il buon giornale, l' ESTENSORE DELLA LETTERA E LI DIFENDA A SUA POSTA, IO TENGO CHE IL TORTO SIA DAL CANTO DEI VALDESI. DIFATTI, PIETRA-MARAZZI HA I SUOI TEMPLI, I SUOI PASTORI (e che pastori ! !) E LA SUA RELIGIONE GIÀ STABILITA : DUNQUE ESSA NON HA D'UOPO CHE I VALDESI VADANO A PREDICARE IVI IL VANGELO. Ma che sorta di ragionamento è questo : e dove fa consistere l' OPERAIO la libertà di coscienza ? Stando sul terreno della libertà religiosa e non su quello delle leggi ANTICHE GOVERNATIVE, noi diremo : che i Valdesi hanno lo stesso diritto di predicare il vangelo a Pietra-Marazzi ed altrove, che hanno i nostri missionari di predicarlo nella China e nell' America. La libertà di coscienza non è rispettata e si fa atto di GUERRA APERTA e di VERA USURPAZIONE, quando le credenze religiose si vogliono imporre colla forza, come ha sempre fatto la corte di Roma colle torture e coi roghi e colle persecuzioni che si praticano tuttora negli stati papali : e come sembra voler fare l' OPERAIO colle sue LEGGI GOVERNATIVE, coi suoi AFFITTAMENTI di nuovo conio e colle sue tendenze per gli SFRATTI più o meno forzosi. Ora è un fatto che i Valdesi, come gli Evangelisti, non costrinsero mai alcuno colla forza a sentire le loro lezioni religiose : va chi

vuole alle loro sedute e chi non vuole se ne rimane a casa.
Dove sta adunque l'attentato alla libertà di coscienza? Se poi
gli abitanti della Pietra sentono volentieri i Valdesi, segno è
che la religione cattolica non è tanto STABILITA nel nostro
paese come crede l'OPERAIO. In tal caso, chi viola il principio
della libertà di coscienza non sono i Protestanti che predicano
a chi vuole sentire: ma quei preti e quei cattolici PURO SANGUE
che usano tutti i mezzi leciti ed illeciti, non escluse le sassate
dei birichini di piazza, per cacciarli dal paese di viva forza.

L' abbiamo detto e lo ripetiamo: coloro che accusano i
Protestanti della decadenza della nostra religione confondono
l'effetto colla causa. Il protestantismo non farebbe progressi
se non trovasse il terreno preparato. E chi ha preparato il
terreno? È la corte di Roma e il clero colla sua ignoranza,
colla sua avarizia, colla sua intolleranza, col suo spirito anti-
liberale ed antinazionale: chi rovina la nostra religione non
son i Protestanti, ma il papa colla sua massima gesuitica SIT
UT EST AUT NON SIT: che è quanto dire guerra e guerra
implacabile alla civiltà ed alla libertà.

VIII.

LETTER FROM SCIPIONE BARSALI TO DR. STEWART, GIVING AN ACCOUNT OF THE FIRST INTERVIEW HE HAD WITH CARDINAL CORSI.

SIGNORE,—

Mi avrà forse in concetto di testardo, giacchè malgrado
i consigli amorosamente da V.S. somministratimi, sono andato
a parlare col Cardinale a Pisa. Ma come potevo io plausi-
bilmente esimermi da ciò fare, dietro tante e replicate chiamate?
Una aperta negativa, sarebbe stata una aperta ribellione alla sua
autorità, e forse interpretata come un' audace disfida da provo-
care il tremendo, implacabile sdegno Pretino, a danno ancora
degli altri miei confratelli. Vi andai, ed il Cardinale mi accolse
affabilmente, dimostrandomi molta benignità; ma il risultato
del lungo dialogo con esso tenuto, fu ch' io rimasi qual ero, ed
egli qual era. Solamente ebbi a promettergli di ritornare da

lui. In quel Signore più che il teologo trovai un astuto giureconsulto. Lasciai che sciorinasse a suo talento, tutte quelle stiracchiate ragioni, che ho udito le mille volte da altri preti, con le quali tentava d' indurmi a credere, e piegare il capo, alle decisioni della sua dispotica chiesa ; ma si avvedde Egli stesso che quelle allegate ragioni rimasero senza effetto, poichè mi protestai, che nessuna impressione facevano sull' animo mio, le induzioni dell' umano razionalismo, e che la mia credenza aveva per base la Santa Scrittura. L' astuto prete mi dimandò se sinceramente credevo in Dio, e nella Santa Scrittura, *oppure ero indotto a professare la religione della Bibbia dal convincente argomente dell' interesse che potevo ricavare da una delle molte società segrete di forestieri che per nostra disgrazia inondano la Toscana, e profondono enormi somme per fini, i quali io poteva ignorare.*

Le risposi che la mia professione religiosa è figlia del più intimo convincimento, e che la sola Parola di Dio mi aveva consigliato ad adottare i principj religiosi da me professati. Troppo mi renderei prolisso se dovessi narrare tutte le parti di questo dialogo : mi limiterò a dirle, che sua Eminenza con la sua logica dottorale si provava a farmi comparire la Bibbia un libro di fantasia a un dipresso come l' Orlando furioso dell' Ariosto. Ma io le dissi : Signore se Ella mi atterra la Bibbia, dove poserà la sua Chiesa infallibile? Sulla tradizione? instabile fondamento, che ancora questo ha bisogno d' avere per appoggio la Bibbia, perchè io credo che i tradizionali non la pretenderanno ad essere della Bibbia più autorevoli. Insomma, la conclusione fu che ci separammo amici e la nostra discussione rimase aggiornata. Ma io non vi andrò fino a che non mi abbia ripetutamente chiamato.

Intanto fra noi si vanno intelaiando dei matrimoni ; come faremo quando dovranno effettuarsi? Iddio provvederà !

Riceva i saluti di noi tutti e mi creda di V.S.

Umilissimo Servo,

SCI. BARSALI.

Butler & Tanner, The Selwood Printing Works, Frome, and London.